Magic Sk

Zan

《 Rec

D1556942

The electricity released from her blade circled around her to form eight orbs, each about the size of a human head. Yellow sparks cutting through the sky rose up into the golden orbs.

They twirled above Cayna's head as if they were singing and dancing—as if they were alive. Cayna aimed at the rock golems, and with a murmur of "Go," the spheres whirled higher and higher.

Cayna then swung her electric sword toward the ground like a conductor's baton, and pillars of lightning came crashing down from the orbs and onto the rock golems.

"…Hey now…"

Cayna furrowed her brow at this holier-than-thou attitude that had just blown away every bit of her battle fatigue. It was clear from her expression that she was wondering what kind of weirdo would have a Guardian like this one.

"I'm the Third Skill Master, the high elf Cayna. Whose tower is this?"

CAYNA

IN THE LAND OF LEADALE

2

Ceez

[ILLUSTRATION BY]

Tenmaso

YEN ON

NEW YORK

L IN THE LAND OF
EADALE 2 Ceez

Translation by Jessica Lange
Cover art by Tenmaso

This book is a work of fiction. Names, characters, places, and incidents are the product of the author's imagination or are used fictitiously. Any resemblance to actual events, locales, or persons, living or dead, is coincidental.

RIADEIRU NO DAICHI NITE Vol. 2
© Ceez 2019
First published in Japan in 2019 by KADOKAWA CORPORATION, Tokyo.
English translation rights arranged with KADOKAWA CORPORATION, Tokyo through
TUTTLE-MORI AGENCY, INC., Tokyo.

English translation © 2021 by Yen Press, LLC

Yen On
150 West 30th Street, 19th floor
New York, NY 10001

Visit us at yenpress.com
facebook.com/yenpress
twitter.com/yenpress
yenpress.tumblr.com
instagram.com/yenpress

First Yen On Edition: February 2021

Yen On is an imprint of Yen Press, LLC.
The Yen On name and logo are trademarks of Yen Press, LLC.

The publisher is not responsible for websites (or their content) that are not owned by the publisher.

Library of Congress Cataloging-in-Publication Data
Names: Ceez, author. | Tenmaso, illustrator. | Lange, Jessica (Translator), translator.
Title: In the land of Leadale / Ceez ; illustration by Tenmaso ; translation by Jessica Lange
Other titles: Riadeiru no daichi nite. English
Description: First Yen On edition. | New York, NY : Yen On, 2020.
Identifiers: LCCN 2020032160 | ISBN 9781975308681 (v. 1 ; trade paperback) |
    ISBN 9781975308704 (v. 2 ; trade paperback)
Subjects: CYAC: Fantasy. | Virtual reality—Fiction.
Classification: LCC PZ7.1.C4646 In 2020 | DDC [Fic]—dc23
LC record available at https://lccn.loc.gov/2020032160

ISBNs: 978-1-9753-0870-4 (paperback)
        978-1-9753-0871-1 (ebook)

10 9 8 7 6 5 4 3 2 1

LSC-C

Printed in the United States of America

·IN THE LAND OF· LEADALE

2

IN THE LAND OF LEADALE CONTENTS

ILLUSTRATION BY Tenmaso

The Story Thus Far

After a terrible accident, Keina Kagami was only able to live off a machine.

With so much free time on her hands, she started playing the VRMMORPG *Leadale* and quickly became addicted to the joy and physical freedom it gave her. Along with Kee, the AI assistant her uncle created for her, Keina made a name for herself as a *Leadale* powerhouse. In the world of the game, she was a member of the rare high-elf race and a Skill Master who had obtained every possible skill.

One day, as her uncle and cousin's care for her weighed particularly heavily on her mind, a power outage shut down the equipment that was keeping Keina alive, and she soon perished.

…Or so one might think.

For reasons unknown, she awoke in an unfamiliar wooden room in the body of her game avatar. Naturally, Keina couldn't hide her confusion at suddenly becoming Cayna, her *Leadale* character.

Here she met the plucky yet motherly inn proprietress, Marelle, and her cheerfully helpful daughter Lytt.

After talking with the two, Keina realized she was in one of the inn towns of *Leadale*'s former White Kingdom. She was surprised to learn that there were now three kingdoms as opposed to seven and that this town was nothing like it had been in the game; instead, it had become nothing more than a poor, remote farming village. She decided to stay there for a while and used this time to improve the local water supply, take down some bears, build a public bath, and then take down even more bears.

Just as Cayna was thinking about moving on to a bigger town, a wagon caravan of merchants came to the village. She used her superior Magic Skills to heal a badly wounded mercenary guard traveling with the caravan, and her extraordinary healing prowess caught the eyes of the mercenary captain, Arbiter, and the head of the merchant caravan, Elineh.

The caravan had plans to go to Felskeilo, a main distribution point for goods, located in the center of the continent. Cayna decided to accompany them, all the while learning basic knowledge about this new world. During her travels, she reunited with her youngest son, Kartatz, who worked as a shipbuilder, got caught up in the capture of a prince, and made connections to a marquis.

Cayna then reunited with her daughter, Mai-Mai, headmistress of the Royal Academy, and was astonished to find she was already married. This rash of incidents led her to believe it might be the wrath of her terrible friend.

She discovered a Guardian Tower while taking on a request from the Adventurers Guild and subsequently discovered that there were no longer any other *Leadale* game players left, the shock of which caused her to hole up in her room at Marelle's inn.

However, her eldest son, Skargo, now a powerful High Priest (a title that really must have been some sort of sick joke on the Admins' part) and master of bizarre Effect Skills, soon came calling. His incredibly impactful visit relieved Cayna of her worries, leading her to have an honest conversation with her three children and forge new (for Cayna, at least) familial bonds.

She then met up with Elineh, who asked her to serve as a guard on the caravan's journey to the northern nation of Helshper, which was currently overrun with bandits.

On the way there, they stopped back at the inn town where Cayna rescued a lost mermaid from an underground water vein and left her in the villagers' care.

When the caravan arrived at the Helshper border, Cayna and her allies soundly defeated a group of bandits disguised as sentries. The whims of an unknown individual brought her to cross swords with Arbiter, but by reaffirming the extent of her own physical abilities, Cayna managed to swiftly deal with the issue.

However, the flickering shadow of a certain player deepened her suspicions.

Prologue

After the mock battle with Arbiter that reaffirmed Cayna's battle prowess, Cayna found that her mind was spinning for the rest of the trip to Helshper.

The primary source of her consternation was the psychological magic that an unknown figure had used the other day at the campground. Since Cayna herself hadn't been affected at all, she was under the impression it was a low-level attack.

However, her magical resistance was so strong that no one in the entire continent could ever hope to match it. More importantly, this attack seemed incredibly effective on the mercenaries and ordinary citizens. As proof of this, Arbiter and his men simply thought they got a bit carried away last night without actually understanding the reason for their elation.

The spell's effects also seemed to center around the group that had focused on Cayna. Everyone else in the caravan who had remained a distance away and the Flame Spear co-leader who had been watching over them didn't seem the least bit affected.

"Nghhh…"

"Hey, miss. You tired from using too much magic?"

"Pardon?"

Arbiter must have taken her yawning and glum expression as a sign of magical overexertion. Cayna had been continuously using Movement Up ever since they crossed the border, and a lot of people in the caravan were worried about her.

It wouldn't be unusual for most mages to collapse under the stress of maintaining such a spell for even half a day. Of course, for someone like Cayna with MP in the tens of millions, it would be surprising if she used up even 1 percent of her magic after going the whole day like this. She'd been using the skill MP Healing since the very beginning of the trip in order to stay fully replenished, so it really wasn't the least bit of a burden.

"No, no, I'm just fine. This is way easier than Attack Magic."

"...Yeah, but still, y'know?" Arbiter said as he looked out over the caravan.

The mercenaries were keeping a close eye on their surroundings. But they weren't the only ones affected by Cayna's Movement Up spell; it affected *everyone*.

Take the horses, for example. And the wagons and carriages. And the families of the merchants who were relaxing inside those carriages. With all these subjects under the effects of the spell, anyone would wonder if the caster was exhausted.

Arbiter looked reasonably doubtful as he tried to glean Cayna's condition from her expression.

"I'm okay, really. I'll be sure to let you know if I'm getting tired."

"But weren't you zoning out just now?"

Bull's-eye. Cayna averted her gaze.

"There's just a little something I've been worrying about. It has nothing to do with our journey, of course."

Cayna insisted fervently that her uneasiness was completely unrelated to their travels. Arbiter nodded reluctantly before leaving her side, and Cayna stroked her chest.

Yikes, that was terrifying! Arbiter was staring me down.

"That is to be expected of a mercenary leader. He is extra-ordinarily perceptive."

Kee made a good point, but it wasn't like she could always keep up with every mysterious behavior.

They hadn't seen any signs of bandits since entering Helshper, but they weren't out of the woods yet.

Cayna put "that idiot" out of her mind and instead focused on strengthening the caravan's defenses.

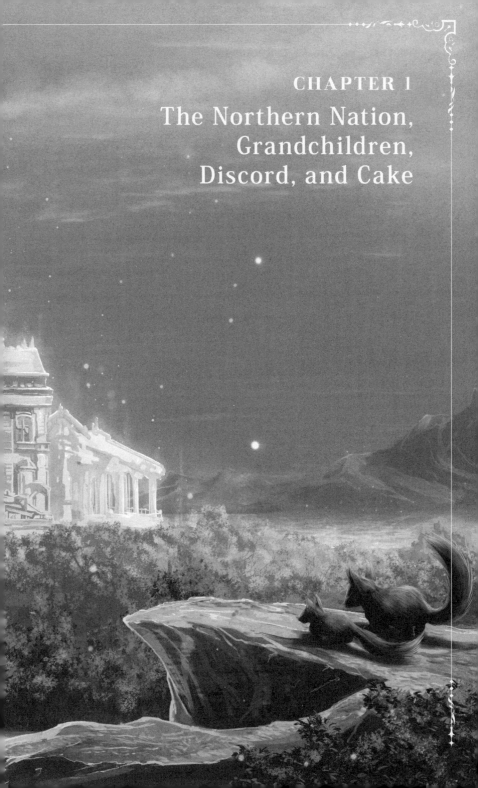

CHAPTER 1
The Northern Nation, Grandchildren, Discord, and Cake

Despite Cayna's and Arbiter's various doubts, they did not run into any more bandits before reaching the Helshper capital. There were a few monster attacks, but the mercenaries were able to easily drive them off thanks to Cayna's magical support.

Such enemies were no big deal for her, but for those who traveled for a living, even a single horned bear posed a credible threat. With the boost of a single Buff spell, the mercenaries' faith in Cayna as a mage increased by the day.

Although it had been a bit of a wild ride, the caravan reached Helshper's royal capital about eight days after departing the remote village.

Entering the country with a crimson pig (piglet, rather) seemed like it might be problematic, so Cayna dispelled it just before they arrived at the border. She further lightened the load on the wagons and horses; once the caravan replaced the horse they'd lost earlier, they wouldn't need the crimson pig on the return trip.

Unlike Felskeilo, Helshper's capital was built at the base of gently sloping mountains. The royal castle, surrounded by forest, overlooked the town. One might think this setup would be detrimental to the capital's defenses, but the forestation was actually intentional. Apparently, the castle guards would be notified the moment any suspicious person entered the forest and could swiftly apprehend them.

Of course, the castle wasn't the only place with greenery. The town itself was verdant as well, with the dense woods characteristic of Swiss villas or the Japanese city of Takayama. Countless carriages came and went as the sweet scent of fruit wafted along the breeze. Various fruit-bearing trees had been planted throughout the town, and people were free to pick whatever fruit they wanted. The only rule was that you couldn't litter the area with any of the seeds.

"This region is known for its fruit. I'm sure you'll take a liking to it, Lady Cayna," said Elineh.

"Do all the trees on those slopes bear fruit?"

"Yes, I believe so. The fruit are all the same variety, but there are many ways to eat them, whether raw or made into jams. You ought to go take a look for yourself when you have the chance."

Regardless, Cayna was getting a good view of the trees as they spoke.

She felt there was something odd about the imposing, blindingly white castle that loomed over the town. The fact that the ramparts were made from Western-style stone blocks the size of a human being was fine enough. However, the radiant, towering castle building was Japanese—it looked exactly like Himeji Castle. Furthermore, on either side of the structure were two enormous windmills that were even taller than the castle itself.

"Wowww, what's up with *that*?"

Cayna could only manage a smirk as she took in the sight of this haphazard fusion of East and West. It was anyone's guess as to what era and what world such chaos even came from.

Of course, Cayna was the only one who held this opinion.

"Ah, come to think of it, that castle is quite similar to one that used to be in the Felskeilo scrapyard. I never noticed," Elineh noted.

"Oh yeah, that thing," said Arbiter. "I heard it was once a Helshper fortress."

"A fortress… Maybe it belonged to the Purple Kingdom's Heartbeat of the Dawn guild? Those guys were always big on making all their stuff samurai-esque, weapons included."

As Cayna dug deep into her Game Era memories, the capital guards wrapped up their inspection of the caravan, which then passed through the gate into the capital proper. From there, Elineh's group continued down the central road that split the town into north and south.

Unlike Felskeilo's capital, this road here could accommodate horse-drawn carriages. After all, aside from the paths set into the slopes and those used to connect the eastern and western gates, everything else was undulating hills. If a horse could no longer support its carriage's load, it might run wild downhill. Once that happened, there'd be no stopping it.

On the northern side of this road were merchants' shops and the noble district; to the south, the marketplace and the residential district with its expansive Grecian-style townscape that continued all the way to the foothills. The numerous lakes and tributaries surrounding the district made for a lush, refreshing vista.

As Cayna stared awestruck at the brilliant contrast of blue and green, Elineh and Arbiter called to her in turn.

"Come to think of it, Lady Cayna, you were asked to deliver a letter to someone, correct?"

"You know someone around here, miss?"

Cayna tried to recall the name Mai-Mai had mentioned.

The name was—

"The name is Caerick of Sakaiya, Cayna," Kee answered without a moment's delay.

Since he remained quiet until needed, she often forgot he was there.

She gave a silent thank-you as she replied to Elineh and Arbiter. "They go by the name of Caerick, from a place called Sakaiya."

As soon as she said the name, Elineh looked astonished. Arbiter, on the other hand, accepted it in stride.

"I dunno whether nothing surprises me anymore or if I just don't have it in me to be shocked," he said.

"Even your circle of acquaintances is extraordinary, Lady Cayna. In that case, I have business to conduct with this individual as well. If it is not too much trouble, allow us to accompany you."

"Thanks, I appreciate it."

Cayna bowed her head, and the rest of the caravan set to work. Some went to get carts to transport the luggage while others began to check the luggage itself. Others still unhitched the horses and took them to their boarding stables. Arbiter left half of the mercenary squad behind to guard the carriages, then went to secure lodging for everyone at the local inn.

"Well then, Mr. Elineh, I'll reserve your usual place. You'll have your own room as well, miss."

"Thank you, Arbiter."

"No need to thank me. You're one of us now. We're all in this together through thick and thin." He scratched at his cheek with a wry smile.

Since they were headed to the same place, and there was little chance of getting into a fight in town, Cayna was entrusted with escorting Elineh.

She was indeed the strongest among the group, but...

Once Elineh left the caravan with Cayna following close behind, she was so pumped up that she couldn't focus. Other towns had plenty of changes since the Game Era themselves, but here the difference was like night and day.

Her reaction was the same as when they'd arrived in Felskeilo. Elineh grinned.

"Ah, I'm sorry," said Cayna. "I'm supposed to be guarding you, yet my focus is all over the place..."

"As long as you watch out for pickpockets, that will be enough. It seems that you truly don't know much about the modern world, Lady Cayna."

"It's embarrassing to admit, but I really am more of a country girl."

As they headed toward the Merchants Guild, Elineh explained some of the capital's intricacies—in particular, the line connecting the windmill on the gently sloping hill next to them with one of the lakes. It appeared to be a mere line upon first glance, but Cayna's Eagle Eyes noticed it was some sort of log shape. She couldn't make out the details, though.

"The Helshper capital is also known as Windmill City and the City of Skills. Since the water source is so low, the windmills draw up water-filled tubes made from logs and use that water to supply each part of the city."

"Hmm. Don't they have wells?"

At Cayna's question, Elineh pointed to the conspicuously large two-bladed windmills on either side of the castle.

"That's what those are for. I hear they reach unfathomable depths."

"...Whoaaa..."

Cayna was deeply impressed by the industriousness this required. She recalled the passionate technicians she'd once met at Marelle's inn and regretted not taking them seriously enough.

"I'll give a proper explanation next time I see them...," she mumbled.

Elineh gave a pained smile as he wondered if the girl was too much of a bleeding heart.

The Merchants Guild was a pure-white dome-shaped building that was evocative of a white *daifuku*.

17

Once inside, Elineh and Cayna informed the receptionist of their business and handed over the personal effects of the Helshper guards who had perished at the hands of the bandits to a guild employee. The employee hurriedly reported this to their superior, and the two were led to another room. It was here that the elderly white-haired head of the guild entered with his secretary.

"I've heard quite the unbelievable tale. So it was you?"

"Bless my soul, if it isn't the head of the guild himself. What an honor."

If Elineh was even acquainted with the head of a foreign guild, there was no doubt he was an incredible merchant. Elineh took a seat on the sofa while Cayna, impressed anew by his prowess, stood behind him as his escort.

He proceeded to explain to the guild leader at length the incident with the bandits at the eastern border: their numbers, how they were dealt with, and how the mercenaries had taken express care to bury the murdered border guards.

Just to be safe, Elineh made no mention of Cayna's magic. After all, once she'd defeated the bandits' mage, he'd melted into nothing more than a stain in the ground. They had no way of proving what had happened.

As the elderly man listened, he had the secretary write everything down. The crease across his brow deepened. Finally, Elineh said, "This is what the perpetrator wielded," and placed the wand of the defeated bandit leader on the table. Elineh and Arbiter had decided to hand it over to the nation of Helshper.

Arbiter had thought the wand might prove to be a secret weapon for the mercenary group while Elineh felt it might make a fine addition to his wares. Alas, its origins were just a bit too eerie. Holding on to the wand would run the risk of miring the caravan in a scandal, so they decided it was best to turn it over to Helshper officials as evidence.

Items from the Game Era seemed to be considered Artifacts in this world, and the guild leader immediately contacted his higher-ups to properly deal with the situation. Before long, the Helshper knights would be dispatched to the border. The guild leader also asked Elineh to recount the details of the bandit incident to Helshper government officials.

"We're going to have to report the same thing to a lot of people, aren't we?" Cayna said to Elineh.

"Well," he replied, "that's simply how bureaucracy works."

Cayna could only sigh at the thought of having to repeat the same story over and over. Elineh was the one who'd have to deal with all the questioning, but she wondered if maybe there was some sort of magical copy machine they could use.

"Now then, our next stop is Sakaiya, correct?" Elineh asked her in confirmation. As soon as they left the Merchants Guild, he stretched and gave his shoulders a good thump. The guild leader's unexpected appearance seemed to have left him mentally drained.

He then led Cayna to a wide, imposing building that stretched out to the left and right. Even for a mercantile house, it took up a huge amount of land. It was about five times the size of an average house. It also had a different design compared to the surrounding buildings. The plain white walls were the same as the others, but it had a tiled isosceles triangle roof. Set up by the side of the road were the sort of small tents used by the Romani people, which seemed to be temporary storage space.

A large group of people—either vendors or laborers, Cayna couldn't tell—were carrying items back and forth between the building and tents. Their chorus of chanting and clapping alone was rather boisterous.

The group contained a hodgepodge of races: a human shouldering four boxes at once; a dragoid performing calculations on an abacus; several kobolds pulling a cart; a werecat sitting cross-legged atop a pile of packages while smoking tobacco from a pipe. It was a scene that gave one the vague impression everyone knew exactly what their roles were.

"What's with the East-meets-West deal here…?"

"East meets West… That has an interesting ring to it."

Elineh tilted his head at Cayna's exasperated murmurings. Unsure of how to answer, she tried explaining that the phrase was used to describe the mixing of two different cultures. He considered this carefully, looked at the building once more, and nodded deeply.

"Yes, I see. East meets West. I've thought for some time that something seemed off. That must be the reason. I understand now."

Wait, what?

Cayna had been certain he would have wanted a more elaborate answer, but he'd been quick to accept her explanation. It was kind of anticlimactic.

Elineh easily slipped past a dragoid laborer and some dwarven and kobold apprentices darting about with various packages. Cayna tried to follow, but he was so short that she worried she'd accidently kick him.

Finally, Elineh found the main entrance where the vendors were directing the laborers back and forth.

"Cayna, do you know anything about Sakaiya?"

"Not one bit."

"……"

Perhaps it was because she'd answered with such brazen honesty that Elineh grew speechless and put his head in his hands. Adventurers depended on the famous Sakaiya for tools, since it had branches in every nation, as well as guards to protect them. The fact that this self-proclaimed country bumpkin didn't even know that much was rather pitiful.

"In my entire life as a merchant, I've never met someone who hasn't heard of Sakaiya."

"Huh…?"

According to Elineh, Sakaiya was a mercantile house that was absolutely vital to the nation of Helshper. Its reach extended across the continent, and it touted a long line of merchants who had significant influence in the Merchants Guild. In fact, one might say Sakaiya *created* the Merchants Guild. The company dealt in practically everything under the sun, from a single grain of wheat to magical tools.

The last thing a merchant ever wanted was to fall on Sakaiya's bad side, so all dealings were conducted with extreme prudence. Since Cayna admitted she didn't know any of that, Elineh decided it was best that she stay quiet and concentrate on her guard duties so as not to further blow her cover.

He couldn't let anyone find out about the massive bomb he was keeping under wraps.

As they approached the entrance, Elineh stopped an elf boy who was running errands for the merchants.

"Might I have a minute?"

"Oh! Why, Master Elineh, it's been some time. You wish to see the young master, yes? I will call for him, so please wait just a moment!"

Elineh nodded in satisfaction as the very sight of him caused the elf boy to run inside and fetch the owner.

After seeing how her kobold partner could obtain the audience of a high-status individual by his very presence, Cayna felt with internal trepidation that he probably wasn't someone she wanted to mess with.

"Oh my, Master Elineh. Considering the state of things this year, how in the world did you make it to Helshper?"

"I've made quite a few valuable connections. Friends truly are a blessing."

The man known as the young master, who exchanged pleasantries with Elineh before moving to the business at hand, was a dignified-looking elf. Although most elves had gold or silver hair, his was a rare black, and he had brown eyes.

Meanwhile, Cayna listened in and resigned herself to the fact that she'd never have gotten this far if she had just shown up on her own.

The conversation continued in this vein until finally they exchanged a firm handshake, putting an end to their negotiations.

"Is the master here today by any chance?" Elineh asked. "I have a letter for him from Felskeilo."

"A letter? Would you mind if I took a look at it myself?"

"Not at all."

Elineh handed Cayna's letter to the elf. He turned it over, and his cheek twitched the moment he saw who it was addressed to.

"One—one moment, please!"

Despite having been the picture of tranquility just seconds before, the elf tossed all that out the window in a fluster. Elineh and Cayna exchanged bewildered looks.

After waiting for some time, the elf came racing back. It must have been an unusual sight, for the other people inside the shop appeared equally bewildered by his demeanor.

Elineh and Cayna were urged farther into the store and led through a long hallway into a quiet room full of subdued furnishings. They took a seat on the sofa as indicated and once again tilted their heads in astonishment. Before them stood a handsome male elf even more dignified than the previous one.

Being an elf, his youthful looks were a given, but there was something about him that was leagues more impressive than the elf they'd just spoken with. This one had the dark hair and eyes typical of a Japanese person. His familiar coloring put Cayna's mind at ease.

"Well met, Master Caerick. It's been quite some time."

"It has indeed, Sir Elineh. I hear your wiles are as sharp as ever."

Elineh went to rise from the sofa and give a deep bow, but this man known as Caerick raised a single hand and implored him to relax. Caerick seemed to represent Sakaiya itself.

Everything was proceeding smoothly until the dark-haired elf suddenly stepped in front of Cayna and bowed deeply. The shock of it all nearly made Elineh's heart fly out of his chest.

Caerick of Sakaiya, who was considered to be something of a god among merchants, had established the Merchants Guild one hundred years prior and set up trade routes among the three nations. He had been an acquaintance of Elineh's father and had mentored Elineh in the ways of business. As far as Elineh knew, aside from royalty, Caerick bowed to no one.

Having heard all this on the way to Helshper, urgent alarm bells were now blaring inside Cayna's mind.

With no time to react, his next words swept away all thought.

"It is a great pleasure to meet you at last, Grandmother. I am Caerick Sakai, the son of your daughter, Mai-Mai."

".........Pardon?"

"Mother has told me much of your renown. It is a true honor to meet a treasured Guardian such as yourself."

Elineh was struck dumb by this sudden revelation, overcome with almost the same amount of shock as when he learned Cayna was a mother of three.

Speechless and wide-eyed next to him, Cayna was even more panicked.

If he's Mai-Mai's son, doesn't that make him my grandson?! I'm seventeen years old and already have a grandkid— Hang on, this means

Mai-Mai's probably been married once before, so chances are good that there's even more grandkids, and great-grandkids are gonna pop up one after the other, and if Caerick's already got kids, that'll make me a great-grandmother... Ah-ha, ha-ha-ha...

She remained frozen stiff as sweat poured down her like a waterfall.

Since it was his second time going through this, Elineh managed to recover and curiously glanced over at the wordless Cayna. Naturally, her condition was not lost on Caerick, either.

"...Lady Cayna?"

"Grandmother?"

Elineh thought it strange that she didn't move even the slightest muscle, and he took the liberty to wave his hand in front of her eyes.

No response.

After a forceful rap on the shoulder, she instantly came back to her senses. Cayna took a single deep breath and once again turned to the elf merchant.

Silky black hair and a deep, dark gaze. His eyes were reminiscent of Mai-Mai more than any other feature. Cayna said nothing as her expression twisted, and both Caerick and Elineh frowned.

"I knew it—you've exhausted yourself from continuously using magic on our way here, haven't you?"

"My, how terrible! You must be weary indeed! I shall prepare a room for you that is much finer than anything a shabby inn might offer, so please do have a rest."

"Ah, no, I'm all right. I just wasn't expecting this sort of shocking revelation... I'm not letting Mai-Mai off the hook this time..."

Now that she had recovered, Elineh sensed a dark aura coming from her and averted his gaze.

For some reason, Cayna was suddenly emitting an incredibly overpowering force from deep within. Struck with the full brunt of her malice, Caerick stood there petrified. Even Elineh could tell that much.

"Besides, I feel much more comfortable in a shabby inn, so please—*don't worry about it.*"

As someone who knew Cayna better than Caerick did, Elineh recognized the thorniness to her tone.

Her grandson Caerick's simple statement had set Cayna off, and a storm now roiled within her. Kee was able to pacify her to some degree, allowing only the overpowering aura to manifest physically.

Cayna was extremely fond of both Marelle's inn and the cheap lodgings in Felskeilo, so she was very much looking forward to staying at a foreign inn—the unassuming yet delicious food, the banter among adventurers, and the students working to put themselves through school. For someone like Cayna, who had spent over half her life unable to feed herself, visiting the local marketplace with its traditional blue-collar charm to enjoy the food was something of a pastime of hers.

Marelle's slow-simmered vegetable soup in particular had the comforting flavor of a home-cooked meal. Hearing all these things disparaged as shabby really ticked Cayna off, even if it was rather childish of her to react that way.

It didn't matter that Caerick was a merchant of significant renown and influence. Nor did it matter that he claimed to be her grandson. To Cayna, he was an absolute stranger. Mai-Mai had kept the existence of her son a secret and tried to surprise her mother with a face-to-face meeting. But even Mai-Mai couldn't have anticipated that Caerick might say something so offensive that Cayna would immediately come to dislike him.

And that was precisely why Cayna was so grumpy. Even though his first chance encounter with his grandmother should have been an emotional, heartfelt one, Caerick cowered under the pressure of Cayna's Intimidate skill that automatically kicked in. In the bedtime stories his mother had told him, Cayna was one of the thirteen Guardians of old—and a most wicked executioner who would "blow even her own kin to smithereens if wronged in any way." (These were all just stories Mai-Mai made up to frighten him into behaving.)

Caerick began to panic as he wondered where he had erred.

Stuck between the two, Elineh had no choice but to somehow intervene. He whisked the irritable Cayna away from Sakaiya as fast as his legs would carry him.

There was no chance of calming her without first knowing the cause of her ire. Elineh took Cayna, still trembling with anger, over to an inn he always stayed at whenever he visited Helshper.

"Oh! If it isn't Sir Elineh. Now we can really get things started!"

"Come join in, too, miss!"

The Flame Spears were throwing a drinking party in broad daylight to recover from the trip. This happened all the time, so it wasn't a particularly unusual scene. What *was* different, however, were the three knights interviewing everyone in the caravan. Elineh and Cayna had apparently been at Sakaiya so long that the Helshper knights had already arrived to begin questioning.

An associate of Elineh's who had joined the caravan pointed the kobold out as he entered the inn. The knights nodded and walked over to him.

Of the three, their captain seemed to be the elf woman. For some reason, she kept glancing over at Cayna.

"Are you the one supervising this caravan?" she asked Elineh.

"Ah, you must be the knights the Merchants Guild spoke of. It's a pleasure to meet you. My name is Elineh."

"I am Caerina of the Helshper knights. I apologize for my brevity, but I wish to ask about the incident at the eastern border."

"Yes, I would be happy to answer any questions you may have. First…"

Cayna left his side and headed toward the merrymaking mercenaries. She plopped down in an empty seat. Even though she was trying to keep it under wraps, anyone could tell from her intense brooding that she was in a bad mood.

"What's up, miss? Someone in the crowd cop a feel on ya?"

"Kick the bastard right where the sun don't shine!"

"Don't tell me ya let yer magic loose on someone, did ya?"

"No, I didn't! Someone made fun of the things I love. I'm just mad, okay?!"

"Well, I bet a good meal will fix that right up. Hey, over here! Proprietress! Bring this li'l lady some of your famous fixin's!"

Surrounded by trusted friends, Cayna was finally able to quell her turbulent emotions. After a single taste of the stew the mercenaries had ordered, her mood improved in the blink of an eye.

Once it was clear that Cayna had returned to her usual mild-mannered self, the mercenaries heaved a sigh of relief. After witnessing her incredible magical prowess just the other day, they knew her true strength was no joke. As kind and good-natured as she normally was, Cayna was downright scary once you set her off. Cayna's rage was terrifying to behold—all the more so if a third party incurred her wrath.

Cayna herself had no idea that everyone present was merely placating her with food.

"Mmmm, that was amazing!"

"Pardon me for interrupting your meal, Lady Cayna, but might you come with me for a moment?"

Just as Cayna had her fill of a simple yet satisfying stew, Elineh finished his initial conversation with the knights and called her over. She did as requested.

Among the three who had initially approached them, only the captain, the female elf Caerina, remained.

Of the continent's three modern nations, Helshper was home to many races both human and nonhuman. The nation's royal family was human, but elves in particular held positions of power. Of course, dwarves and dragoids served important roles as well, but not quite as often as elves.

This knight named Caerina was one such influential elf. The moment Cayna sat down next to Elineh, Caerina got to her feet before kneeling and bowing her head. There was no question it was an outlandish gesture that shocked all present.

Cayna was reminded of the incident back at Sakaiya and held a hand to her forehead as if she could sense another oncoming headache.

"H-hold it. Why are you bowing all of a sudden?!"

"It seems that my younger brother has displeased you greatly, so I shall apologize in his stead! Please forgive him, Grandmother!"

"Huh…? Uh…what?!"

Being called Grandmother twice in one day left Cayna at a loss for words. When she took a closer look, she did notice that Caerina bore a striking resemblance to Caerick. She was pretty sure not many elves looked so Japanese.

"You're related to *that jerk*, right?"

"Correct. I am Caerina Sakai, Caerick's elder twin sister. Still, to call him '*that jerk*' is quite something… My brother must have offended you greatly."

Caerina stood up, crossed her arms, and heaved a sigh.

Her reaction to Caerick's behavior was rather swift, even if they were siblings. Elineh had some questions. After all, the time it took

for Cayna and Elineh to return to the inn after visiting Caerick and the amount of time Caerina had been here at the inn didn't match up.

"You certainly seem well-informed, even though the incident only happened a short while ago... Did you stop by Sakaiya on the way here?" asked Elineh.

"No, it's simply because we're twins. We can communicate with each other even from far away."

"Ah, so you're using Special Skill: Telepathy...," said Cayna.

"Indeed, Grandmother. Mother has called the ability by such a name."

Even for a Skill Master such as Cayna, there were skills even she could not pass on to others with Special Skill: Scroll Creation. Telepathy was one of them.

In the world of the game, this was a joke skill that allowed either siblings or parents and their children to message one another in seventy-five characters or fewer.

The process you had to go through to get the skill was a real pain. First, you and a good friend had to decide what your relationship would be, then you had to contact the Admins. This was a mechanism that ensured Telepathy could only be used between two consenting parties who established a fictional blood relationship. Basically, it was like making a blood promise, entering a sister pact, or swearing an oath in the Peach Garden.

Cayna had formed contracts with "siblings" in the game, but her Telepathy hadn't shown any signs of communication from them since entering this new era.

Of course, she hadn't tried sending them any messages, either, so she couldn't just arbitrarily decide that they'd broken off contact with her.

It was a little baffling that her children somehow had this skill, even though she had no memory of ever using it with them. When

31

Cayna had first reunited with Skargo and the others, they had whined about how she didn't answer their messages, but since she'd never made the pact with any of them, she'd had no way of responding. Back then, she had no choice but to play it off with a plausible lie.

All three of them totally believed that lame excuse that I forgot to respond because of the Isolation Barrier...

Caerick had been the one to incite Cayna's fury, so she had no intention of taking her anger out on Caerina. The sister wasn't the least bit responsible for her brother's rudeness, so Cayna accepted her apology fully.

Caerina looked extremely relieved to hear this. Curious, Cayna asked why.

"My mother used to always tell us of your demonic wrath—or how you'd blow your own kin to smithereens if wronged in any way..."

"I most certainly do not!!"

Despite this strong denial, the peanut gallery—Elineh and the mercenaries—chimed in.

"Miss... That's pretty awful."

"To think Lady Cayna used to do such terrible things..."

"I—I didn't!! Do I really look like some monster who just murders people on a whim?"

The mercenaries, however, exchanged glances, and after a beat, they agreed in unison:

""""What about those ice flowers?""""

"*Come onnnn!* Why're you all ganging up on me like that?!"

Cayna's flustered reactions were so funny that Arbiter and his men couldn't help teasing her a bit to lighten the mood.

...However, it wasn't long before their teasing went too far. They soon unleashed her imperial wrath and opened the gates of hell.

"HA-HA-HA! SO THAT'S HOW IT'S GONNA BE, HUH?! I CAN GET MAD NOW, RIGHT?!"

"Wait! Calm down, miss! Gently put down that thing in your hand!"

"Where'd she even get that giant snowball?!"

"Huh? Uh, what?"

Snowballs the size of a person's head popped up all around Cayna. Apparently, hell had frozen over but was still hell, nonetheless.

"It seems that everyone here is drunk. I hope one drop will be enough to wake you all up."

"Just look at us! We're all obviously sober!"

"That ain't one drop at all!"

"Hey, boss, why don't you do something…? Damn, he's gone!"

"He saved his own hide!"

"Now firing."

""""GYAAAAAAAAAAGH?!"""""

Needless to say, the mercenaries in the inn all turned into snowmen. Furthermore, the tale of how Caerina got wrapped up in it all is a story for another day.

◆

Elineh and his caravan would be in Helshper for ten days to conduct their mercantile business. During this time, the Flame Spears would work in shifts among small groups of escorts. Cayna's assistance would be needed only for the return trip, so until then, she could do as she pleased.

"You may go sightseeing, do work for the Guild, or anything else that suits your fancy."

That was what Elineh had told her, but since Cayna had plenty of money left over from her gaming days, money really wasn't an issue.

Just then, one of Elineh's apprentices, a young merchant in training named Lidy, came back with bunches of firewood.

"Hi, Miss Cayna. I went and bought ten bundles of firewood for now."

"Ten?!" Her eyes widened at the stack of lumber.

"Well, it is what it is. You said so yourself that it's not as if we can make them ourselves whenever we please."

"I guess I did say that... How many logs are in one bundle?"

"Good question. I'm not really sure," he replied brightly as he unveiled one pile of wood after the other.

There were sixteen or seventeen logs in each one. The inn had been cleaned out of firewood, and the logs collected by Elineh's caravan piled up on the dining hall floor.

Cayna took one and cast Craft Skill: Processing: Buddha on it.

A small green tornado completely enveloped the log that was about the width of a person's arms, and in an instant, it created an exquisite wooden image of Miroku Bosatsu. She then cast the same spell on another log to create Yakushi Nyorai.

Cayna went on picking up one log after the other and placed the finished products on the tables around her. Soon enough, the tables were buried under her series of Buddha statues. Lidy and his companions organized them by type and gently packed them away in boxes. About an hour later, 160 pieces of wood had been turned into Buddha statues.

"Phew, I'm beat!"

"Good work, Miss Cayna."

"That was a fine job, Lady Cayna. You can expect a forty percent share of the profits."

"You think people will actually buy these, though?"

Cayna was following up on Elineh's suggestion of selling the statues after he first saw her create them in the remote village. The process hardly left a dent in her MP, nor was it physically taxing, but the idea of putting them up for sale stressed Cayna out. Her main concern was what they'd do if the statues didn't sell, let alone even catch people's attention.

"How much will these go for, Elineh?"

"Five silver coins for a single statue, I'd say."

As soon as Lidy heard his price, he shouted "That ain't cheap!" and Cayna couldn't help but smirk.

A single piece of firewood cost eight bronze coins. Ten bundles of firewood cost eighty bronze coins. If they sold their entire stock, it'd be at least 850 silver coins. Even for easy money, it was a ridiculous amount.

"No need to worry, Lady Cayna."

"Huh? What do you mean?"

"We'll market these as deities revered by the high elves. You won't find such a unique item anywhere else on the continent."

As Elineh said this, Cayna regretted not explaining the statues more carefully.

"...Still, what am I supposed to do, really?"

Armed with the map that a mercenary she'd befriended on the way to Helshper had drawn for her, Cayna headed to the Adventurers Guild in search of possible work for the day. Her goal had nothing to do with finances; she simply wanted to kill time.

"Whenever I look at this map, I get the distinct feeling I'm being sent on a fool's errand."

It was hard to say what this world's literacy rate was like, but the simplified map of the capital in Cayna's hands was a series of lines and dots. However, this wasn't the real issue. The real problem was that everything from ADVENTURERS GUILD to LODGING and MARKET were all in hiragana. It had the childish feel of a TV show that follows people with a hidden camera.

Helshper's Adventurers Guild was situated in a two-story building facing the main road in the residential district. As if it were some sort of established rule, it had the same exact three-tower formation as the guild in Felskeilo. The interior was also very similar, with the lounge located right at the entrance. Farther in was the reception area, and to the left was the signboard.

Just like any other guild, the board was filled with requests. A good third of them were merchants asking for someone to drive off the bandits along the outer western trade routes.

Since this was related to merchants and the story Elineh mentioned to her before, she tried gathering information from the fellow adventurers present.

There was a gray-scaled dragoid in heavy armor who carried a giant two-handed ax on his back. Next to him was a lightly equipped woman who carried a saber at her waist and a whip around her arm. Cayna called out to them.

"Um, excuse me."

"Hmm? What's up, little miss? You're pretty tiny for an adventurer."

"Everyone looks tiny compared to you," his partner added.

The two seemed to be working together. Cayna had fully given up on dealing with the whole "little miss" issue. Perhaps thinking she might be more comfortable talking to another woman, the dragoid's partner turned to Cayna.

"I haven't seen you around these parts before. Did you just get your license?"

"No, I've come from Felskeilo."

"Considering the situation going on right now, it's pretty amazing you made it all the way here. Did you use the outer trade routes to the east? Seems like the bridge there collapsed, though."

"We were able to cross the river without a bridge."

"Well, it certainly sounds like you know what you're doing. So what can we help you with?"

CHAPTER 1

"I heard there's a castle in the middle of a lake somewhere in Helshper. Do you know where I might find it?"

The dragoid warrior responded by pointing to the map on the Guild announcement board to the right side of the room. It was a simplified, portrait-style map of Helshper. Several small lakes and narrow rivers were marked here and there south of the capital, and below this was a red line. It seemed that about 30 percent of the entire map was marked as dangerous.

"Ah, you must mean Crescent Moon Castle. If that's what you're looking for, they say it's controlled by a den of thieves. It's off-limits, so you can't go in now. It should be south of that red line."

"Why is it called Crescent Moon Castle?"

"I'm not entirely sure, but the entire castle shines on the night of a full moon. There's rumors that it hides a vault of ancient treasures, but the old fogies are downright terrified of the place. They call it the Hall of the Guardian."

This was exactly the kind of info Cayna had been looking for. Of course, an over-two-hundred-year-old elf like herself would know more about this Guardian Tower. On the other hand, if further people learned she was the Silver Ring Witch, that would only cause her greater trouble. Therefore, Cayna had no choice but to avoid prying any further. She wanted to know more of the details, but this tidbit was fortuitous enough.

"Thank you very much." Cayna bowed her head to the pair in gratitude.

"No worries. I mean, this stuff's all common knowledge anyhow."

The woman smiled and waved at Cayna. Her dragoid partner, however, was studying Cayna's face intently.

"Um, is something the matter?" she asked.

"No, it's noth— GWAGH?!"

37

The dragoid man was about to say something, but the sudden elbow strike from his partner stopped him in his tracks.

"Don't mind this guy. He's just a creep who has a bad habit of staring at girls until his eyes bore straight through 'em."

Even Cayna was naturally put off by this.

"Huh? Uh, oh, I see."

She looked at them both with an uncomprehending, troubled expression and left the Adventurers Guild.

As the woman waved good-bye to Cayna, her dragoid partner finally caught his breath and sighed.

"No matter how you slice it, she's definitely a suspicious one," she stated.

"*Cough*... What was that for, idiot?!"

At any rate, the angry dragoid protested no further and merely crossed his arms. A dragoid's face was hard to read, but he was clearly dissatisfied.

"Don't just randomly accuse me of bein' a creep."

"Sorry, my bad. But I had to say somethin'. You were bein' rude."

The woman's sisterly tone from earlier was completely gone. She now sounded more like just one of the guys.

"Kinda feels like I've met her somewhere before...," the dragoid commented.

"Sheesh, what's with the cheesy pickup line? She's an elf. Obviously, she's gonna be pretty."

The dragoid tilted his headed and insisted that he wasn't trying to flirt and really had thought he'd seen the girl somewhere before. However, his partner paid zero attention to this and replied, "You *always* go for the elves." The dragoid finally gave up and slumped his shoulders. "Your true self is showing," he cautioned in earnest, not as a means of payback for her rudeness.

Just as she was about to retort, she clapped a hand to her mouth and began mumbling, "I'm a woman, I'm a woman, I'm a woman…" This was a ritual that occurred each time her true colors slipped, but to her partner, who knew the situation, she was only getting what she deserved.

There was no question it was a truly unfortunate scenario that was more than "Something unfortunate happened." However, there was nothing anyone could do about it, so he had to just let her be.

Once the dragoid saw that she'd recovered from her self-soothing, the two of them left the Adventurers Guild.

They were also losing work from the recent issues with bandits. And yet, hoping others would do something about it only made them keenly aware of their own incompetence.

After leaving the Guild, Cayna wandered aimlessly around town wondering what she should do. A one-way trip to the castle in question would take about two days by horse, but if she used any of the options in her arsenal, she could arrive that same day.

At any rate, she had heard that the bandits were successfully evading the knights. Were Helshper's knights really that incompetent? Caerina was by far among the strongest people Cayna had met in Leadale. It was hard to believe that a bunch of bandits would get the better of her.

That said, the rest of the Helshper knights were slightly weaker than Arbiter. Cayna surmised that this brought down their abilities as a whole.

"Still, since this isn't the game anymore, I doubt anyone will quickly respond to a request to take the bandits down."

Cayna's concern was how people would react if she herself dealt with them.

Sudden betrayal was a painful thing.

After she became a Skill Master, she'd received proposals from people outside her Guild, like the players she hit it off with in the fields. They'd say, "How about giving me preferential treatment if we split the handling and referral fees?" Their aim was to accept quests and get the payout. This annoying occurrence had followed Cayna wherever she went.

She was already known as a Skill Master by that point, so she couldn't afford to be careless when dealing with players who flocked to her. However, whenever she asked players she had trusted about what she should do, that had been their answer every time.

The shock of it left her speechless. As a result, she retreated into the most remote regions and avoided any large gatherings of people outside her own Guild. It was probably preferable compared to her friends who fell into nervous breakdowns if they stopped playing.

Nevertheless, just because she'd had such experiences in the game, it was no reason to believe the people here would be the same. Befriending people like Elineh, who understood her aversion to being the center of attention, and Arbiter, who cautioned her to keep her immense power at bay, was truly a blessing, one she was extremely thankful for.

I bet even a merchant like Caerick has heard about this bandit situation.

"Is that really a wise decision? You shut him down pretty hard."

True… I feel guilty for snapping at him. Plus, it'd be in bad taste to see him right after what happened yesterday. Maybe I'll pay him a visit tomorrow and bring an apology gift.

"Wouldn't food be more appealing than an item?"

Oh yeah, the Merchants Guild already has everything you can think of. Maybe I'll get some fresh ingredients.

Cayna kept talking with Kee to keep herself from having any bad thoughts and headed toward the market. It was time to pick out a gift.

◆

Meanwhile.

In Skargo's office in the capital of Felskeilo, a completely worn-out, dead-eyed Mai-Mai collapsed on the table. Skargo's sister's condition obviously concerned him, and he thought about what he could do for her. However, if his mother, Cayna, was in any way the cause of her consternation, in his eyes, the scales would fall in his mother's favor.

There was indeed a reason for Mai-Mai's bewildered state. She had received a Telepathic message from Caerina the evening before. Excitedly thinking, *My children in Helshper must have had a touching first meeting with Mother,* she glanced over the brief missive.

However, what she actually found was: *Caerick made Grandmother angry. His life has just barely been spared. What should I do?*

Mai-Mai's sudden, violent fall from cloud nine filled her with despair, and the terror of an enraged Cayna returning to Felskeilo gripped the elf. Unable to keep still, she had rushed over to her older brother's place.

Upon hearing her explanation, Skargo's expression shifted as he considered whether defending his sister would direct their mother's rage toward himself.

Naturally, as someone who knew his sister had her reasons for coming to Felskeilo after leaving the children in Helshper, he had no intention of turning her away. Nonetheless, their mother's anger was a force of nature.

It'd be one thing if she was simply angry, but mix in Intimidate, and a person's mind was likely to break.

Had Cayna taken all that into account, Skargo and the others wouldn't be on such an emotional roller coaster.

Skargo placed a hand on the shoulder of his comatose sister and gave a refreshing smile of his pearly whites.

"I can only say you are reaping what you sow. Well, in any case, I shall apologize with you, so take heart."

"R-right. Thanks, Skargo."

Mai-Mai was rarely so honest and timid, and Skargo thought

that there was some cuteness to her after all. Simultaneously, Skargo's encouragement strengthened Mai-Mai, and she saw him in a slightly more brotherly light.

From their point of view, they would have liked to hear more of the details from Cayna herself with Telepathy, but since their mother lost the skill, there was no way to reach her. It wasn't known exactly how she lost it, but her children were convinced something must have happened two hundred years prior. Whatever the reason, Cayna had finally left her hideaway in the forest and reunited with them. Her three children hoped that from now on Cayna could live as she pleased.

◆

"Hey, you lot! How dare you!"

"Hmm?"

Cayna had just finished buying up all the Cooking Skill ingredients the Helshper market had to offer, and it was only by coincidence that she heard the angry voice call out.

Since money was no object to her, she had picked out everything from large bags of wheat to fruit used in recipes. This was exactly the type of market-destroying behavior Elineh had been concerned about.

As small business owners smiled tightly at the customer who bought up everything left and right, a commotion broke out on a corner of the main road lined with street stalls. Cayna put her purchases away into her Item Box one after the other and looked back at the source of the noise. She'd just leave things be if it didn't have anything to do with her, but it'd be another story if the street stall in question was lined with Buddha statues.

As she approached, an elf with a bow strapped across his back was parked in front of the stall. Spit went flying as he yelled at the troubled shop owner. People surrounded them at a distance. Half were worried observers, while the other half were amused onlookers.

"Who gave you permission to use the high elves' illustrious name?! This is an insult to my people!"

The elf pointed to several signs hanging from the tent poles. Written in huge letters were slogans like DEITIES REVERED BY THE HIGH ELVES and YOU WON'T FIND THESE BEAUTIES ANYWHERE ELSE!

Considering how personally the elf was taking this, elves must have still revered the high elves as they had back in the Game Era.

"I did get permission…"

"Liar! The high elves would never leave their village for the outside world!"

The vendor, a merchant like Elineh, couldn't win no matter what he said. The shop apprentices already spotted Cayna, and their eyes begged her to save them.

This is definitely gonna suck.

"It cannot be helped."

Kee gave her no choice but to intervene, and Cayna resigned herself to it. She approached the ranting elf.

"Hey there."

"Whaddaya want?! This ain't got nothin' to do with you, so get los…?!"

She called out from behind him, and as he turned around to look at her, the Active Skills Intimidate, Evil Eye, and Fear hit him like there was no tomorrow.

Alas, their difference in power was far too great, and the elf stopped in his tracks with wide eyes.

Cayna brushed back her hair and showed him the trademark short, pointed ears of a high elf before questioning him.

"I was the one who made the statues and allowed him to use the slogans. Is there some sort of problem?"

His eyes popping as far as they could go and his jaw slack, the elf man began to act strangely. His face grew paler and paler, he held his cautious stance without moving a muscle, and he said nothing.

As both the onlookers and Cayna tilted their heads in confusion, it was then that she realized the problem.

"...Maybe he can't breathe?" someone offered.

"Ah...!"

As Cayna hurriedly fixed her blunder and halted the Active Spells, the elf collapsed and began coughing violently.

The reason for this was the Evil Eye and Fear that had been cast on him. Evil Eye had a Faint effect. Even though the effect was called Faint, it was more like completely conking out. Fear paralyzed the target. With both of these in tandem, it had apparently restricted the elf's breathing.

He took deep gulps of fresh air and rejoined the world of the living, but Cayna felt sorry for him as he flinched back at the revelation that she was a high elf.

"I-I'm terribly sorry for my shameful actions before your great countenance, Lady High Elf! Please punish me however you see fit!"

"Uh, right. Be more careful next time, okay?"

After the elf prostrated himself and bowed so many times his head might have fallen off, he ran from the scene in a hurry. Such a sequence of events brought out a bit of villainy in her as she contemplated keeping everything that just happened hush-hush.

Unable to bear the weight of the onlookers' gazes, she gave up on the rest of her shopping and returned to the inn.

"So what'dja buy, miss...?"

The unwieldy items and those that she bought in bulk were stored away in the Item Box. With a dead-tired expression, Cayna returned to the inn with several bags. The mercenaries who greeted her were red-faced from liquor.

"Are you still drinking?"

"Well, duuuh. That's what we guards gotta do while we're in town. Dis is the only way anyone not on duty gets to relaaax."

Although Arbiter loudly touted his reckless principles, a vein rose to the temple of the second-in-command behind him. Cayna avoided his haunting gaze and started putting her purchases on the table. The objects that came from the paper bags were clearly anything but natural. Even so, Arbiter and the others were so wasted that they didn't even notice anything was off.

"There were quite a few useful-looking ingredients, but I wonder if I bought too much."

"Well, let's have a look-see… Ruche fruit, eggs, sheep's milk, and sugar? You gonna make somethin'?" Arbiter asked.

"It sure does seem like it, but what?" Kenison chimed in.

"I was thinking either a pie or a cake. Hey, why do you all look like you've just witnessed some natural disaster?!"

Arbiter, Kenison, and the other mercenaries were wide-eyed and speechless, and Cayna protested their dramatic reactions. Arbiter and Kenison seemed to be engaged in a silent conversation of "But still, y'know?" and "Yep."

Since they'd never seen Cayna in charge of cooking during the journey, they figured she had no knack for it. And this was indeed her first time, so they probably weren't wrong, either.

"What?! Well then, please wait right here! I'm about to blow you all away!"

Arbiter and the others watched with mystified expressions as Cayna gathered up her items and headed to her room on the second floor. She had intended to borrow the inn kitchen, so she wasn't really sure why she had retreated to her room.

However, less than ten minutes later, Cayna came back downstairs with a sweet-smelling pie stuffed with red ruche fruits.

"Already?!"

"What's goin'. on now?! Wasn't that *too* fast?!"

"Oh-ho-ho-ho-ho! Behold my true power! Now eat!"

She borrowed a knife from the proprietress who had been lured over by the aroma and cut a piece for everyone present. Of course, both the proprietor and proprietress of the inn soon partook as well.

Everyone took a timid bite, and their eyes nearly popped out of their sockets at the invigorating flavors. They quickly ate with relish.

"This is amazin'!"

"It's so tasty, Miss Cayna!"

"Yes, yes, it *is*, isn't it? Heh-heh."

"Wait, how in the world did you make it?!"

"...Hmmm. It has a mellow sweetness, the fluffy ruche fruits have remained intact, and the pie dough is neither too hard nor too soft. The crisp, crunchy texture adds a whole other layer, and the mix of flavors fills your mouth with subtle harmony..."

It wasn't long before the proprietor was singing her praises. Naturally, such an abnormality left Arbiter and the others with questions as well.

In the game world of *Leadale*, items made with Cooking Skills provided all kinds of temporary support effects and stat boosts. She hadn't been totally sure what it would end up tasting like, but since it seemed to be nothing outside the "pie-like flavor" eaten in the game, Cayna put her hand to her chest in relief that her massive bluff had worked.

She herself was shocked it had come out so well.

Pie-type cooking raised your magical power. A ruche pie would increase it by 3 percent. Even if Cayna used this pie for a magic boost, she'd deal just an extra thirty-three damage points.

According to Elineh, pie was often seen in home cooking, but cakes were reserved for royals and the nobility by specialty bakers, so not many commoners knew what they tasted like.

In addition, Cayna made a cake with leeberries, which were very similar to strawberries. This was a big hit among everyone, and it all too swiftly disappeared into their stomachs. The proprietor kept asking Cayna for the recipe, but she had used a skill to make it and had no idea what the process involved outside the ingredients. She didn't think she'd be able to pass it on to average people with a Scroll Skill, either.

Since her biggest concern was the large amount of sugar in the recipe, she calculated the unit price for a single slice and realized it would be a high-cost product. When Cayna told the proprietor this, he admitted that was beyond his reach and gave up.

It seemed that, according to Mai-Mai, things made from Cayna's Scroll Creation were not "read" but rather "understood." There was quite a big difference between the two, but in this modern era, one wouldn't have much luck finding people who could tell them apart.

Cayna eventually got caught up in everyone's excitement, and she started showing off one dessert recipe after the other. Word traveled among the friends of the merchants and mercenaries, and they gathered around. As everyone rolled over on their sides like full seals, the stock of ingredients dropped to less than half.

"We can sell this, Lady Cayna," Elineh proposed with smudges of white cream around his mouth.

"Since they're fresh, they can't be lined up in a storefront. Plus, we have no way to keep them cold…," said Cayna.

Even without refrigeration, she could maintain freshness by either putting them in the Item Box or making them on-site. However, creating it in front of people presented its own set of challenges.

How many would really be okay with eating something that just appeared out of nowhere? And how many would accept ingredients that were swallowed up by strange orbs and whirlpools right before their very eyes? Treating players and the people of this world the same way would invite serious misunderstandings, so Cayna completely rejected the idea of selling cake.

She went to buy more ingredients. As she took a look around, Cayna incidentally wondered if she could do meat or fish dishes. By the time she returned to the inn, she was once again laden with goods.

The next day, she went all out and made a two-layer cake usually saved only for special events. There was a possibility it might get crushed in Sakaiya's constant flow of traffic, so she put it in the Item Box and set out.

Cayna had been worried about not having an appointment, but these fears were unfounded.

The elf known as the young master who Elineh had done business with the other day was apparently Caerick's son. He ushered her inside as soon as he saw her.

After being led to the same room as before, the son went to call for Caerick without having any idea of the circumstances.

"Please wait here a moment, Great-Grandmother. I shall hurry and call Father."

"Oh, sure. *(He's…my great-grandson…)*"

The chances of seeing her great-grandchild at her age was nothing short of a miracle.

Just as Cayna began to seriously worry that it was more of an accident than a miracle, she heard a loud cry of "What did you say?!" followed by hurried footsteps coming from deeper within the residence. The door opened with a bang, and the handsome elf Caerick appeared.

He was flustered and panting, and his eyes bulged at the sight of Cayna. Suddenly, he fell prostrate to the floor.

"Huh? Uh…Caerick?"

"I AM SO VERY SORRYYYY!!"

Before she had the chance to say a single word, Caerick apologized as he readied himself for anything and pressed his head to the ground.

Except for his initial statement, he seemed to think nothing he said would ever be enough. Cayna gave a heavy sigh.

After some time, her trembling grandson lifted his head to peek at her. Cayna made a bright smile and put her hands on her hips.

"At any rate, stop groveling and sit in a chair!"

"Y-y-y-y-yes!!"

As Cayna watched Caerick jump up and sit down across the table from her, her shoulders relaxed. Caerick prepared himself for some sort of divine punishment, and his grandmother shook her head with a sigh.

"Well, first of all, I'm sorry."

"…Huh? What? Uh, what about 'blowing your own kin to sm—'"

"Who said anything about that?! It was Mai-Mai, wasn't it? She told you, didn't she?!"

She switched gears and scolded Caerick for doubting her honest apology. Dark storm clouds roiled behind her as she watched her frightened grandson yelp and give a timid nod.

"My stupid daughter is really in for it now… Oh yeah. Caerick."

"Y-yes, ma'am?!"

"You can use Telepathy, right? Could you send a message to Mai-Mai for me?"

"Y-y-y-yes! Wh-what shall I write…?"

"Ask her which she prefers: the iron maiden, the guillotine, aerial sepulture, being buried alive, or being burned alive."

Later on, a trembling Caerick told his sister Caerina of how dead serious their grandmother's eyes were in that moment.

Incidentally, he never got a reply from Mai-Mai.

Cayna somehow calmed the terrified Caerick with her smile and words, then brought out the cake from her Item Box. Having finally regained his composure, he looked at the giant, sweet-scented cake and once again bowed to his grandmother. She accepted this and proceeded to explain why she had been so offended.

"As a merchant leader who delivers goods to everyone, my comments were shameful. I am terribly sorry, Grandmother."

"It's okay; you've apologized enough. I was also wrong for getting so childishly angry."

After many twists and turns, what it really came down to was that Cayna had been venting. She was relieved that they were finally able to talk normally.

Seeing his grandmother smile and relax with no ill will, Caerick called for a servant to bring tea. The two of them each took a slice of cake for themselves before having the rest of the cake taken away. Cayna was surprised to find that it took two people to move it.

Upon taking a bite of her own creation, Cayna said, "Yes, this turned out good," with a satisfied nod. After tasting it himself, Caerick's eyes went wide. He quickly began to eat it up voraciously.

"You're just like Arbiter and the others. Is cake really that uncommon?"

"No, I've eaten some at parties before, but I've never had anything like this. Hmm…"

"Please don't tell me *We can sell this* like Elineh did, okay? I really don't feel like going down that route."

"I see. That's too bad."

What continued afterward was your usual chitchat. She gave a simple summarization of events from her time in hiding to the present.

"So that is how you became an adventurer, Grandmother?"

"I did it two hundred years ago, too. When I couldn't believe the seven nations disappeared without a trace and didn't know what to do, the caravan I'm with now took me in and taught me what I needed to know. I'm no match for Elineh and the others."

Tossing away her past fame and living as a humble adventurer really was interesting.

Caerick accepted his grandmother for who she was and gave up on the favor he had considered asking when they first met. He shook his head to clear his thoughts but noticed her smirk and grew nervous.

"Wh-whatever is the matter, Grandmother?"

"I can tell by the look on your face that you want to ask me to take care of the bandits. Am I wrong?"

"No, you are correct. However, you appear unenthusiastic about taking on any large jobs. It seems I should let the matter drop."

"You've got good intuition. It's not so much that I don't want to do it but that I'm afraid of other people's responses afterward. Imagine the rumors that would spread if one little girl beat those bandits with ease when the knights struggled to keep up with them. I'd go into hiding again. I might even prefer keeping the cat in the bag by wiping the country off the map."

"Y-you're joking, right?"

Caerick gulped at her mischievous expression paired with completely serious murmurings. He gave a sigh of relief and put his hand to his heart when the dangerous glint disappeared from her eyes, and she said in all sincerity, "Yes, I'm kidding." The mere fact that she had the power to do these things was enough cause for concern when the joke wasn't immediately obvious.

"Sorry to change the subject on you, but I heard from Elineh that this country has a place called Crescent Moon Castle. I learned more about it from some people at the Adventurers Guild, too."

"Ah yes. It's a source of tourist revenue, but it's currently within the bandits' territory."

Caerick took out a map that was more comprehensive than the one Cayna saw at the Guild and proceeded to explain the area in greater detail.

Due south of the capital past the lakes and marshes and over two bridges was the knights' garrison.

Farther south was a boundary line where the Helshper knights were just barely keeping the bandits from moving northward. It took two days by horse to reach this boundary line and another to reach the castle in question.

"Hmm. The bandits' hideout is even farther south. If their reach extends that far, I wonder if they really know what this castle is?"

"Um, Grandmother? What is that castle?"

"Looks like a Guardian Tower."

"What?!"

Shocked, Caerick recalled the mythical stories Mai-Mai used to tell him as a child. The thirteen towers were said to be the foundations of the world gifted from the heavens. They were mysterious places that held wondrous treasures, but only a chosen few could enter.

Caerick excitedly went on and on about the swirling rumors, and Cayna gave a mixed look of exasperation whenever that information was wildly wrong. This was what a two-hundred-year-old game of telephone could do.

"I'll have to awaken the Guardian and strengthen its defenses before the place gets destroyed. I guess I'll go tomorrow."

"But wait, Grandmother. There is a knight garrison right in front of it."

"It's no problem; I've got plenty of ways to get around them."

"I'm pretty certain there are also bandits around the castle…"

"Ah, that does sound like trouble. I'll have to give 'em a push if they get in the way. Plus, if they retreat, we'll be able to use the sea route and transport goods, right?"

Caerick gasped at what she was implying. He had failed to notice before, but if the bandits in that area disappeared, fishing villages in the danger zone could send ships to Felskeilo. Cayna was essentially saying that while she had no intention of getting rid of the bandits, she'd at least help out enough to get trade flowing. If she was going to go that far, Caerick could do something, too.

"I understand. My sister should be arriving there on business sometime today. I shall have her ensure that the path is clear for a single adventurer."

"Oh? Is it really okay for the world-famous Sakaiya company to help one measly adventurer?"

"It's no trouble. After all, that same adventurer will be fulfilling an important task for Sakaiya by delivering supplies to the knights' garrison."

"Heh-heh-heh. Sakaiya has a dark side, too, doesn't it?"

"No, we could never compare to you, Grandmother."

"Heh-heh-heh-heh-heh-heh……"

"Ha-ha-ha-ha-ha-ha……"

The servant who came to bring more tea heard their creepy, simultaneous giggling from the other side of the door and ran away in shock.

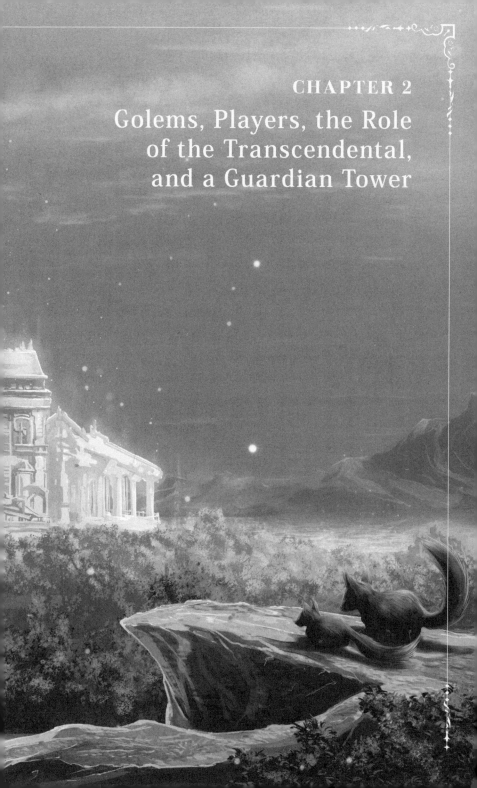

CHAPTER 2
Golems, Players, the Role of the Transcendental, and a Guardian Tower

It was their fourth day in Helshper. Cayna told Elineh and the others that she would be away for two or three days.

"A request?"

"Yes. I'll be delivering goods to a knight garrison for Caerick."

"I see. Well, I'm certain I don't need to worry about you, Lady Cayna, but do be careful. I'm relieved to hear you two are on good terms now."

"Yeah, ah-ha-ha-ha… I'm sorry I caused you so much trouble, Elineh."

Elineh looked as if a heavy burden had been lifted off his shoulders. Cayna could only give a dry laugh in reply. After all, the relationship between Helshper's most powerful merchant and one of Felskeilo's most influential adventurers had gotten into an argument. From his point of view, watching them fight for reasons unknown to him must have been unbearable. The news that they had resolved his biggest fear harmoniously was bound to bring out such a reaction.

"This is Miss Cayna we're talking about, so I really doubt anything's gonna happen. Can't be too careful, though."

"We'll need your talents on the way back, Lady Cayna, so please take care."

"I will. Thank you, Elineh, Arbiter."

Everyone saw her off warmly, and Cayna headed to the western gate. Caerick had informed her earlier that he'd send a supply wagon for her in the early morning. In any case, even if half the story was a front, she really *was* going to deliver supplies.

When she arrived, the gatekeepers and several merchant carriages that traveled between the capital and the nearby fishing villages were standing outside the western gate. Many of the fishing villages' residents had been displaced by the bandits, and the number of marine products entering the capital was on the decline. Cayna had heard that they couldn't enter the city and instead lived together in a huddle outside its walls. As long as they were in close proximity to the capital, the soldiers would notice any monsters or beasts and drive them off, but it was still dangerous.

It wasn't as if she was brimming with a sense of justice, but this news made Cayna feel like tackling the bandits for real.

Mixed among the carriages by the western gate were small, simple wagons covered with canopies pulled by short, stout donkeys. The snug, compact look was similar to a handcart.

Waiting next to it was the young master of Sakaiya, Caerick's son, Idzik. When he spotted her, he gave a deep bow and greeted her.

"My sincere apologies, Great-Grandmother, for having you come all this way so early in the morning…"

"It's not early at all. The sun is already pretty high up. If anything, I think we're getting a late start."

Based on the sun's position, it was probably around seven. If this were during a journey, everyone would have eaten and set off in the carriages already, so one might say it was rather late in the day.

"No, my father spoke out of turn and caused you much distress, so this is the least we can do to apologize. Thank you very much for accepting our request."

"I guess it's hard to find someone willing to take on this job…"

"No one can say what will happen during the journey, after all. Many adventurers hesitate to get involved with the knights and Sakaiya, so it's been a bit of a struggle for us."

The young master's pained smile told her of the suffering he must have gone through, and she instinctively patted his head. Idzik only knew about Cayna from the basic outline he'd heard from Caerick and fearfully shrunk in on himself.

"Well, I know I'm just an outsider, but even if you fail, sometimes not taking a job too seriously can be a good thing as long as it doesn't affect the next one. Hey, there are people above you who can take responsibility, right?"

"Ah yes… Although I cannot say doing so would be an easy feat."

"Well, I'm off."

"Thank you. Do take care."

As the guards at the gate and Idzik saw her off, Cayna gripped the donkey's reins and headed south down the hill away from the capital. The well-trained animal followed her commands even without the use of her Beast Master skill. It matched her walking pace and clopped along with her.

Perhaps it was due to the abundance of lakes and wetlands, but a mist began to roll in after about an hour of traveling downhill. It wasn't thick enough to impede the path ahead, so they wouldn't fall into any water as long as they didn't go off course. When the trail continued along a mostly even surface, she looked back and saw the just-barely visible walls of the capital.

As they kept at a steady pace, Cayna thought, *I have to go two days like this? I bet it'll be faster with a straight path.*

The time between thought and execution was about ten seconds.

In that same instant, a giant red crab appeared from the summoning circle beneath her. Even its width reached eight meters across. There were four legs as thick as human arms on each side for a total of eight, and it had two pincers on each side that were huge enough to easily cut an adult torso in half.

It was a crab monster known as a veldocancer. This one was about level 180. They mostly lived in rivers. In the Game Era, the ones in what was currently the area near the Ejidd River served as prey for players who were more than beginners but not quite midlevel yet.

Cayna thought the donkey might run away or go wild with fear, but it was a calm soul that did nothing more than utter a *hee-haaaw.*

"Think you could give us a ride, veld?"

Although the veldocancer hadn't moved a muscle since being summoned and merely frothed from the mouth, it heard Cayna's request and popped out its multiple eyes up and down in understanding. She picked a good spike on its shell and fixed the cart's wheels in place.

Cayna then cast the spell Field and gave it a range that was only five meters in diameter. This magic would create a barrier that could make even a little ledge on a cliff or a boat rocked about by angry waves an incredibly comfortable experience. Aside from the fact that it consumed MP every ten minutes and had a narrow range, it was rather effective.

Even though it was an uncomfortably tough shell covered in spikes, it felt as if she were sitting on a smooth floor. Once Cayna got the donkey unhitched from the cart and settled in, she pointed the veldocancer in the direction she wanted to go. This path was a direct line on the map, and although they'd encounter some lakes and rivers along the way, it was no problem at all for this monster.

Cayna gave the go signal, and the veldocancer began to scuffle along, not sideways but facing forward. As long as they avoided the main roads and continued along the largely undulating, lake-filled regions, their chances of coming across eyewitnesses were slim.

"...Grandmother. Caerick informed me through Telepathy today that since you are delivering supplies from him, he would like us to let you proceed as you please. However, considering that you should have only left early this morning, why have you arrived just before evening? Might I hear the reason?"

The knight garrison Cayna had reached was nestled in a narrow valley and surrounded by cliffs. Looking at the sentries stationed there, the cliffs seemed to act as a natural barricade with the fences that had been erected. The main road that normally had nothing more than inspection points had been turned into a line of defense against the bandits.

Several rows of bungalows to the north served as the main headquarters and housing for the commanding officers. The average soldiers appeared to be staying in large tents.

Cayna had arrived in the early evening of the same day she left the Helshper capital's western gate. She had lessened a trip that usually took two days on foot by twenty-eight hours.

To say nothing of Caerina, whom Caerick had informed ahead of time, the other knights who had heard when the supplies were scheduled to show up were also shocked to see Cayna and rushed to greet her. Several garrison servants unloaded all her luggage and made sure the donkey was cared for as well.

Cayna was then led to the true master of the garrison, or in other words, Caerina, and questioned in an interrogation room they referred to as the parlor.

Before her stood Caerina and her second-in-command, a werecat man.

"I hurried all the way here to bring the supplies you so wanted, and this is the thanks I get?" said Cayna.

"This isn't a criticism of you in any way...," Caerina began.

"You know this adventurer, Captain?"

"Yes, she's my grandmother. Not that she should receive any special treatment."

".......What?!"

The co-captain's eyes grew wide, and he looked back and forth between the still-baby-faced high elf in her late teens and his stoic commanding officer.

Here we go again, thought Cayna. If anything, she considered Caerina as more of a sister. And naturally, any outsider would see Caerina as the elder and Cayna as the younger.

As if attempting to hide her embarrassment, Caerina put her hands on her hips and changed the subject. She once again asked Cayna for an explanation.

With a wry smile of *Guess there's no getting around this*, Cayna openly confessed how she had traveled there.

"You summoned a monster and rode it here?!"

"I sure did."

From the perspective of a player, it wasn't a big deal in the least, but the co-captain let out a frantic shout at the news of this abject bucking of societal norms. No one had ever heard of someone summoning a monster and controlling it. The werecat's normally stoic expression grew increasingly suspicious, as if the person right before him were spreading wild rumors.

"Such falsehoods will hurt your career as an adventurer."

"Huh?"

Cayna looked surprised. She certainly hadn't been expecting that kind of response. Since the only knights she'd ever met were the self-important, arrogant chumps in Felskeilo, she was touched that one of Helshper's own would express concern about her potential career.

The werecat's expression grew troubled, but as soon as Caerina shot him a look, he reluctantly stepped back.

"Be that as it may, I would prefer greater discretion when it comes to fulfilling Caerick's self-indulgent requests," said Caerina.

"Ah, I knew it."

In Cayna's opinion, such a cookie-cutter response only proved that bureaucratic red tape was the same no matter where you went.

The moment she decided to bulldoze her way through this completely anticipated reply, a commotion suddenly came from outside. It sounded like a bunch of people madly running around. Loud, angry voices were throwing out orders left and right. Just as the three of them went on high alert, a soldier came rushing through the door without so much as a knock. Not even waiting to catch his breath, he clutched his chest, gave a bow, and quickly issued his report.

"Reporting! It's an attack! There are nine enemies! We believe them to be rock golems!"

"What?! Prepare a counterattack!"

Accepting her orders, the soldier did a right about-face and fled the room. The co-captain's red-lined cape fluttered as he hastily followed.

Just as Caerina was about to join them, she turned back for a moment and pointed at Cayna.

"You will quietly remain here, Grandmother. All right?"

"Really? Oh dear, whatever shall I do?" Cayna wondered dramatically. She tilted her head and gazed off in no particular direction.

Caerina watched this act with a pained smile, said "It's not my fault if you get hurt," and left the room.

"Aren't you going to help?"

"Seriously, what do I do now?"

At Kee's question, Cayna sat with her elbows on the back of the chair, bent backward, and looked up at the ceiling. She'd cast Search on all the knights and soldiers as soon as she arrived and felt it would be too difficult to watch. Even if she did, Caerina was the only one with any decent fighting power.

Even the co-captain wasn't as skilled as Arbiter and probably served as nothing more than a burden. The rest of the knights were so low-level that it was painful to watch. At this rate, she surmised that it really would have been better to bring the Flame Spears along.

Using the attack as a chance to cross the defensive line was one option, but that would mean abandoning her granddaughter. This left a bad taste in Cayna's mouth.

Feeling a sense of nostalgia as the atmosphere grew more similar to battles from the days of old with each passing moment, she stood from her chair.

As evening dipped the grassland in orange, nine shadows sluggishly walked toward the defensive line. One was particularly large compared with the rest. The other eight were the size of human adults, while that single shadow was about the size of a cavalryman.

Several more of these cavalrymen were located just behind the group. According to initial sentry reports, they had changed their course in the garrison's grounds.

Caerina and the other knights moved to high ground and looked in the direction the sentries had indicated. They groaned. Sure enough, step by step, nine human-shaped figures were awkwardly lumbering toward them.

Be that as it may, the only humanoid beings taller than two meters were the dragoids, and this enemy's physique shared nothing in common with them. Creatures that looked like people yet were made of boulders and stone were known as rock golems.

Eight of the nine were human-sized, but the last one stood two heads taller than the rest. Caerina silently analyzed it and clicked her tongue quietly enough so her subordinates wouldn't hear. There were many reasons for her displeasure, the first one being that her knights were at an overwhelming disadvantage. The second was that without hammers and maces, it would be impossible to deliver any decisive damage to this kind of foe.

Even so, as knights serving their country, they couldn't exactly say, *We're in trouble, so let's get out of here.* It was frustrating for the subordinates to know that they'd most likely sustain serious injuries, but they had to risk their lives and fight on.

"Don't let them advance any farther! Archers! Fire at will!"

From high above, the prepared archers nocked their arrows and released simultaneously. Bolts from powerful crossbows shot straight, and fire arrows released from longbows created a parabola across the sky. Perhaps the soldiers really did have talent; 80 percent of the arrows struck directly between the stones and boulders or in the rock golems' faces.

However, that was all it did. The crossbow bolts struck the enemy with a dull *thud!* and bounced right off. The fire arrows merely scraped the surface, fell to the ground, and burned a section of the field. The knights let out mumbled curses of "Shit!" but this did nothing to quell the rock golems' advance. They'd been hit with enough arrows to make anyone else look like a porcupine, but that didn't stop the golems for a moment. Their force could rip through the garrison's simple fence like paper.

"Captain! Let's get out there!"

"Yeah! We can't let those things take one step farther!"

The hot-blooded subordinates each shouted their counsel. Caerina understood where they were coming from. She truly did, but she didn't believe they stood a chance against these foes.

Even so, they were running out of time. If the rock golems breached the garrison, not only would the knights' morale plummet, but many noncombatants would be harmed as well.

"All hands, draw your swords! Don't let them get any closer!"

""""Right!!""""

Her mind made up, Caerina drew her sword from its sheath. As she did so, the knights serving her followed suit and lifted their blades high. The orange sky rang with the sound of scabbards, and each person gave an inspiring war cry.

"For Helshper!"

"We won't let 'em get the better of us!"

"Victory is ours!"

"I raise this sword to the captain!"

"Huh?! Dammit, that's low!"

"The winner always makes the first move!"

"I raise my sword to the captain, too!"

The latter half of these cries were probably supposed to lighten the mood, but...

"Everyone, stay sharp! Chaaaaarge!!"

On the co-captain's orders, the roaring knights faced the rock golems as one and rushed forward.

Fewer than twenty knights were stationed at this encampment, meaning there were about two people for every golem. The high-pitched clang of metal against rock immediately rang out across the battlefield. No matter how the knights cut and sliced, their blades proved worthless. They merely wedged into the rock and stone with a spray of sparks.

The fists of the slow-moving rock golems couldn't keep up with the nimble knights and struck the air. Neither side was able to get a decent hit on the other.

However, the side with the real disadvantage was the group of knights who didn't want to lose their position. They kept clanging away at the enemy with their bronze swords, but the golems steadily closed in on the defensive line. The knights scrambled to react, but they had already lost their cool.

One frustrated soldier aimed for a golem's glowing red eye and stabbed with all his might. A conspicuously loud clang followed as the blade pierced through the glowing cavity.

…Or so it appeared.

The sword was merely stuck there. The rock golem had no sense of pain and couldn't even feel the slightest itch.

Conversely, the knight got the impression his attack had worked and stopped moving. Anyone would see that he'd left himself open. A single forceful blow pummeled his head and crushed his helmet. He went slamming into the ground and passed out without even the chance to let out a scream. A thick, pillar-like foot then proceeded to kick him out of the way. The knight's body flew into the air like a rag doll and rolled away limply after it fell back down to earth.

A comrade quickly rushed to the injured man's side and saw that his breastplate had been crushed. His breathing was faint, and the knight lifted him on his shoulders to take him from the battlefield. He continued to call out to him in a loud voice, but the man's intermittent breaths gave no answer.

"Dammit!"

With the loss of a single member, the knights' coordination began to crumble. The previous heroic atmosphere had disappeared.

Caerina and the co-captain managed to destroy one leg of the biggest golem and further slow its movements.

Then, as she finally checked the situation around them and saw another two subordinates go flying in arcs through the sky…

The rock golem began pursuing the two injured soldiers further.

"Captain?! Please wait!"

Ignoring her co-captain's admonitions, Caerina raced toward the rock golem and imbued her raised sword with magic. The surrounding knights voiced their awe and admiration at the red magic she wielded.

An instant later, the crimson magic blade transformed into a large flaming sword.

"HYAAAAAAAA!!"

With a mighty shout, Caerina swung her sword and released its energy.

Weapon Skill: Fire Blade

The red semicircular slash cut a straight line through the air and pierced the rock golem's chest. A large explosion followed, and the golem did a somersault before toppling to the ground with an earthquake-like tremor.

""OHHHHHH!!"""

"That's our captain!"

"Take that, you rockheads!"

The knights cheered and shouted with glee. Caerina, meanwhile, was drenched in sweat and breathing hard. She leaned against her sword to forcefully keep her knees from buckling.

"Captain!"

"I'm okay. But it might be hopeless…"

As Caerina and her co-captain murmured quietly, the newly beaten rock golem before them began to slowly move. Bigger than all the rest, it regenerated its broken knee and stood up.

The knights' numbers were diminishing while the enemy's were still in fighting form—there was hardly a scratch on them.

The wide-eyed knights looked over at Caerina in shock. Just as she was about to say they'd have no choice but to retreat, she heard a laid-back voice from behind her.

"That was fantastic. If being self-taught has brought you that far, then color me impressed."

Weapon Skill: Zamzer Blade

A crescent moon–shaped bolt of lightning raced right past Caerina. The very next instant, the threat before them was cut diagonally from the right shoulder to the left hip. The knights didn't move a muscle as they watched the rock golem begin to crumble apart from where it was struck. It was reduced to mere stones and boulders that rolled along the ground.

When Caerina looked back in astonishment, she found Cayna kicking a pebble beneath her feet. In her right hand was a short sword emitting sparks of electricity.

Upon the arrival of the sudden new intruder, the knights stepped away from the rock golem she had done battle with and regarded Cayna with suspicion.

"It's good to have a well-rounded education," she said.

Not paying the least bit of attention to the ten or so swords pointed at her, she raised her shining golden blade to the sky.

Magic Skill: Zan Ga Boa: Ready Set

The electricity released from her blade circled around her to form eight orbs, each about the size of a human head. Yellow sparks cutting through the sky rose up into the golden orbs.

They twirled above Cayna's head as if they were singing and dancing—as if they were alive. Cayna aimed at the rock golems, and with a murmur of "Go," the spheres whirled higher and higher.

Cayna then swung her electric sword toward the ground like a conductor's baton, and pillars of lightning came crashing down from the orbs and onto the rock golems.

The sound was loud enough to make everyone present drop their weapons. The light burned their eyes, the vibrations rumbled through their very cores, and the thunderous roar left them momentarily deaf.

The hammer-like lightning attack split the rock golems clean in two. Afterward, the remaining pillars of light that towered over them annihilated the reforming stones until nothing remained.

Covering their ears against the close-range explosions, the knights stood there dumbfounded. All too quickly, a single person had obliterated something that had threatened their very lives.

As the knights murmured "What in the world is she...?" among one another, Caerina was able to speak up and get them to sluggishly move. They hurried to the aid of their comrades and were shocked to find even those on the verge of death from rock golem–related injuries sleeping with peaceful expressions.

"Oh, I healed them for you," Cayna said with a grin that she covered as if she were a precocious child.

The knights eyed her dubiously.

They had no idea how they were supposed to react to such an impossibly quick full recovery.

"Grandmother. Thank you very much for helping my subordinates."

Caerina stood up shakily, then gave a simple bow with her hand to her chest.

Cayna cast a gentle gaze on her granddaughter and put her electric short sword back in its sheath. She stroked Caerina's cheek.

"You gathered up a Fireball into your sword and attacked just like that, right? It's a good concept, but I'm guessing that on top of not being able to do anything else in the meantime, you use up too much magic and can't go on afterward?"

"It is shameful."

The co-captain looked at Cayna in utter shock as she completely saw through the workings of Caerina's most secret technique with ease. After all, he had never heard of a mage who could unleash a skill two or three levels higher than Caerina's own with no side effects and perfectly wield high-density magic singlehandedly.

Cayna eluded his gaze with a bright smile, looked at him for a moment, then turned to the rock golem she'd just taken care of.

"Looks like the sun will set soon."

The only orange left in the sky was over by the trees across from them. Up above, a deep indigo-blue night was fast approaching.

"You all should take the glory for this. Or should we report that a little girl saved the nearly annihilated knights all on her own?"

Cayna put a hand to her grinning face and squatted down to look up at Caerina, who bit her lip. She appeared insulted at the idea of giving up any achievements.

"Tch… What do you want in return?"

"What I said from the very beginning. I wish to pass through here. You're okay with that, right? I'll pick up the donkey and cart on my way back, so look after them for me, okay?"

"…Please do as you like. However, proceed at your own risk. We knights want no part of what you're up to."

"Unfortunately, risk comes with being an adventurer. Thanks for your consideration."

Having said all she wanted, Cayna turned away and headed south toward the plains. After wordlessly seeing her off, Caerina dropped her tense shoulders and patted the dumbfounded co-captain's own.

"Ah… Wh-who in the world was that adventurer just now?"

"Probably the strongest person on the entire continent. Notify the others without telling anyone of what you've seen here. It'll be trouble if someone out there learns of her existence. If we're not careful, it may cost us Helshper entirely."

"That can't be…"

He and the other knights who were listening were dubious of the exaggerated future Caerina spoke of.

"Remember this well: There are monsters in this world that can destroy a city in a single magic strike."

A few gulped audibly at Caerina's dead-serious eyes and stern voice. The truth was that the knights understood what she meant by the quick preview they just witnessed. They put their hands to their chests and took Caerina's warning to heart.

"Next, send a messenger to request more personnel. We'll leave the defensive line in this state and send several people out to do reconnaissance. It's a good opportunity to prove my words true. Take a good look around. We can ascertain whether she left behind anything in her wake."

Her tone made it sound like they were talking about something from legends and fairy tales that trampled down armies. Chills ran down their spines.

In order to get Caerina's plan moving along, the co-captain dashed over to the garrison. A fed and watered horse was brought out, and a messenger soldier was sent to the capital with a missive. The knights who had been injured by rock golems were carefully moved to the tents. These survivors were given nothing more than dry meat and stale rye bread before being split into those who would remain behind on defense and those who would be part of the scouting team. Preparations were soon underway.

The opportunity for Caerina to prove her claims would come sooner than expected.

It happened as evening shifted even further into the dark indigo of night, and a chilly air filled the garrison. A thick pillar of light rose up without warning in the direction of the southern sky Cayna had run toward.

Everyone froze, mouths agape as they stared up at the beam of light cutting through the darkness. An instant later, a half dome in gradating reds appeared at its base. It took up a greater part of the night sky and illuminated the meadow in twilight.

Just as it seemed as if the long shadows created by the trees would reach the garrison, there was a subtle tremor beneath their feet, and a noise echoed with a *BWAAAM!*

The red dome was absorbed into the darkness, and it disappeared just as suddenly as it had shown up.

"That grandmother of mine isn't very subtle. She has absolutely no concept about doing things in moderation…"

Caerina's mother once told her as she put her to bed: *"Your grandmother can blow away an entire city with one hit of magic."*

What Caerina just witnessed was surely that very power.

"Is…is a *person* doing that?"

Caerina nodded deeply while her co-captain appeared speechless. As she watched him immediately go pale, she thought it might be too cruel to tell him that likely wasn't the full extent of her grandmother's power.

She pointed out that there was still a possibility of surviving enemies and sent out scouts to check.

During the recent battle, Cayna had noticed several cavalrymen observing the garrison from the rear. She also noticed how they became flustered and ran off when she defeated the rock golems, so she sent a Wind Spirit after them.

When it turned out that the camp they'd fled to wasn't even a half day's ride by horse, she was both surprised and exasperated.

"Did the knights not notice them, or are they just blind?"

"The caster was present but cleverly hidden. The fact that they do not appear to be among this group only proves that."

73

From what she could tell, the escapees were your garden-variety bandits. Even from her hiding place, Cayna could hear them shouting things like "Contact the boss!" and "Man, no one ever told me those things would go down *that* easy!"

Since fighting the bandits individually would have been a pain, Cayna used magic to cloud their minds and make them pass out. She then burned the camp to a crisp with the biggest and farthest-reaching Flame Magic she could muster, leaving behind a massive, deep crater. Finally, she used an earth-based spell to form holes in the crater and buried the bandits up to their necks.

Cayna figured that the enormous magic display she just pulled off would attract enough of Caerina's attention that she'd send scouts to investigate and take care of the matter. Interrogating petty bandits for decent info wouldn't do Cayna much good.

After that, she called upon three Brown Dragons with Summoning Magic: Dragon. Since her summoning strength was set to level 2, the Brown Dragons that appeared were about the size of large dogs. Their ochre scales designated them as earth types, and they were as ferocious as the ankylosaurus dinosaur. Like the Blue Dragon species, it was also one of the seven types of dragons that couldn't fly. However, it boasted the greatest defensive and physical power of them all.

Cayna devoted two of the dragons to leading the way south through the night. The third dragon stayed slightly ahead of her and kept a close watch on their surroundings.

As she followed, Cayna thought about the rock golems.

"Hmm, there was something weird about the level of those golems... Kee?"

"Eight of them were level 43, and only one was level 172."

"In that case, based on the limits of Summoning Magic, the caster split one golem into eight and split four into one. That equals

twelve. It fits perfectly. Huh… Could that mean there are other players besides me around?"

*"If the game's original settings are still in place, I believe
dwarves, elves, demons, and high elves can easily live two hundred years."*

Summoning Magic had a specific rule: If you wished to call upon
multiple of the same creature, it could only be a maximum of nine,
and your summoning strength had to equal a total of level 12.

Monsters and animals had their own elemental attributes, each
of which were closely connected. These attributes were split into
groups along the lines of the five basic elements. In Leadale, four of
the groups were Earth, Water, Fire, and Air, while the other two were
Light and Dark.

The groups possessed special values: If you called upon an Earth-type
monster, you couldn't call a Wind-type one. If you called upon a Fire
type and a Water type at the same time, the Fire type would automatically weaken the Water. If you called upon a Light type and a Dark type,
they would clash with each other and get out of control. And so on.

The recent rock golem battle followed these rules perfectly. At the
very least, it was proof that a player had been the one to send them.
Namely, it meant that the bandits' boss was a midlevel player. From
Kee's analysis, Cayna figured they had to be around level 430.

"They're pretty strong, then. Skargo and his siblings, let alone
Caerina, would be no match for them."

The whupping the knights had gotten made this very clear. The
other question was, how had a player slipped into a world abandoned
by the Admins? Cayna had a hard time believing this person went
through the kind of freak accident she had. In which case, that also
raised the question of how much of the Admins' influence remained
in this world. There was certainly no end to the mysteries.

"Either way, I guess I don't really have any other option but to go and ask this person myself."

The night was wearing on, so Cayna called back the two Brown Dragons leading the way. Their mission had been to search for the individual who created the rock golems.

Since the camp had been full of nothing but low-level bandits, Cayna thought maybe the golem's caster hightailed it out of there after making the rock golems. That was why she'd kept to the main road, but apparently her guess had been off.

After deciding that any further searching was useless, Cayna settled in for the night until morning came. She had the dragons stand watch as she slept, when she was most vulnerable. Cayna also had her Pervert Blocker arm bangle and Kee, more importantly. Either of the two would immediately alert her if anything was amiss.

She never slept outside during the Game Era, and naturally she didn't have the tent that had usually been considered more of a gag item. When she summoned a small Fire Spirit in place of a bonfire, a fiery monkey appeared and sat down cross-legged.

Wrapping herself up in a blanket and her cape to form a simple sleeping bag, Cayna used one of the Brown Dragons as a pillow and let herself relax. It wasn't long before she was fast asleep.

The next morning, Cayna woke up refreshed. She gave a big yawn and eyed her surroundings with a weary smile. Two of the Brown Dragons had gathered around the one she'd been using as a pillow. She should have been sleeping on the ground, but since they'd huddled together, she was up on its back as if it were a pedestal or altar.

After cleansing herself with Purity, she made a sandwich with her Cooking Skills and had breakfast. Luckily, since she bought vegetables, meat, and bread along with the cake ingredients, she could always have a hot meal.

After putting away her blanket in the Item Box, she switched gears and once again headed south. Now far from the Helshper capital, the scenery changed from blue waters to a stretch of green. The lakes and marshlands decreased while the grasslands and wilderness increased. The flat terrain continued on, which made it simple for her to spot any bandits. Then again, she was likewise easy to spot as well.

Even with full knowledge of this, Cayna made her way forward while looking neither left nor right. Finally, she sighted a building. It stood on the small island in the middle of the lake, just as Elineh had spoken of. This was most likely the aforementioned beautiful castle and what the adventurers at the Guild had called Crescent Moon Castle.

There was something dignified and solemn about its presence, however. It strongly reminded her of those random palaces she'd see while surfing the Internet.

Whether it was a castle or a palace was neither here nor there; the real issue was the people camped out right in front of the lake. Several paddleboats were bobbing along the shore, and a rough-looking crowd who may as well have been screaming *We're about to loot that palace!* had gathered. There was no mistaking that these were the bandits causing so much trouble for Helshper lately.

Seeing as there was no form of coverage on the grassland, once Cayna noticed them, they naturally noticed her, too. She soon heard shouts of "It's an enemy attack!" "Tell the boss!" "Isn't it just one little girl?" and "We can handle 'er on our own."

"Ignorance is not bliss."

Kee sounded exasperated. If he had a body, he would have surely shrugged and shook his head hopelessly.

The three Brown Dragons were still by Cayna's side, and she asked them to take care of the bandits. Glad to be of service, they let out a squeal in unison and charged at the enemy.

The bandits must have thought the dog-sized, armored beasts were some subspecies of wolf monster. Archers fired their arrows, but these tragically bounced right off the dragons. The dragons looked hardy enough, but at that size, anyone was bound to underestimate them.

There were only three Brown Dragons and over twenty bandits. As puny as the three were, however, they were still dragons. Furthermore, a single one was level 220.

The Brown Dragons charged into the bandits headfirst without ever slowing down and completely trampled them. The sound of broken bones followed as the bandits went flying through the air from a dragon head-butt. The lightest swish of the creatures' tails bent the men in half and left them immobile. Their Sand Breath clung to a person's body and instantly solidified them into sandstone sculptures. In a matter of minutes, the bandits were falling to the ground like wailing works of art.

Cayna, meanwhile, was up against a figure in full armor who appeared out of nowhere. Their azure outfit had spikes on the shoulders and elbows, and they seemed to be staring at her.

"It looks like you've taken good care of my subordinates."

"No need to thank me."

When Cayna used Search to check their stats, she could only confirm their level. Just as she'd surmised earlier, her foe was level 432.

She knew the armor was preventing her from getting any more details. Only one piece of equipment used an open-winged Blue Dragon as a helmet. Cayna was annoyed that they seemed to be heading in the direction of hand-to-hand combat. The black horns protruding from the helmet only added to her frustration.

She could also tell from her opponent's voice that he was surprisingly young, at least her age or maybe a bit younger.

"You look like nothing more than an adventurer, so what's your business here?! Don't you think it's a bit harsh to toss my men around like rags?!"

"Huh? …Weren't you the one who sicced those rock golems on the knight garrison?!"

"What? Ah, that was a nice display. I didn't have a hand in it, though."

"Huh?"

Cayna instantly narrowed her eyes at this extremely odd statement. Her foe seemed to at least value the lives of the bandit underlings. And yet he didn't appear to care at all about the knights who'd had the stuffing beat out of them.

By saying the rock golems did it, was he trying to insinuate he only gave the order?

The sheer recklessness of this person left Cayna incredulous.

Maybe he thought he was still in the world of the game?

"This is *Leadale*, but it's also not, y'know."

"Are you nuts? Now that the Game Masters are gone, player killers can do whatever we want. Isn't it awesome to watch your level skyrocket?"

From regarding his words and actions alone, Cayna immediately realized this was just a normal kid who hadn't come to grips with reality. Although he looked grown, on the inside he was a child with poor morals. That said, Cayna didn't consider herself an adult, either, and all desire to capture her opponent went out the window.

"This is reality. You can't just selfishly decide who lives or dies."

"The heck are you talking about? This is a game, ain't it? I can take people down and level up all I want."

Cayna withdrew the magic staff she wore as an earring. She spun it in her hand once, and it instantly extended to nearly two meters in length. At the same time, all her combat-oriented Active Skills automatically kicked in. If the average person so much as even approached her, not only would her vicious nullifying abilities take effect, twelve different skills, such as Menace, Intimidate, Attack Support, Defense Support, Bonus Damage, and Reduced Damage, would also solidify her presence.

"I'll prove you're wrong. This is the real world."

"Quit bein' stupid. I told you—we're in a game. Maybe you oughtta upgrade your operating system!"

He unsheathed the large sword on his back. Its upper half was split into fangs, and the blade itself gave a screech of "*Geh-geh-geh-geh.*" It was the gag weapon known as the Hungry Like the Wolf Sword that ripped and broke apart any average weapon the moment they made contact. Her foe's Supreme King of Fools Armor had absolutely no magic effects cast on it, either. At this rate, he was practically screaming, *Look, I'm a player!*

"Don't think you stand a chance against a player. You dunno who you're messing with!" the bandit leader spat.

"I'm gonna make you eat those words."

The unexpected meeting that resulted in a fight to prove one's own doctrine was about to begin.

The signal to start was a high-pitched shriek of metal. The Wolf Sword and magic staff clashed violently and set off sparks.

"Tch!"

With a click of his tongue, the bandit leader quickly withdrew from their point of contact and created distance. Cayna swung the staff in her hands and boldly probed his movements. His eyes bulged in their sockets, and he looked between his own weapon and hers.

"For cryin' out loud… This thing can't destroy it…?"

"Aw, that's too bad. The Hungry Like the Wolf Sword is supposed to be great at destroying weapons—well, except for rare and EX Items. Guess you've got some more studying to do, huh?"

"Tch. So you're a player!"

"You're a bit slow on the uptake. Didn't I *just* say things that only a player would know? Weren't you even listening?"

Not happy with her breezy, condescending attitude, the bandit leader poured magic into his sword. As the blade's fangs clanged away, it shone and transformed the magic into a blue light. He raised the sword above him and began swinging it in a figure eight.

Cayna didn't earn her Skill Master title out of stylishness or on a whim. She already knew exactly what attack he was about to unleash.

Keeping in time with him, she poured magic into her own staff. The ochre-colored power transformed into a shining arrowhead at the very tip.

Weapon Skill: Sword Specialization: Destruction Hurricane!

The bandit leader became cloaked in a gale-force wind. When combined with his glowing blue sword, it created a massive tornado that swayed back and forth. The wind became a sharp knife that tore through the sky and scraped the ground as it headed straight for Cayna.

As soon she saw this, she took her glowing ochre staff and stuck it into the ground.

Weapon Skill: Cracking Earth Hammer!

Suddenly, the earth beneath the windless space where the leader stood within the tornado collapsed. Raging wind and all fell into the cracked basin-shaped hole in the earth.

"Uwagh! That's just— GW-GWAAGH?!"

"Pfft—"

Cayna burst out laughing as she listened to his pathetic screams as he was knocked around. The tornado was called off halfway and disappeared all too quickly. The toppled bandit leader was stuck in the deep, round hole.

As he crawled out, and his face popped out over the lip, Cayna took a side swing at it.

Clang!

A metallic sound rang out, and a blue head went flying through the air. Or rather, a blue helmet. The rest of the armor was covered in mud, and from the neck up, there was a tan head with twisted horns growing out of the bandit leader's temples. He was a demon, one of the game's overpowered, balance-breaking races. They were stronger than the well-rounded human race, and it was said during beta testing that they had the ability to completely annihilate players.

Lots of people chose this race at first, but since it was pretty difficult to play as one, their numbers soon dwindled. In the end, they fell to "least popular character" right behind high elves. A demon's ability score was twice as powerful as a human's, but overall, demons simply had far too many drawbacks. They could only belong to the Black Kingdom, and the NPCs of other nations held them in great contempt. The prices in stores were twice as high for demons, and they couldn't sell anything. And finally, even Non-Active monsters (monsters that didn't attack as long as you left them alone) picked fights with them.

If they'd been at the same level, he would have posed a serious threat to a high elf like Cayna. Even if he'd had a 50-level stat boost, the two of them would've been evenly matched in close combat. From what Cayna could tell, his basic swordplay was subpar. He'd lose in a fight if he let up for even a moment.

Although Cayna was also a member of the Black Kingdom, she hadn't known everyone there. Anyone with an attitude as bad as his would be the subject of many rumors. Since she'd never heard of this gag weapon maniac, he was probably a player who'd entered the game after Cayna died.

"Shit! I never heard of a skill like that. Also! You've been hidin' your stats this whole time. Quit playin' dirty, dammit!"

Sheesh…

"What a child…"

Still on high alert, Cayna was almost as exasperated as Kee.

The demon, who had clearly flown off the handle, slammed his sword into the ground and unleashed his rage.

"That's what everyone who rushes through the tutorial says," Cayna told him. "But the fact is that you can't see the stat details of a higher-level player so easily."

"What was that?! You seriously think someone like you is higher than me?!"

The leader struck at her while continuing his stream of complaints. Cayna spun her staff, repelled it outward, and returned a hard strike straight into his chest. The magic within the Supreme King of Fools Armor merely nullified it. Physically, its defensive power wasn't much different than steel armor.

At the same time, she released the low-level electric attack she'd been holding in one hand. It skimmed along the ground, flew upward, and should have continued into his torso. However, just as it was about to make contact with the armor, it bounced off unnaturally and disappeared.

As soon as the demon saw this, he gave a look that said *Well, duh* and smiled scornfully.

"Ha! My armor nullifies magic. Betcha didn't know that, loser!"

"I know all about it! It didn't work in the game, and that's not how it works here in reality!"

She pointed the end of her staff at the demon and displayed the true power of her Special Weapon.

Upon its master's cry of "Extend," the staff instantly grew longer into infinity, and the astounding phenomenon stopped the demon in his tracks. It struck his chest and sent him flying backward.

"WHA—?! GWAGH?!"

"This Golden Hoop Staff weighs more than seventeen thousand pounds. Ever heard of it?"

The magic staff returned to its normal height, and she stroked it in her hand. She twirled it as she confirmed that the flying demon had landed in the recently made basin-shaped hole.

Magic Skill: Ohta Laga

A water attack slammed into the hole.

If this were the game, water would flow from the space above the caster's head and form a large orb.

However, there was a large source of water right by her. A pillar of water lifted from the lake made an arc through the sky and poured down on the demon stuck in the hole. He clearly sounded like he was drowning, but what he was saying probably translated to something like *Why?! Magic isn't supposed to work!*

Paying no attention to his discomfort, Cayna cast more magic in rapid succession.

Magic Skill: Zan Laga

A bolt of lightning descended from the clear sky like a spear, missed the wide-eyed, sinking demon, and shot straight into the water. The shining yellow electric phenomenon was in no way good for the eyes, and the demon convulsed as he thrashed about.

His eyes still wide as he suffered from the electric shock, he somehow managed to pull his limp body over to the edge of the hole. He was wearing his heavy armor, so swimming with it on was no easy task. His HP had fallen into the red zone; one more hit, and he'd be done for.

Cayna froze the water and encased his lower half in ice. Upon confirming he was stuck there, she leveled herself with his forehead and dropped the magic staff.

The demon woke with a groan of "Gwegh" that sounded very much like a toad being crushed. His eyes darted about as he realized his situation.

"Dammit! What'd you do? This freakin' hurts!"

"It does hurt, doesn't it? Why can't you see it's real pain?"

Even though pain had existed in the game, it had amounted to not much more than the prickle of feedback along the surface of your skin. Excluding the more eccentric types, no one was likely to consider removing their limiters so they could experience a full range of pain.

The demon player had almost drowned, felt electric shocks throughout his whole body, cried out from the cold and frostbite, and now turned a ghastly blue. He trembled further with fear as Cayna loomed over him mercilessly.

He then began to spew a stream of incoherent excuses.

"It-it's a lie... Th-this is a game... If I die...I can just reset, right...?"

"If you die, that's it. No continues. No extra lives. No reset button. My deepest condolences."

"Th-that's... H-help me! I'm just a kid! If you kill me, the police will...!"

"There are no police. This is retribution. You have to take responsibility for your actions, okay? Do you know how much trouble you've caused for others as the leader of the bandits?"

The chill in Cayna's voice surprised even her, and the demon player began to sob.

"*Sniff...* Uwagh! H-help me. Please help, uwagh... WAAAAAAGH!"

With a murmur of good-bye, Cayna raised her magic staff overhead.

*　　*　　*

The very next instant, Cayna obeyed her Intuition skill and jumped back. An arrow flew between the demon player and where she had just stood.

"Kee! Why didn't you warn me?"

"It did not seem as if such an attack would harm you in any way."

Cayna hurriedly looked behind her and saw several cavalrymen racing toward her. She initially thought she'd taken too long and that the bandits' reinforcements had arrived, but Caerina seemed to be at the forefront, and she soon grew wary.

As if realizing the armed-and-ready Cayna couldn't be taken lightly, the other knights stopped and stayed where they were. Only Caerina alighted. She stayed out of Cayna's range (not that this would stop the magic staff), fell to her knees, and bowed her head.

"My apologies, Grandmother. These are my colleagues. Please, be at ease."

"What do the knights want with me? I was just about to finish him off, but…"

The one to answer her was not Caerina, but a human knight with a goatee and a dignified presence who came from behind.

"Unfortunately, we wish to judge that criminal by Helshper law."

Since the other knights had different crests on their armor, Cayna assumed he was a leader of these knights. However, she frowned at his incomprehensible statement.

"Are you crazy? You think you can handle him? Even Caerina would be no match for this guy."

The other knights looked at Caerina with shock. The knights' leader also turned toward her as if to ask *Is that true?*

"I have never actually crossed swords with him, so I cannot confirm for certain…but if my grandmother says so, then that must be the case."

Cayna mysteriously wondered how Caerina could be a captain despite admitting this so openly, but she didn't have time for compassion. Demons had the unique ability of Passive Skill: Continuous HP Regeneration, so they had to condemn him before he started healing.

As Cayna went to once again swing her magic staff, the faces of the knights immediately shifted, and they all unsheathed their swords.

The demon's sobs echoed as the situation intensified.

Reorganizing her priorities, Cayna determined that messing with the nation of Helshper wasn't necessary at the moment. She shrank the staff and affixed it to her right ear.

Caerina put her hand to her heart at this. After all, she knew that if Cayna got serious, she'd destroy the knights' most elite forces as if she were taking candy from a baby.

The mages who were among the knights melted the ice and pulled the bandit leader out of the hole.

Cayna took a black collar out of her Item Box and walked over to the demon despite the knights' threats. She affixed it around his neck with a *clack*. A moment later, all his armor was unequipped and stowed in his Item Box. The Supreme King of Fools Armor disappeared.

Now left only in his black underwear, he looked down at himself in surprise. A stats screen popped up in midair, and his jaw dropped when he saw it. In the Equipment field, it said the item around his neck was called a Punishment Collar, and it reduced his stats and level to 10 percent.

"Wait—if you have that collar, then…that means you're… NO WAAAAY!"

"Too bad. It might've been easier if I'd finished you here and now. Good thing you understand our difference in level, huh?"

The Punishment Collar was a warning item put on players who committed illegal or intolerable acts. The only ones who could use it were the Game Masters and the twenty-four Limit Breakers who passed the Transcendental Quest. In actuality, there was also a personality test one had to take, and if you failed it, you couldn't pass the quest. The Limit Breakers had the ability to supplement the understaffed Game Masters, and when the Admins made this wish known, it shocked all involved.

The Punishment Collar was a restraining device removeable only by Game Masters and Limit Breakers. The wearer lost a tenth of their level and stats as a result. Wearing it a second time, however, labeled the user as a troublemaker who needed constant surveillance, and their account was effectively terminated.

At this point, the demon finally realized who Cayna was.

Like NPCs, the Game Masters were easily recognizable because they didn't have a level, but Limit Breakers were different. He was reluctant to call her average, but she was indeed a player.

"You should be able to handle him now. Be careful, though, or he'll trip you up, okay?"

"Understood. I shall take that to heart. Thank you very much, Grandmother."

The demon was taken away with a stunned expression. The collapsed bandits were also captured and stuffed in the jail carriage. The knight leader began to say something, but at Caerina's protest, he closed his mouth, unwillingly nodded, mounted his horse, and departed. He probably wanted to ask her to accompany them as a witness. Caerina had made certain this didn't happen.

"I'm not really sure if it's a good or bad thing that I turned him over… I guess only god knows, huh?"

Cayna looked back on her actions with a sigh and shrugged. She then took the Guardian Ring out of her Item Box so she could finally accomplish her initial goal.

Sure enough, it began to sparkle with a green light. She chanted the standard password without much thought. However, the ring did nothing more than glow. Silence followed.

As soon as Cayna tilted her head at this lack of reaction, a black hole opened up like some sort of trash chute beneath her feet, and she fell in.

"Wha—?! Hey, what is this...?"

After letting out a loud yell, she suddenly realized she was on hard earth and sighed. She looked around speechlessly.

Ruins spread out before her. It had a templelike atmosphere and was washed in a pale-green light. The marble floor was cracked, and thick granite columns had broken and toppled with several still remaining upright. The sun continued to shine at its zenith overhead, but the green filter gave the impression that it was only a shadow of its former glory.

Cayna stepped down, and right before her was a throne with a skull on it. She approached the skull, being careful not to step on any of the other bones, and picked it up in her hands before giving it some MP.

Realizing nothing was happening, Cayna switched her attention to the throne. An instant later, the seat that had been previously dyed in the surrounding colors changed to velvet with gold trimming.

At the same time, the skull began to rattle and float in midair, and the bones around it came flying in. When they all formed together, a full skeleton wearing a crown appeared. A velvet cape that seemed to materialize out of nowhere was fastened over its forearms.

"Oh, so this is the Guardian, huh?"

As Cayna nodded in understanding, the skeleton before her pulled a feather fan out of nowhere. It flicked it open to hide its mouth and put its left hand on its hip.

"I see you have the audacity to come to this remote place.

**Hmph, nothing I can do about that, I suppose. I shall welcome
you. Do show proper appreciation."**

"...Hey now..."

Cayna furrowed her brow at this holier-than-thou attitude that
had just blown away every bit of her battle fatigue. It was clear from
her expression that she was wondering what kind of weirdo would
have a Guardian like this one.

"I'm the Third Skill Master, the high elf Cayna. Whose tower is
this?"

**"One of the master's comrades, are you? Ah well—I shall
tell you! The great Opuskettenshultheimer Crosstettbomber is
the keeper of this tower. Are you an acquain...? O-oh?"**

As soon as she heard the name, Cayna lost all strength and collapsed on the ground. Unsurprisingly, the skeleton had no idea how
to react to this and hesitated. Cayna trembled for some time before
giving her head a single shake and standing up. However, her expression still held a look of resignation.

"Opus... *Sigh*... This weird thing makes total sense, then."

**"Who is weird?! Who, I ask?! You will never find a more
noble skeleton in this world than I."**

No matter how you looked at it, the only appropriate words to
describe it were *bones, bag of bones, doctor model*, and *science class mystery*, but it'd probably be a losing battle if she pointed that out.

Opuskettenshultheimer Crosstettbomber, aka Opus, was one of
the few demon players and the Thirteenth Skill Master. He was originally the Fourteenth, but since the original Thirteenth had suffered a
mental breakdown and quit the game, he moved up a slot.

He and Cayna had been hopelessly and begrudgingly connected
since the days of beta testing and even joined the same Guild. He

only ever spoke openly with Cayna and the other Guild members. He was also incredibly arrogant, loved tricking people, and had too many quirks to count.

In short, he was an idiot. And an oddball. An absolute genius who would either go on talking forever if you let him, boast random and useless knowledge, or pick up radio waves.

However, no one could match him when it came to battle strategy, and other nations dubbed him *Leadale*'s Kongming. A good example of this was the one time only four level-1,000 players, Cayna included, won against the Purple and Yellow Kingdoms under Opus's orders. He had laughed loudly, but Cayna and the others had their magic to their limits and ended up dead tired.

Furthermore, he was both a terrible friend and a mentor to Cayna. She couldn't even read a book on her own and didn't know how to use a computer, but after she met him in the game, she'd gained all sorts of knowledge. When she thought about how she'd never hear him speak again, a tinge of loneliness raced through Cayna's heart.

"Honestly, I ask that you not suddenly become depressed in someone else's tower! It is rather unpleasant!"

The self-proclaimed skeleton Guardian complained while Cayna sank into dejection. The inflection at the end had an echo of worry in it. It simultaneously handed her a bound red book and a ring.

"...Huh?"

"My master was certain you would come here and entrusted me with these. Come now, express your gratitude."

"Th-thank you..."

Still a bit shocked, Cayna accepted the ring and book. Feeling light, she opened the latter's pages.

And quickly closed it. The relief that had been on her face moments before was gone.

The skeleton looked at her questioningly.

"What is the matter?"

"...How should I put this...?" she answered with a trembling voice as she opened the book once again.

When looking past the cover, it was normal to see an end-paper and title page. However, this object only appeared to be a book but was something else altogether. Upon opening it, Cayna found a box-shaped cavity with a tiny girl inside. She was just under twenty centimeters tall.

The girl had light-green hair and large bright-blue eyes that gazed at Cayna. She wore a thin, billowy dress, and growing from her back were four light-green transparent wings. This little girl who stared at Cayna for some time was known as a fairy.

The fairy didn't move while her and Cayna's eyes were locked, but when she did stir, she kicked off from the inside of the box and fluttered upward.

"Whatever are you keeping the book open for?"

The skeleton Guardian looked at Cayna's hands curiously. Apparently, she (?) couldn't see the fairy.

The fairy herself clasped her hands in front of her chest in a gesture of prayer and gave Cayna a fleeting smile. A memory of someone else's smile vaguely floated into her mind, and her heart skipped a beat.

The fairy floated up toward her, planted a kiss on her cheek, and settled on her right shoulder.

"Who are you?"

"...?"

Despite Cayna's question, the girl merely continued to smile as she lightly shook her head. It was as if she were saying *Don't ask that yet*. Or maybe even she didn't know.

Cayna didn't know the answer, but Opus had given this girl to her. She'd at least figure out why.

Cayna wasn't exactly sure what to do with the book she had found the fairy in, but it seemed like it would probably be useful for something. She decided to put it in the Item Box.

Noticing that Cayna seemed to have calmed down and was feeling a bit better, the skeleton Guardian covered her mouth with her fan.

"Hoh-hoh. Finally, a decent expression. Honestly, I do wish you would not wander about my master's tower with such a dark look. My master also informed me that you may use his Item Box as you please. It is all yours."

Having said what she wished, the skeleton Guardian elegantly walked over to the side of the throne. That seemed to be her usual position.

Cayna checked the tower's Item Box and gathered up the plant and mineral materials she didn't have yet, since she'd been more or less given them. There were no weapons, defensive equipment, or even anything practical. This was just like him, and it made her slightly happy.

The Guardian here was a bit strange, but like her terrible friend, she was also oddly considerate of others. Cayna took a liking to her and poured almost the rest of her MP into the throne.

"Well then, I guess I'll be going. If you start running low on MP, either use the Ring to call me or contact the Guardians in the Ninth or Third towers."

"Oh? Yes. I—I suppose it cannot be helped. You are my master for the time being, so do call upon me should the time come."

The skeleton had turned away as she said this. Cayna gave a small wave and headed outside.

It was once again heading toward evening.

"I didn't think we were inside *that* long."

"Look at the fairy. She seems quite content, so might that be the cause?"

Upon hearing this from Kee, she looked at her right shoulder to find the fairy sitting there and swinging her legs.

When she met Cayna's eyes, she gave a smile that was like watching a flower bloom.

"I guess our first goal should be to figure out a way to understand each other."

Cayna had to ask the fairy about Opus's whereabouts, but this all-important source of information only smiled and said nothing.

"Let's take things slowly."

"Right."

Since they didn't have any clues to go on, Cayna gave a tired sigh that said the road ahead was going to be long and bumpy.

The Brown Dragons, who had gotten her there and who she'd left behind, were all gathered. She'd given them plenty of MP so they could stick around and handle the long journey, and it looked like they could still move.

Her MP was recovering bit by bit, but since she was hoping to fill it back up, Cayna decided to spend another night by the lakeshore. She lit a bonfire, had a light meal, and filled her stomach.

As the sight of the three dragons rolling around and playing together soothed Cayna, she looked back over her shoulder.

It wasn't a full moon at the moment, so the palace-like tower wasn't all aglow. However, since the lake surrounding the tower emitted a faint light, a silhouette of the palace stood out against the darkness.

"So this is Opus's tower. It's my first time seeing it, but is it really the House of Murder and Malice...?"

Cayna's cheek twitched at the unsettling moniker and thought maybe it was better that the bandits hadn't entered it that afternoon.

Even their leader himself would have certainly been killed if he had stepped inside.

The House of Murder and Malice was the infamous nickname of the tower Opus controlled. This was because it was packed to the brim with lethal traps.

For example, there was a written covenant on the door with a standing signboard that said ALL VISITORS, PLEASE SIGN YOUR DEATH WARRANT HERE. If you approached clumsily, the iron-plated oath that was sharp as a razor on all four sides would come flying at you endlessly and slice people up.

Furthermore, there was a lion-headed door knocker that visitors would use. When they did, the handle would draw the hand into the lion's mouth and fix it in place. The gap between the front of the doorway and the door would drop a sharp guillotine, and the visitor's one arm would be cut off.

She had heard of these brutal traps and many more from the creator Opus himself. Everything from the walls, floors, pillars, and stairs to the furnishings and flowers inside vases were deadly traps meant to put an end to anyone who walked in.

No one could fathom why anyone would voluntarily go waltzing into the infamous tower. In another sense, though, plenty of players would go on the forums and proudly talk about how they died.

At any rate, that was the sort of history this Guardian Tower carried. Even those who approached it out of curiosity would realize how dangerous it was the second they saw the sign out front. It wasn't Cayna's job to worry about people who lacked any common sense.

She looked out upon the palace tower for a while before deciding to call it a night. Taking care not to crush the fairy, she rolled up in her blanket.

Thinking it'd be nice to see her detestable, terrible friend in her dreams, she closed her eyes.

CHAPTER 3
A Bridge, Laundry, a Queen, and a Bear Hunt

After spending a night in front of Opus's Guardian Tower, Cayna picked up her cart and donkey from the garrison and returned to Helshper. The knights trembled in fear at Cayna's presence and stayed out of her sight. She merely thanked Caerina for watching over her things.

Cayna's trip home was also through unconventional methods, and she roared down the main road. This may or may not have created a new urban legend.

When she made it back to Helshper, she immediately went to see Caerick. He had apparently already been informed about the capture of the bandit leader and showed his thanks with an exaggerated bow.

The remnant bandits in the fortress still hadn't been swept out, so the outer trade route to the west wouldn't be safe to open until a force was sent out to suppress them. According to Caerick, that subjugation would be a joint force between the Helshper and Felskeilo knights.

Then, the next day...

"*Sniff.* Ngh..."

"Why are you moaning like a ponsu, miss?"

As she wrestled over whether things were fine the way they were, Arbiter gave an odd look and called out to her. Incidentally, the ponsu was a popular fish similar to a catfish that lived in the Ejidd River. It was a home-cooked staple that could be either baked or boiled.

That aside, Cayna was a bit concerned over whether she could talk about it. However, since news of the bandits' subjugation was already spreading across town, it was only a matter of time before Arbiter got wind of it. She didn't think he was the type to disclose secrets indiscriminately, so she went into the details of the bandit leader's capture the day prior.

"Hmph, so that's what he was like? Sounds like he acted like a little kid... I've never met a demon, but I've never heard of 'em being that terrible."

She obviously couldn't tell Arbiter that, despite looking like a young man, the demon was actually a child player.

"I myself have a demon acquaintance, but someone so pompous isn't a great reference to go off," she said, using Opus to dodge the issue.

In this world of Leadale, demons were treated no differently from the other races and didn't suffer much open discrimination.

"Well, it's not like I was there, but wasn't your decision the right one?"

"Huh? But I'm a bit worried about letting him live and handing him over..."

"Hold on a sec. Didn't you go there to fulfill a request for fresh supplies? Even if the master had intentions of his own, it's our job as adventurers to accept those requests. The clients who submit the requests are the ones who make the judgment calls."

"Is...that so?"

"The country is hurting either way. You weren't wrong for passing him over to the knights and letting Helshper decide his fate. When it comes to what you *should* be worried about, you're barkin' up the wrong tree. If you got involved and killed him without even being asked to help with the subjugation, it'd be a complete loss of face for the nation."

She hadn't planned on discussing the discord in the nation, but simply talking to someone and not being told she was wrong dislodged the splinter in her heart.

Arbiter grinned when he saw her expression clear up.

"I'm sorry, Arbiter. Thank you for talking with me."

"No problem, even the words of a senior adventurer can help out sometimes. You can pay me back with some cake."

"You've really grown quite fond of it, huh?"

Taken in by his laugh of "Wah-ha-ha!" as if he were trying to dodge the question, Cayna smiled. The fairy next to her had been looking worried for some time, but once the weight had been lifted off Cayna's shoulders, she smiled as well.

When she had arrived back in Helshper, Caerick never asked about the fairy, either. In fact, when she returned to the inn, neither Arbiter's mercenaries nor Elineh said anything, either. The only other one besides Cayna who recognized the little girl's presence was Kee.

When she did ask Kee about her, he replied, *"She is probably an ariel,"* and spoke as if he knew Opus. When Cayna tried asking again, he remained silent. It seemed like she was better off not expecting a clear answer.

In the meantime, she was a bit worried about how low they were running on cake ingredients and decided to go to the market. Just as she was leaving, a mercenary returning from the outside called to her.

"You've got a guest, Miss Cayna."

"Who, me?"

He pointed behind him to Caerina, who wore her knightly armor.

"Caerina…"

"Grandmother..."

"Ah, you should probably find a room if this is going to be a deep conversation, right?" Arbiter suggested as the two stared at each other motionlessly and murmured each other's names.

"First, please accept this."

Since they had a lot to talk about, Cayna decided they should head out into the city rather than somewhere within the inn. When they made their way past the crowded main road and to the corner of a quiet residential street, Caerina held out a small bag. It was surprisingly heavy, and Cayna took a look inside. It was filled with silver coins.

"What's this for? Is it the delayed payment Caerick talked about yesterday?"

The amount was excessively large for a bandit-removal request disguised as supply replenishment. Altogether, it came to around two gold coins.

"I heard the payment the Adventurers Guild has offered you. It seems my simpleton brother has kept you as an unnamed, charitable third party and now has the merchants wrapped around his finger. As a result, they are raising a toast of gratitude to the unknown adventurer."

"Uwagh, I better avoid the taverns, then."

If she ran into anyone toasting her in congratulations, Cayna was pretty sure her face would burst into flames from embarrassment. Just the thought of the signboard that had been 30 percent filled with PLEASE DO SOMETHING ABOUT THE BANDITS requests made her visibly uncomfortable.

When Caerina saw that her grandmother seemed hesitant to accept such an exorbitant reward, she too began acting strange and started babbling without a second thought.

"That is actually the only congratulations we have planned, Grandmother. We considered giving you a thank-you letter from the nation but decided to forego it. We realize you have no desire to be famous."

"Thanks, Caerina. I wasn't sure what I'd do if I suddenly received a summons."

"However, the king, the prime minister, and the knight leaders know of you. I informed them that you have a close connection to the Guardian Tower and strongly dislike dealing with people of influence, so I am quite certain you will rarely be bothered with nonsense. Even so, you would do best to be careful."

"Right, got it."

Given the large number of elves in Helshper, there was no shortage of anecdotes about the Guardian Tower from days past. Many of these stories were strange, but considering Opus had been in the area, Cayna was certain most of the rumors were true.

Some said the castle used to turn into a carriage and race around.

Others said an actual ghost that screamed, "The forest is for rest!" haunted within.

Others still said that on the night of a full moon, golems and dragons would come bearing clubs and continuously hit them against cylindrical trees.

Each story was enough to give her a headache.

"By the way, what happened to the demon I captured the other day?"

"He's locked away in a dungeon under strict security. According to the guards, something seems to have stunned him, and he's completely motionless. What is the purpose of the collar you put around him? We can't seem to remove it no matter what we try."

"I'm pretty sure only one other person besides me can remove it. Think of it like this: Take it off, and it'll be like blowing away the castle and all."

105

Cayna couldn't be completely sure, but it was safe to say anything Opus left behind was meant only for her.

"I understand. I shall inform everyone of this."

"There's one thing I should warn you about, though. The collar reduces his abilities to ten percent, but you can't let him mess with his Item Box. Someone at his level probably has some explosive items, so I recommend keeping him tightly bound so he can't move."

"Ah, I see. Understood."

There was a set minimum level at which items in the game could be used, armor and weapons included. The Supreme King of Fools Armor couldn't be equipped unless you were at least level 150, which is why it instantly vanished when she put on the Punishment Collar. It was most likely stored away in his Item Box. There were all sorts of recovery-type items that even the lowest players could use, and Cayna had no idea how many of them that demon possessed. There were also plenty of attack and support items and many more that even two-digit levels could use. Even the stun bomb she used on Skargo and Mai-Mai to make them pass out could be handled by a level-30 player. For those who saw power as the name of the game, you could round up small-time punks pretty easily if you were in a single room.

Of course, none of these would create a huge fuss, but it was better that she warn them. She needed to consider the possibility of a jailbreak where he used charm-type items on the guards and quickly used a transportation-type item to escape somewhere.

Since he could get to his Item Box if his arms were free, the easiest solution would be to stick him in a barrel of concrete and let it dry.

Caerina seemed to think he was so dazed he wouldn't even consider a jailbreak, so Cayna decided to just let the government deal with him.

"By the way, Caerina, what's your rank like among the knights? You're stronger than the leader, aren't you?"

She couldn't say "What level are you?" anymore because such a system didn't exist in this era. It seemed like most people just recognized whether someone was stronger or weaker than them.

"I'm a captain of the knights, but I'm actually an instructor. The current leader is my pupil."

"Ah, so once this ridiculousness with the bandits started up, they pulled you into their ranks in a hurry, huh?"

Cayna nodded with an "I seeeee." That way, the average knights would be extra respectful of her, and the leader would obediently do as she said. In Cayna's personal opinion, Caerina was far stronger than the national average. Arbiter was right below her, and right below him was Helshper's leader of the knights.

When you boiled things down, the lack of real battle experience was clearer in knights than adventurers and brought weakness upon them.

"The knights can't compare to adventurers both then and now, huh?"

"Yes, I'm sorry to say." Caerina bowed her head in shame.

Cayna had only mentioned the past so there'd be no misunderstandings, but Caerina understood the truth of the situation and didn't make much effort to object.

"Did you devise that flame sword yourself, Caerina?"

"I am terribly ashamed of it."

Cayna had asked so suddenly because she was curious about the move she'd used to attack the rock golems.

"Long ago, I had seen an adventurer utilize a similar technique, and I used that as a reference to create my own. Naturally, the adventurer who allowed me to take notes was much more powerful than I."

Clearly a player, Cayna thought.

"That sounds like Firemoon Flower Iyah La Doul. Several crescent moon–shaped blades go flying when you swing the sword down, right?"

"Yes, that's it! That's exactly it! If you know of it, that must mean you can use it, Grandmother!"

"Well, I *am* a Skill Master."

Cayna puffed out her chest as if it were nothing. The fairy on her shoulder did the same, but Caerina didn't see this.

Even so, when Caerina asked almost apologetically if Cayna could instruct her, Cayna couldn't give an immediate nod. After all, no matter how closely they were related, it didn't seem like she could use a Skill Scroll on a nonplayer. Not only that, as a Skill Master, she couldn't give a Skill Scroll to anyone who hadn't cleared her tower.

"If you want a Skill Scroll, you'd have to complete the trial at the tower. It's not something I can give away easily."

"By *tower*, you mean the Crescent Moon Castle…"

"You absolutely must *not* go there! You'll be walking to your own death! Don't pointlessly throw your life away!"

"I understand. I will be sure to stay away."

"Perfect."

Cayna's attempt to instill the fear of the castle within her granddaughter was even more terrifying, and Caerina apologized with dead, emotionless eyes.

The two engaged in small talk for some time until another knight came calling for Caerina. She took her leave.

"Well then, Grandmother. I must bid you farewell. I fear other matters have arisen, and it seems as though the caravan whom you travel with will soon conclude their business. This will likely be the last time we are able to meet before your departure."

"Aw, that's too bad. Well, as long as it has nothing to do with power plays, you can always contact me via Mai-Mai if you need anything."

"From Felskeilo to Helshper? That's quite a long trip. I imagine it would be hard on you."

"Oh, it's no problem at all. If I input this capital into my Teleport, I can go back and forth in an instant."

"I see... Wait, you can Teleport?!"

Cayna never meant to sound so outrageous, but Caerina quickly wished she'd never asked. She'd always known her grandmother was the greatest mage in existence, but her grandmother kept dropping words far beyond normal logic into casual conversation as if it were nothing.

Eager to protect her mental health, Caerina hurriedly ended the conversation and went off with the knight who had called for her.

As she watched her granddaughter grow flustered and rush off, Cayna thought that serving the court really did seem like a tough job.

I don't even mind being called Grandmother anymore. It's amazing the things you can get used to.

She turned on her heel and started heading back toward the inn. Thinking she'd take her sudden easy money (though the amount was no laughing matter) to buy some of the capital's famed alcohol as a souvenir, she made her way to the market.

She also tried asking the fairy if there was anything she needed, but the little girl merely shook her head sadly. Now that Cayna thought about it, she couldn't recall ever seeing the fairy eat anything, either. She was probably the sort of creature that absorbed mana from the air for sustenance.

Like NPCs, the fairies in the game world of *Leadale* primarily existed to aid you on quests. Thus, she didn't remember hearing many details about them as a race.

So far, she'd been using facial expressions and gestures to communicate with Cayna. Cayna determined that she'd made a concentrated effort to talk to the fairy and deepen their understanding of each other.

That day, she bought only edible ingredients, including those needed for cake, and returned to the inn. When she got back, Elineh gathered everyone around and explained the schedule for their remaining time in Helshper.

Since the bandit leader had been captured, their outstanding business negotiations were now proceeding smoothly. The caravan would leave Helshper within a few days. However, the western outer trade route was still impassable thanks to the remaining bandits, so they would once again pass through the eastern trade route.

"So I guess you'll be needing me again…?"

"We're counting on you, Great Nameless Adventurer," Elineh said with a crafty smile as he pushed up his glasses.

Cayna's cheek twitched. It wasn't a secret anymore; it was apparently completely out there in the open.

After that, Syrus, one of Elineh's subordinates who was traveling with his family, gave Cayna a small pouch. Inside was another large sum of silver coins.

"This is your current share, Miss Cayna. We also sold all those statues."

"Um, how many did I make again? I just remember there were ten bundles of wood."

"There was a total of one hundred and sixty-two. We sold each and every one. A single statue costs five silver, thus we earned a total of eight hundred and ten silver coins. You had a forty percent share, so your total comes to three hundred and twenty-four silver coins."

"In that case, it'll be one thousand six hundred bronze coins, which will equal eight hundred and ten days at Marelle's inn…"

If she included the money Caerick gave her for taking care of the bandits, she could double that number. Incidentally, Kee was doing all the math.

Cayna was the only one who took great delight in the fact that she had saved up enough to pay for Mimily's room and board.

Incidentally, she tried to avoid using the money that had carried over from her game without good reason. This was because the cost of living in this world was so affordable that she could get by comfortably without needing to tap into it.

However, those listening to them turned to jelly and dropped in shock at her excessively shabby conversion methods. Cayna tilted her head as everyone looked at her as if she were a fish out of water.

"...Uh, wait, hold on. Is that how you're converting that huge sum of money...? You really are a strange one, miss...," Arbiter began.

"That's for sure... Maybe there's a more solid method...?" Kenison chimed in.

"Th-this is Lady Cayna at her finest... I'm unsure whether I should follow her example or be exasperated..."

Unaware they were saying whatever they wanted about her, Cayna passed out the collection of candy and snacks she had bought at the market to the caravan's women and children.

Then, the day before they were set to leave Helshper...

Cayna went to Sakaiya and met with Caerick.

"Your work the other day was splendid, Grandmother. We cannot yet open the western trade route, but knowing there is now hope has made a world of difference. Allow me to express appreciation on behalf of my fellow merchants. Thank you very much."

"I've heard you a million times alreadyyy."

"No, merchants must properly repay their debts in one form or another. Until I have reimbursed you in full, please allow me to thank you as many times as necessary."

Caerick was both more conscientious and more stubborn than she thought. However, his insistence on paying her back also made it easier for Cayna to ask for help in the future. Caerick had likely anticipated this and said it on purpose.

"Um, well, there is some information I'd like to ask about. Do you mind?"

"Please, ask away. If it is for you, Grandmother, I shall go through both fire and water."

"I haven't even said anything yet. Well, I guess it does involve water, though."

"Uh, what?"

Cayna wanted to ask about Mimily. If there was someone who could tell her about a village connected to mermaids, she wanted their help.

Although the continent of Leadale was surrounded by water on three sides, finding one single mermaid village across such a vast area was nearly impossible. The ocean was both wide and deep, and land dwellers couldn't move within it freely. Although Cayna could handle the task with her skills, accomplishing this on her own would take an outrageous amount of time.

Mermaids weren't particularly hostile toward land races, so she thought there might be a friendly face out there who would accompany her.

"A mermaid... I haven't heard much, but this is none other than a request from my grandmother. I shall make full use of my information network and aid in your search."

"Thanks. I'll probably cause you a lot of trouble, but please help me out."

"Not at all. Do pay Sakaiya another visit."

"Right. I'll be sure to come back."

Cayna gave him a cake as thanks, said her good-byes, and left.

Nothing of special mention happened on her way back from Helshper, and everything proceeded smoothly. The caravan found another horse to replace the one they'd lost, so there was no need for Cayna to summon any more beasts.

Cayna spoke more at length with the fairy, or at least enough that she didn't unsettle anyone. Although she'd never left Cayna's shoulder before, on the fifth day, the fairy started flying around her. Even so, she was wary of other people. When others approached, she would quickly return to Cayna's shoulder and hide in her hair. Cayna started calling her Li'l Fairy. This came about because she figured Opus had given the girl a name as well. If she ever met with him face-to-face, she'd ask what the fairy's name actually was.

The group passed the now properly guarded border and approached the Ejidd River. Arbiter and the others noticed the knights and soldiers gathered by the riverbank. There was a large mountain of lumber along the bank as well, and they seemed to be preparing to build a bridge.

Despite this, there were no visible laborers. Elineh stopped the caravan to see what was going on. The knights noticed them as well, and a leader-type figure approached. He reminded Cayna of an admirable knight she had met once on the battlefield, and she quickly hid in the shadows of a carriage. For some reason or other, she had felt like trouble was brewing.

But even if she didn't want to get involved, that trouble was coming toward them anyway.

After Elineh spoke with the knight, he informed the rest of the caravan that bridge construction would start from that point forward.

"Now? How?" Cayna asked.

"How come I don't even see any workers or tools, then?" Arbiter questioned.

Cayna had a good guess as to how there could be materials but no personnel. A player with specialized building skills could do so.

Or rather, perhaps not a player, but someone she knew very, very well who was more than qualified.

She looked out around her from the shadow of the carriage and spotted her youngest son sailing across the river on a small ship.

"Kartatz!"

"! Mum! What are you doin' here?"

As the familiar dwarf came ashore and raced toward her, Cayna thought, *I knew it,* with a sigh of relief.

Commotion stirred among the knights, who were not aware of the situation.

Elineh, Arbiter, and the other Flame Spears had been told of Cayna and Kartatz's relationship beforehand, so no one batted an eye when he called her Mum. However, seeing the two next to each other like that did feel incredibly weird, and they all simply face-palmed.

One was a beautiful teenage elf girl. The other was the complete opposite—a rugged, full-bearded dwarf.

"I know we were told already, but maybe there's been some sort of mistake?"

"They're mother and son…? The Seven Wonders of the continent might have a new member."

Kartatz did run a workshop, but since he was also one of the nation's full-time building engineers, the knights were there to protect him.

To prevent any misunderstandings, he explained to the knights that he was Cayna's son. As soon as they fell back, he clarified to Cayna why he was there.

"Ah, you're building a bridge here since the outer western trade route can't be used?"

"Well, it looks like the bandits' boss was captured before we even started. Both Helshper and Felskeilo are sending out soldiers to take care of the rest of 'em. Doesn't change my job, though."

"I'll blow away anyone who tries to pick a fight with you, Kartatz!"

"Why so violent, Mum?! Even if you're kidding, don't turn the Ejidd River into the Ejidd Lake!"

Any third party listening knew Kartatz meant this as a joke. However, for Arbiter and the others who knew even the slightest bit about what Cayna's magic could do, there was nothing funny about it.

"Now that we have the chance, let's build it together as mother and son," said Cayna.

"Ah, no, I appreciate it, but aren't you working as a guard for the caravan?"

"I can't do my job if there's no bridge. Arbiter! Elineh! You don't mind, right?"

"Sure, why not? Go for it."

"I will not pay you for the hours spent working on the bridge."

"I'm not that greedy!"

Cayna and Kartatz laid a rough map on the ground and began talking it over.

The captain of the knights then approached Arbiter and his group, and they began conversing as well. Arbiter was famous within the Adventurers Guild, and he'd once been a knight long ago, so he was an easy person to talk to from the current knights' perspectives.

"Sir Arbiter, is it true that the elf girl is Sir Kartatz's mother?"

"I swear it on my spear. It's true!"

Several of the soldiers widened their eyes at his bold declaration.

It was a well-known fact that Skargo, the High Priest of the church, Mai-Mai, the headmistress of the Royal Academy, and Kartatz, the boss of the shipyard, were all siblings. But to think that elf girl was the mother of the famous threesome… They all stared at her unblinkingly, but even as they watched her speak with Kartatz, none could believe their eyes.

"I don't see a single worker with him. How's the bridge supposed to get built?" Arbiter questioned.

"Yes, well, Sir Kartatz possesses deep knowledge of ancient arts, which allows him to build without aid. As long as he has the materials, there is no issue at all."

"Oh yeah, Miss Cayna used those techniques, too. Guess the apple doesn't fall far from the tree, huh?"

As the two nodded at each other congenially and continued to converse, Elineh nudged in from the side.

"Things aren't looking too well over there."

""Huh?""

They answered him with mystified expressions, and their faces further tightened when they noticed the dangerous air swirling around what should have been a friendly conversation between mother and child.

"I'm *saying*: Why not build the bridge right along the shore?! If you put a higher hill there, it'll be hard for the carriages to go over and put a strain on the poor horses!"

"Mum, if we do it your way and keep the bridge right above the surface of the water, it'll get washed away as soon as the river floods! You need space between the bridge itself and the river!"

"First of all, why would you use this much material for a pier?! You can reduce it and save some for the walkway!"

"You're not taking rivers seriously enough, Mum! You can build the walkway again as long as the scaffolding is still there! That's the only part of the bridge they can rebuild without having a specialist like me around!"

Rawr! Hissss!

The merchants, mercenaries, and knights blankly looked on at the catty war of words they couldn't do anything to stop.

After receiving a look from Arbiter, Kenison went to intervene, then backed away. He couldn't refuse an order from his leader, but a host of voices admiring his courage rose up from the soldiers.

"Um… Uh, why don't we, um, all calm down a li'l? How about talkin' it over?"

"Quiet, Kenison!" ← Combined with Intimidate

"This ain't got nothin' to do with you. Get lost!" ← Combined with Glare

"…Uh, yes, I beg yer pardon."

However, he was quickly done in by their intensity and forced to retreat. The soldiers booed, and Kenison snarled a "Why don't you guys try it, then?" in reply.

Despite normal (?) appearances, it was a level 1,100 versus level 300 battle, and the tension in the air was anything but ordinary. It was the type of heavy atmosphere that seemed like it would crush the average person flat if they weren't careful.

"Starting the bridge before the bank starts sloping will put it farther from the surface of the river, right?!"

"Like I said—if we do that, we'll run outta materials!"

"If you're short on materials, that's what a craftsman's fo… Ah!"

"Huh? What is it, Mum?"

As she was about to speak, Cayna noticed something and suddenly froze. The onlookers who had been watching over the proceedings sighed in relief that the battle between monsters had quieted without need for further intervention.

Unsure of what put a halt to the fight, they were all giving mystified looks when iron balls the size of barrels appeared from the empty sky and rained down around Cayna.

Rumble, rumble, rumble. There were twelve total. Each was a lethal weapon that could easily kill someone in one strike, and everyone around them ran for cover with a scream.

Cayna looked at Kartatz's twitching expression with a satisfied smile and happily explained.

"See what I mean? Go ahead and fill the pier with iron. If you need more material, you can just get it someplace else."

It was at this point that the onlookers wanted to ask "Where'd she get all that?!" However, Cayna appeared ready to murder someone, so they said nothing at all.

The truth was that these iron balls had been stored in the Item Box belonging to Opuskettenshultheimer Crosstettbomber, aka Opus. Since she had his permission, Cayna had humbly and unreservedly borrowed anything that seemed useful. At the time, the Guardian had said with some disgust, "This is rather like robbing a house that has burned down," but to Cayna, this was in one ear and out the other.

She once again pulled her son back as he tried to retreat, opened her Skill Formation screen, and continued with her lecture.

Although iron was iron, this was a special variety of Opus's making. Thus, only Cayna could use Building: Bridge. With her in charge of the pier, and Kartatz constructing the walkway, everything came together well. The bridge planning had been turbulent and full of twists and turns, but once they got moving, things proceeded quickly. The wind whirled, and the river split around the two. Before everyone's very eyes, the materials and iron balls rose up from both sides of the river toward the sky and twisted together. The iron squirmed about like an amoeba as it transformed, pierced the empty cavities of the pier, and slipped into the riverbed like a screw.

The wood materials were split into four categories: girders, floorboards, pillars, and handrails. These all came together one after the other as if they were alive.

While everyone looked on in dumbfounded amazement, a bridge appeared where there had once been only the river's surface. In a little under five minutes, a structure large enough for carriages to pass by with ease had been completed. Mother and child exchanged satisfied looks followed by a firm handshake.

A few moments later, cheers and clapping rose from both sides of the river.

That night, the mercenaries, soldiers, knights, and all held a huge banquet in the camp after they crossed over to the Felskeilo side.

Although Kartatz and Cayna had indeed been the ones to build the bridge, it hadn't taken much effort at all. In fact, those who suffered the most were the soldiers who had to transport the material from downriver.

Since mother and son were finally reunited, a place had been set aside for them to have a pleasant chat. It was away from curious ears and ideal for sharing secrets, so this worked for Cayna.

"He's still alive?!"

"Agh, shhh!"

"Oops. Sorry, Mum."

The conversation inevitably turned to the bandits menacing Helshper. All too late, Cayna realized she'd never asked for the leader's name. When she'd checked his stats, she had only cared about his level and completely forgot to verify his identity. Since the leader was a higher level than her children, she put her hand to her chest in relief that she'd dealt with him before they came across one another.

"Who the hell does he think he is, lookin' down on everyone like that? Why didn't you finish him off?"

"Believe me, I tried. I turned him in because I didn't want to create a mess with Helshper. Come to think of it, I wonder how they'll deal with him? I forgot to ask."

"Geez, you sure are careless. Guess you'll just have to check with Mai-Mai later."

"Oh, now that you mention it, I've gotta punish her, too."

The dark, hair-raising grin that broke across Cayna's face sent shivers down Kartatz's spine.

"Wait, she gave you a huge shock like that?! Sis really is hopeless. She could have at least talked to you."

"Well, I wasn't all that mature about it, either… It nearly turned into a cold war."

"Wha—?! That don't sound good at all… Live your best life, my sister."

Kartatz quickly forsook her and prayed to the stars.

As she watched him, Cayna gave a wry smile and thought how well they seemed to get along.

"Caerick and Caerina are good kids, and I'm glad the relationship between us didn't fall apart. They accommodated me in a lot of ways. It's nice having grandkids."

"A few days into the trip, and you're already a doting grand-mother. What happened?"

Kartatz was shocked as his mother put her hand to her chest and smiled gently. That heartwarming sight alone was like a different world compared to a short while prior, and it put a natural grin on those glancing in on them.

However, since there was never any guarantee of everyone reading a room the same way, Arbiter ignored all this and called out to her.

"Heeey, miss! Come make us that cake you promised before we left."

"…Uh, right now? You really are hopeless, Arbiter. Don't complain if you get cavities."

"Cayk?"

"They won't stop clamoring for it, so I guess I'll make enough for everyone. You have some, too, Kartatz," she said as she stood with a tired sigh and an eye roll that implied *They never change.*

"Nah, I'm not really a fan of sweet things…" Kartatz held up a tankard of ale and lightly dodged the invite.

"*Sniff.* My son has turned down his mother's cooking… What do you think of that, Elineh?"

Cayna hung her head in a false show of gloomy, teary-eyed melancholy in the hopes of getting Elineh to side with her. His reply was dead serious.

"The only punishment is death."

This sentiment spread across the camp and had the soldier and knights rising up with "Sir Kartatz, a man can do no worse than make his mother cry" and "As a son, you should think of your parents." Kartatz finally had enough.

"Agh, okay! I get it! Throw whatever cake or sweet stuff you want at me! Get cookin', Mum!"

"Really? Oh, I'm so happy. If you had said no, I thought I might go crying to Skargo."

"Eeeeek?!"

He could already see it. The vision of his elder brother lecturing him with Special Skill: Oscar—Roses Scatter with Beauty in full bloom put a dejected expression on Kartatz.

Cayna looked at him and burst into satisfied laughter.

As the night went on, a corner of the field glowed bright and rang out with warm smiles even the crackling fire couldn't beat.

On the way back from Helshper, Cayna stopped by the remote village to check on Mimily.

It seemed that the villagers had grown accustomed to life with the mermaid. However, Mimily herself continued to feel the difference in their races and was still having trouble fitting in.

Cayna would have liked to stay a long while and give her the support she needed, but ignoring her guard duties would have been inexcusable. Kartatz and the bridge-building team were also with them, so it wasn't like she could abandon them, either.

Seeing Cayna at her wit's end, Lytt said, "Leave it to me!" and took over with a thump of her chest. "Mimi is a great person, so everything will work out just fine!"

Cayna didn't know where all this was coming from, but she looked at Lytt, who was nodding with full confidence, and decided to entrust Mimily to her.

Of course, Cayna's role as guard ended as soon as they went back to the Felskeilo capital, and she returned to the village to see Mimily that very same day. Such speed astonished even Elineh, who had been considering inviting her along again.

As soon as she rushed back to the village, she was greeted with the sight of Mimily manipulating water in a barrel and twirling it around in a corner of the public bathhouse.

"What're you doing?"

"Hmm? Ah, Cayna. Hello. As you can see, I am doing the laundry."

"The laundry?! Why are you doing that?"

Cayna looked at her with wide-eyed confusion, and Mimily rubbed her cheek and laughed with a "heh-heh."

"It was Lytt who asked me…"

Just as the mermaid was about to explain, Lytt appeared with a mountain of dirty clothes.

"Here you go, Mimi. Oh, Miss Cayna."

"Hello, Lytt. It's been about five days, hasn't it?"

"Thank you, Lytt."

A question mark appeared over Cayna's head. Asking her to "wait just a moment," Mimily took out the clothes from the barrel. After tossing the dirty water from the finished clothes to the sewage line, she added fresh hot water to the barrel. Mimily put the new dirty

clothes Lytt had brought inside it, added detergent powder (sold by Sakaiya), and began to twirl the water around again. She then wrung out the excess water from the finished laundry and handed it to Lytt. The girl put these in a bucket, announced "I'll go dry these!" and left.

"Um, what's going on?"

Mimily gave a wry smile at Cayna's still thoroughly confused expression and with a "Yes, about that…" began to explain.

It all started after Cayna had visited the village five days prior. Mimily had apparently been sulking at her lack of connection with the villagers, so Lytt patiently took the time to talk with her. To spark Mimily's interest, she spoke about everything from her interests to the different exciting things that happened in the village.

Mimily asked no questions, but Lytt told her, "Our village doesn't have much, but there's plenty of fun!" and brought up how she met Cayna as well.

What caught the mermaid's interest was the fact that there weren't many children in the village, so Lytt almost always played alone.

Her circumstances were similar to Mimily's, and Mimily showed her how children played back in her mermaid village. This is where her special water manipulation trick came in.

More than anything else, she seemed eager to show how masterfully she could control the water without affecting any sea creatures, but since arriving in the village, she'd been working with water in barrels.

"Hmm? You didn't do it in the bathhouse?"

"With all due respect, the magic you used to set it in place is so strong that my own power cannot interfere…"

"O-oh. I see…"

Cayna felt bad about unknowingly impacting Mimily's life and continued listening.

Just when Mimily said, "I can control it remotely without looking," and prepared to demonstrate, Lytt's ribbon was blown by the wind and into the barrel. Neither had noticed, and apparently the ribbon stayed there for quite some time after the fact. When Lytt saw Mimily fixing the ribbon she had fished out of the barrel, Lytt proposed, "We should do laundry together!"

Like Cayna, Mimily was initially bewildered. She had no time to react; soon enough, Lytt had brought along the elders of the village and declared, "Mimi can do it!"

"Looks like you underestimated children's energy."

"Yes. It's quite something…"

Mimily said she was shocked by how quickly the seniors accepted the idea. The men of the village, quarreling families, and those whose age prevented them from doing laundry themselves all made appointments with Mimily. In return, the mermaid received one bronze coin per household per day.

Mimily herself jumped at the chance to be saved from her ennui; she thought merely being the recipient of the villagers' daily kindness was regrettable. It was only her second day, but she'd already earned ten bronze coins. She used it to pay for future meals at the inn.

"I'm sorry you went through so much trouble for me, Cayna. I promise to repay the inn cost someday."

"If you've found a path to self-reliance, then more power to you. I already have money, so I'm not expecting you to pay me back."

"Though I cannot promise when, please do expect it someday."

Cayna smiled as Mimily thrust her chest out proudly.

"I've been looking for people with connections to the mermaid village, though. As land dwellers, the ocean is outside our expertise."

"It may be impossible for your kind to fully understand the ocean. I wouldn't get my hopes up."

Mimily put on a brave face and spoke lightly, despite the tinge of sadness in her eyes.

"And to think I went and saved up all that money during my trip so I could help you. I guess things just didn't work out."

"Huh? Please wait. Don't make my debt any higher!"

"Not to worry. I'm simply going to make a small room next to the bathhouse so you can do your laundry. A barrel with a bobbing neck like you see in those bamboo fountains would be good, too."

"Bamboo fountain? Please wait! Hey, are you listening to me?"

"Yes, yes, I'm listening. You've got absolutely nothing to worry about. I'm going to make you a fabulous workplace!"

"Whaaaaat?!"

When Lytt came back with the dried laundry, she was greeted by a new small annex to the bathhouse, Cayna wiping sweat with a sense of accomplishment from a job well done, and Mimily hanging her head limply and murmuring, "I couldn't stop her."

"Hmm. Eeny meeny miny mo..."

With Mimily's place in the village secure, Cayna returned to Felskeilo and resumed her life as an adventurer.

Even without being picky, each and every request seemed like one she could take on. However, Arbiter warned her to resist; after all, doing so would mean she'd leave nothing for the newbies. Thus, she stuck to requests that weren't too difficult yet had no time constraints.

Her main motivation behind that decision was gluttony. She wanted to eat dinner at the inn as much as possible and go hunting for delicious food stands.

Li'l Fairy seemed to fare poorly in crowds; every time Cayna took a step outside her room, she would hide under her hair and peek out. Others couldn't even see her, so what was it that made her so scared?

"There's no way Opus bullied you, right?"

Li'l Fairy shook her head vehemently. Cayna also considered the possibility of a concealment spell that wore off if the fairy was being stared at, but this didn't seem to be the case, either. It couldn't be anything other than a sign of their deepening bond.

"Sheesh, it's just one thing after another, huh?"

Even though adventurers accomplished at least eight to ten requests per day, there was never an empty space on the request board.

The Felskeilo Adventurers Guild had about twenty resident members. It wasn't like each one completed requests every day, but even so, new requests were constantly popping up.

"Well, the more people there are, the more that's needed. If it's not in town, you've got no choice but to go searching outside. The worry never ends."

In one corner where a party with too much time on their hands gathered, a large, well-armored man had heard Cayna mumbling to herself and answered back. As if in agreement with him, his fellow members laughed.

"That's 'cause even if there's work in town, lots of people don't know how to rough it," another party member, a young, fragile, mage-looking man, chimed in. Others nodded along with "Got that right."

It was apparent more than a few adventurers only took on requests within the town. Many of these people were women and children and those with no fighting abilities.

"Like all those requests that say *Find my cat!*—just how many cats do they think are in this town?!"

"Ah, one of those really gave me the runaround. A cat is one thing, but a goretiger? I wanted to tell her, *Don't keep those in town!*"

"The woman who made the request was real nice, wasn't she?"

"So you can keep something like that in town…," Cayna mused.

A goretiger was a giant tiger that was covered in armor from the back of its head all the way down its back. Apparently, more than a few nobles would acquire cubs of the ferocious animals from some-where and keep them as status symbols.

As the group behind Cayna watched her face the board once again, the conversation turned to their struggles as beginners. Think-ing that it felt nice to hear other's experiences, she picked the first request she spotted.

This request was FOOD INGREDIENT COLLECTION: DESIRE HORNED BEAR MEAT. REQUESTOR: THE WHITE-TAILED BLACK RABBIT RESTAURANT. PAYMENT: EIGHT SILVER COINS.

Cayna remembered hearing the name of the restaurant from Kar-tatz before. It was the fancy restaurant where he'd gather with his siblings to dine and discuss any issues.

I'd be interested to know what sort of things they've discussed until now.

After Cayna returned to Felskeilo, she'd asked Kartatz to tell Mai-Mai, "Prepare yourself."

Cayna had yet to meet with her. According to Lopus, who she just happened to see in town, the daily fear of not knowing when her mother would strike had caused Mai-Mai to waste away. Now that Cayna had made peace with her grandchildren, she was no longer motivated to get back at Mai-Mai at all. Instead, she was merely let-ting her daughter stew in her misery as a bit of revenge. If Mai-Mai was now at the point of growing haggard, Cayna thought maybe it was about time to forgive her.

"I guess I can do it after finishing this job…"

She submitted the request to the reception desk, and the familiar employee named Almana took care of it for her.

"Miss Cayna, the ingredients will be delivered directly to the restaurant. Shall I explain where it is?"

"I'm sure I'll be fine if I ask around. Otherwise, I'll drag Skargo out and ask him."

As Cayna gave a bright, carefree smile, Almana thought she could hear the sound of the world lurching.

Using the High Priest as her errand boy... Almana knew what that statement meant, but she couldn't understand it. There were already rumors going around about how the High Priest one day flew into a downtown inn wearing a completely unfamiliar expression, and it was a well-known fact among the townspeople that Cayna was the mother of the famous three. A majority had rejected it with a scoff of "That's ridiculous" and laughed it off as a mere joke.

Still, the Adventurers Guild was considered an infallible source of information. The employees all knew it to be true, but having it once again reaffirmed right in front of her was far too harsh. To make matters worse, the fan mentality of those who knew this young girl to be Skargo's mother and doubted his mother complex, and frequent declarations of her as a supreme being, was unfathomable. It was unclear whether these feelings in the town girls' hearts were of envy or hatred, but Cayna cheerfully and obliviously walked out of the guild and toward the market.

After all, her target was a horned bear.

Cayna had plenty of ways to catch it in her arsenal, but it was a wild animal, nonetheless. She unfortunately (or maybe fortunately?) had two encounters with horned bears near the remote village, but it would still probably take her several days to find one. She planned to buy up ingredients and preserved foods just in case. She'd also have to tell the inn she'd be away for a few days.

On the way, she called out to some boys who looked like they had some free time and gave them a few bronze coins. She asked them to give a message to Kartatz that she'd be out of Felskeilo on work for a while.

Ever since beating Primo, the kids of the town had recognized her as "the scary girl" and couldn't refuse a request from her to save their lives. Since Cayna was unable to use Telepathy with her children, it was a perfect communication method. The inn proprietress told Cayna the children with single parents and orphans of the town took these odd jobs in order to save up money for rent, so Cayna took full advantage of this. After all, even the average person could easily visit the workshop and meet with Kartatz. And since the children had the ability to escape her in a rowboat, she wouldn't have to bother with crossing to the sandbar, either.

As Cayna was shopping, she noticed two girls walking a few streets ahead. She wouldn't normally give them a second look, but if one of them was Lonti, then that was a different story.

Thinking it was some sort of fate, she quickly finished her shopping and chased after them. She called out.

"Heeey! Lonti!"

"Cayna! What perfect timing."

"Huh?"

Hearing Lonti so pleased to see her made Cayna think she might get roped into more escapee prince hunting. However, she looked at the robed girl next to Lonti whose head was bowed toward her and tilted her own head questioningly.

"It's been some time, hasn't it?"

"Hi, Lonti. You're looking well."

"I'm so glad I met you here. I thought I would have to go looking all over for you."

Cayna felt sorry for Lonti as the girl put a hand to her chest in relief, but since Cayna had no idea where this conversation was going, she wasn't sure how to react.

"Allow me to introduce you. This is..."

At Lonti's insistence, the girl removed her hood.

Her light-peach-colored hair was braided and piled up behind her head. She had stern features and willful brown eyes. From what Cayna could see, she was a total beauty. The girl wore white female armor. It had the same design as the Felskeilo knights. She had a thin blade at her side, most likely a rapier.

Cayna would have been able to know her full level and background with Search, but since Lonti was the one who brought her along, she had no interest in checking beforehand. After all, the two were perfectly dolled up, so it was obvious that they were nobles.

People around them looked at the girls but disappeared just as quickly.

"This is my friend from the Academy, um… Mye."

"My name is Mye. It's a pleasure to meet you."

"I'm the high elf Cayna. Nice to meet you."

The girl who introduced herself as Mye exchanged greetings with Cayna and bowed her head. Cayna then smiled brightly, and Mye took a step back in confusion.

Lonti had reacted the same way when they first met. Cayna looked at her and wondered if maybe she was also uncomfortable around high elves. Mye then grew flustered and turned away, red in the face.

Cayna hadn't realized this, but her full smile had been combined with Passive Skill: Charm. Anyone who met her for the first time and wasn't prepared would turn crimson. Of course, Charm did not include the ability to manipulate someone's consciousness and control their will. It mostly just gave a minuscule amount of oomph to first impressions.

Seeing this unfold, Lonti gave a bitter smile that said *She's doing the same thing, huh?* and once again bowed to Cayna.

"I'm terribly sorry, Cayna. I know you are busy, but would you mind if we accompany you for some time?"

"……Huh?"

Cayna looked as if she'd just seen pigs fly, and she stood temporarily frozen at Lonti's request.

She soon rebooted with Kee's prodding and ruminated over this.

"I don't really mind, but…"

"Really?! Thank you so much!"

Lonti jumped with overwhelming joy at Cayna's acceptance, then took the hand of Mye next to her and nodded.

"H-hold on, Lonti."

"It seems that Cayna is all right with it, Lonti. Isn't that great?"

To calm down the strangely and overly enthusiastic Lonti, who was now swinging Mye around, Cayna clapped her hands and temporarily drew the attention to herself. All grew silent.

"I don't mind, but I'm about to leave town on a job request."

""WHAT?!""

This time, it was the two girls who froze. Cayna didn't really know what was going on with them and deliberated over how to deal with the situation. Figuring she should at least hear their side of the story, she decided to push them into the nearest restaurant. Li'l Fairy remained hidden in Cayna's hair as usual.

The eatery was a popular spot among the locals and neighboring towns that was only open during the day and just sold light fare. It was rush hour, but the three managed to find seats in a corner farther inside. They ordered only drinks and waited for Lonti to calm down.

With sweet fruit wine placed on the table in front of them, she finally got ahold of herself and huddled in embarrassment.

"I'm sorry, Cayna. I got carried away."

"It's not really a big deal."

"Lonti. Why don't we listen to what she has to say and rethink the matter?"

Cayna could sense an elegance in Mye's movements and estimated that Lonti's friend must be another member of the upper class.

"Well then, would you mind explaining why you want to join me?"

"That's because…"

Just as Lonti was about to answer, Mye stopped her and turned to Cayna.

"I apologize. She was going along with my wishes. I planned on going outside the walls for the first time and wanted Lonti to come with me. I wanted someone familiar with the outside to accompany us as a guard, but I don't do well with men, so she recommended you."

"I don't really get it, but are you running away from home or something?"

Cayna had been able to guess this with a glance, and the two were stunned into silence.

"I-I'm sorry…," Lonti began.

"I'm the one who is in the wrong for having you come along, Lonti! That's why—"

"Okay, stop."

Mye's sudden panic was starting to draw the eyes of the restaurant on them, so Cayna cast Magic Skill: Barrier and turned them away. Neither Lonti nor Mye had any idea what she did, but all sound around the three was cut off.

"I don't know what you're getting so worked up about, but I'm not going to report you to anyone. Besides Lonti's gramps, I don't have any connections like that."

Skargo and Mai-Mai did indeed count as such connections, but unfortunately, Cayna didn't see them that way.

"So I'm going outside to do a request. Do you really want to come along?"

""What?!""

Both Mye and Lonti had decided to go outside on a whim. Naturally, they did not prepare in the slightest or make the proper provisions. It was obvious from their casual outfits.

Cayna must have appeared the same way to the two, but since she always had a vast supply of goods in her Item Box, she was good to go.

"I should be out there about two nights. If you're running away, people are going to come after you, right? We can give them the slip once we're outside."

"That is true...," Lonti began.

"But the only camping I've ever done has been at the Academy."

"I think you'll be just fine. I can give you a safe place to sleep and delicious dinners."

This world wasn't as relentless as the game, so bringing along the girls wouldn't be an issue for her. It was also proof she lived up to her reputation as a larger-than-life Skill Master on a constant basis.

Mye was reluctant at first, but when Cayna suggested that perhaps she could stay with Skargo at the church, the girl instantly changed her tune.

After paying the bill and leaving the restaurant, they headed toward the eastern gate to leave town. Normally, it was best to set out early in the morning when going on a trip. However, Cayna figured she could use any number of transportation spells and had thus spent the afternoon relaxing.

Unsurprisingly, now that there were others with her, this option was no longer possible. Therefore, in an effort to move the request along, Cayna summoned several Wind Spirits to aid in the search for her target.

"Come to think of it, Cayna, what sort of request did you accept?"

"Oh, right, I didn't tell you. I'm hunting down a horned bear!"

"Oh, I see... Wait, a horned bear?!"

"Yup. The client said they wanted its meat. It was some restaurant called the Something-or-Other Rabbit."

"The White-Tailed Black Rabbit…?"

"Yeah, that was the name."

Cayna hummed a merry tune as she walked down the main road, but Lonti turned pale at the news of this insane request.

A horned bear was a giant bear-shaped monster with stiff fur that stood between three to five meters high and had either one or two horns on its head. They were omnivorous and normally lived in the deeper parts of the forest but would turn up in villages and attack people when they were hungry. To stop them, you often had to delve into the forest, and even adventurers needed to form several skilled teams. They were a formidable enemy that could wipe out parties in an instant, and Academy students could never hope to handle them.

Mye and Lonti summarized all this in a neat explanation, and their faces twitched. However, their leader, Cayna, showed the least amount of worry.

They hadn't seen or heard of the equipment she was wearing, but Lonti and Mye could tell by sight alone that everything was first-rate. Even so, they had no idea what was inside Cayna's travel pack, so her insistence of "Leave everything to me" raised questions.

"Lonti, is that girl okay?"

"Well, even my uncle has endorsed her strength. She's also High Priest Skargo's mother, so there shouldn't be any issues."

"*She's* the High Priest's mother who everyone has been talking about?!"

Mye had sensed a vague air of closeness when Cayna suggested using the church as a day-care center and was openly shocked.

"? Oh, what's that about Skargo now? He do somethin' to bother you, Mye?"

After traveling along the main eastern road for about an hour,

Cayna had turned north down another path. Now the three were traversing through the forest with no trail in sight. Cayna continued ahead of them and occasionally spoke briefly with the trees or the grass. She would then create a path that only fit one person at a time.

When the two first witnessed this, their eyes flew open, and their jaws dropped in shock.

To Cayna, however, she was only using her high-elf powers to communicate with nature. The trees and grasses were just temporarily moving out of the way for her. The way she pulled off these feats with such ease, even though other elves couldn't, put Cayna in a class all her own.

When the two recovered from the shock, they began talking quietly to each other. At one point, when Mye accidentally spoke too loudly, Cayna turned around and looked at the pair. Seeing Mye suddenly clam up made her swell with suspicion, but she seemed to misunderstand something and frowned.

"Did he dare lay a hand on a girl who came to see him?! That damn Skargo! So he's fallen to the lowest of lows and is now the enemy of women. I'll make sure he learns his lesson when we get back!"

"Th-th-th-th-that isn't it! He only advises me on some*zimes*."

Mye grabbed Cayna, who had made a fist in indignation, and frantically explained herself. Apparently Lonti had never seen Mye frazzled, either, for she was completely taken aback.

Mye's fumbled words and flustered red face switched on a light bulb in Cayna's mind, and she smiled darkly. From her crimson mouth cracked like a crescent moon came an even darker laugh.

"Hoh-hooooh. Well then, Mye. Do you have an interest in my son?"

"Eek..."

"Huh? Is that true, Mye?" Lonti asked in disbelief as Mye stood frozen stiff with a face so red it seemed like steam might pour out of her ears. Mye had apparently hidden it so well that she hadn't even told her good friend.

Now a full-fledged neighborhood auntie brimming with curiosity, Cayna crossed her arms and murmured "I knew it" with a deep nod.

"By seeking advice, you could enjoy his gentle admonishment, and along with his beauty, take in his sweet words. Ah, youth sure is great!"

Cayna had already turned into a boorish old man. Mye grew red up to her ears as she bowed her head.

"Why are you reacting like that, Mye?! You were lying about not liking anyone, weren't you?!"

"But how am I supposed to bring up something like that...?"

"In that case, you should have told the queen before the flood of formal marriage intervi—"

"Waaaaaagh?! Shhh! Shhh!!"

"...Ah..."

Realizing that she'd just said something she really wasn't supposed to, Lonti covered her mouth with her hand. However, Cayna had heard all too clearly and looked at the timid pair with a smirk.

"Aghhhh, I've been found out..."

"I'm sorry! I'm so sorry!"

Mye's shoulders slumped, and Lonti bowed her head repeatedly.

So she's the princess, huh?

"I wonder if it is all right that you brought a princess outside the town walls."

I'll go crying to Skargo if that happens.

Cayna's face grimaced as the words *princess kidnapper* flashed before her.

Furthermore, her son was her last resort. She'd said it once, and she'd say it again: Using authority was completely wrong. But in this unacceptable situation, there was a high chance she might be in for some hard labor. To prevent this, it was obvious her cushions, Skargo and Mai-Mai, would be in for some trouble.

"Well, first loves are never all that serious…"

"My feelings aren't so shallow!"

Mye flared up when Cayna suddenly switched back to the subject at hand. However, she saw Cayna's lips twist into a smirk and gasped.

"Nice, you admitted it!"

"I—I—I—I—I did not! That's not what I mean! It's deep affection!"

"There's nothing wrong with that, y'know? I think it's great you didn't really try to deny it."

Mye flapped her arms as she tried to clarify the misunderstanding (?) but Cayna's hands-off attitude threw the already confused girl for a loop.

"I'm not about to get myself involved in my kids' love lives. Plus, it wouldn't be right to take away your feelings. Besides, Mai-Mai is already a loose cannon with a son and daughter in Helshper and a second husband. I wanted to be like, *If you wanna win my daughter's heart, you'll have to at least take me down first!*"

When Mai-Mai later heard this from Lonti, she gave a big sigh of relief that she hadn't waited too long to get married. No matter the heavy hitter, anyone would have turned to mincemeat if they went up against her mother. Since Lopus wasn't a fighter in any sense, she could only imagine the frightful results that would have awaited.

The two girls before Cayna were unaware of her true power and merely nodded with a surprised "Oh…"

Just before the sun set, the three arrived at a simple rest area set along a main road and quickly began to make camp. Mye and Lonti, who had done long-distance marches at the Academy, put simple charms around the area.

Cayna used Summoning Magic to call upon a Flame Spirit (a baby monkey) the size of one's palm, which ran into the night forest to gather firewood. Thinking one could never be too careful, Cayna summoned the cerberus as well.

Mye and Lonti held each other and trembled in fear at the sight of the giant three-headed Doberman pinscher–like creature. Cayna asked it to escort them around the campsite. As long as no all-powerful monsters came along, these precautions were enough to keep them safe. If she saw that the cerberus disappeared into the night forest, Cayna would know there was a terrifying monster out there greater than a horned bear.

Upon seeing Cayna summon and control monsters at will, Mye and Lonti changed their opinion of Cayna; no one without such abilities could have been Skargo and Mai-Mai's mother.

The girl who made them tremble in awe remained blissfully unaware as she doled out courses of meat pie and pizza that weren't even found in the most aristocratic of balls. The shock alone exhausted the two. Cayna watched on gently as they fully enjoyed the unknown flavors and began laying out the dessert preparations.

"Cayna, aren't you afraid of the forest at night...?" Mye asked.

Mye looked around them, jolted at some noise, and trembled as she quickly put the blanket she'd been given over her head. Lonti seemed to be feeling the same way, but she was bravely toughing it out.

"Not really. High elves like me live in the forest. Why be scared of it now?"

Cayna's composure seemed to put the girls at ease, and their shivering subsided a bit. They didn't realize that even the level-480 cerberus that guarded them could be called excessive.

Wow, it's just like Arbiter said.

During his adventurer lectures, he had taught her that the mere presence of a relaxed old-timer was enough to quell the surrounding anxiety. She was rather pleased to see the effect it was already having and feel the trust they had in her.

In any case, she cast Cooking Skill: Pie to ready their dessert. She spread her arms wide, and a giant fireball formed between them. It sucked up the ingredients on her lap, and within a few seconds, she had a ruche pie.

Nodding with approval at the usual pleasing aroma, she noticed that the two were frozen with dotted eyes and open mouths. She hit her fist against her palm in understanding.

"Right, I've only used these skills at the Academy and with Elineh and the others, so this is your first time. I see."

When Cayna tapped their shoulders, and they returned to themselves, she used leaves the tree had given her in lieu of plates and put a piece of pie on each. She passed them to the girls.

They looked between Cayna and the pie, watched the chef eat it with relief, then timidly took a bite themselves.

"Ah, it's delicious…"

"It's so sweet…"

"I'm glad you like it. I made enough for six people, so we can each have two slices."

After eating heartily under the logic that there's a second stomach for dessert, Cayna set her Rune Blade at her waist, stood up, and headed for the small river down the hill. With a quick "I've just got something to take care of," she left.

"I wonder what she's preparing for?" Lonti questioned.

"I have to say, I don't really know what she's thinking…"

It wasn't long before their question was answered.

An impressive *BOOOOOOOOOOM!* rang out, while a roaring *GA-GA-GA-GA-GA-GA-GA!!* shook the air around them.

The two fearfully made their way downhill. Sure enough, they found Cayna. She was standing in front of a thick, cylindrical object made of stone that rose perpendicularly from the ground. She had an expression of accomplishment.

"Cayna!"

"What are you doing?! What is that? A monster?"

"Oh, I thought I'd make a bath. The ground was pretty tough, so I was blasting at it to get it ready. Sorry about the noise."

"Huh?"

"A—a bath?"

Cayna had created a hole with blast magic and used river stones processed into bricks to line the inside. After drawing out water from the river, she then used Warm Water to heat it up. Steam wafted up on the other side of the stone wall she had built to serve as a partition screen.

By this point, the two could only sigh at all the outrageous things she did. Mye thought it was easier to accept than to question, and she pulled Lonti along.

"M-Mye?"

"We're already here, so let's just go in, Lonti."

"Huh? Wh-whaaat?!"

"Well then, I'll keep a lookout here, so go and enjoy yourselves."

"Understood. We'll take you up on that offer."

Cayna waved the two off as they crossed the wall, then leaned against the partition screen and crossed her arms. At the same time, she opened up the Map window, and Kee pointed out the area's terrain.

After confirming that none of the several wriggling light points had red marks on them, Cayna sighed and slumped her shoulders. The wind then twirled in front of her, and three transparent little birds appeared.

These were level-220 Wind Spirits she had called upon that

afternoon to aid in her search. It was apparent that since they were still close to the town, she wouldn't be able to find the horned bear.

"I knew it. We won't have any luck unless we go deep into the forest, huh?"

"There is a possibility that the target is living in terrain similar to that of the remote village. The probability of one inhabiting an area seventeen kilometers to the north is seventy-four percent."

On a map, this was a region right next to the main branch of the Ejidd River. The mere close proximity to water meant more wildlife and more danger. It would be a rough place for the low-level girls, but Cayna had full confidence she could protect them.

In place of bedding, Cayna summoned several six-legged sheep. The girls couldn't get enough of their fluffiness.

The next day, they set out once again on their journey, and Cayna informed them that they would be entering farther into the forest.

Cayna had mostly done her own thing in the Game Era, so to be honest, the girls would only weigh her down. Players, even beginner ones, had at least some degree of understanding and could be left alone. However, this world had no save point you could return to if you died. If someone's life hung in the balance, she'd more or less forfeit her secret doctrine and let the Special Skills fly.

She called three of the Wind Spirits out to search ahead for the horned bear and then two therwolves to guard the girls. The Wind-type white wolves would race with the wind and soar into the sky when needed, so they'd be perfect for getting them out of harm's way.

She had considered both their safety and escape options. Since this option was Cayna's idea, it was exceedingly irresponsible.

Cayna cast defensive spells on the girls and several more layers of protection to back it up.

Asking the trees for directions all the while, they headed deeper into the forest.

"Phew. Looks like I've kicked something boring again."

The horned bear didn't move a muscle; it was covered head to toe in dirt with its limbs twisted in all different directions.

Standing before the expired monster, Cayna brushed back her hair and uttered this samurai-like catchphrase.

"………"

"A-are you okay, Mye?! Hang in there!"

Mye hadn't been able to handle the shock of watching Cayna take mere seconds to silence a monster that even several knights working together could just barely manage. Since Lonti had witnessed Cayna walking on water, she wasn't particularly thrown off and tried her best to call Mye back into consciousness.

The Wind Spirits had searched for the horned bear, and when they found one, they led it to as open a space as possible. Since damaging its fur would lower its selling price, Cayna was careful not to slash or pierce it. Instead, she kicked at it with her usual Weapon Skill: Charge. Cayna also avoided her mistake from last time and took special care not to injure any trees or shrubs.

She then had the Wind Spirits lift the gut-punched horned bear into the sky and let it free-fall.

In other words, she used a kick/fall combo to snuff the life out of it without leaving a single scratch.

When Mye came to, Cayna was starting to dissect the horned bear. The air was thick with the scent of blood, and there was no question that anyone unused to such a situation would grow ill in a matter of seconds. Cayna was controlling the wind for the time being to prevent any other monsters from dropping in, but the stench was incredible. Lonti blanched, while Mye went beyond pale and turned a ghastly ashen color. She covered her mouth as Lonti swiftly led her farther into the forest and away from where the dissection was taking place. Obeying Cayna's orders, the guard therwolves followed after them.

Watching them would only cause Cayna to lose daylight, so she nimbly went about her task. The innards were buried in a hole, the isolated meat was frozen, and the fur was tanned. After the bones had been dried out, they were also added to the Item Box.

Amid the putrefying smell, Li'l Fairy left Cayna's shoulder and moved a short distance away to watch the horned bear be taken apart. Cayna wasn't sure whether her composure meant the fairy didn't particularly mind the smell or if she couldn't smell it at all.

Once Cayna scattered the stagnant air up into the sky and cast Purity on herself, her job was done. Searching for the horned bear had been a major hassle, and the sky was already starting to turn orange.

The journey back to Felskeilo would probably be two days by foot. Using an expedited method when she had the two girls with her would be pretty reckless, so she decided to spend one more night where they were. She told the therwolves to bring them over, and she began setting up camp.

She prepared two barrels and filled one with water that would be used for drinking. For the other, she also filled it with water and cast Warm Water. This would be for washing.

Even for nobles like Lonti and Mye, the bath Cayna had made the night before seemed beyond the realms of normalcy. Although Cayna had been trying to be considerate, it only overwhelmed them. And so today they would be using warm water in a barrel. It was Cayna's way of insisting they scrub to their hearts' content.

When Li'l Fairy got the sense the therwolves would be returning soon, she quickly alighted to Cayna's shoulder. Cayna then called off the Wind Spirits who had searched for the horned bear and instead cast a different summoning spell.

Summoning Magic: White Dragon Level 4

A pure-white magic circle about twenty meters in diameter immediately appeared before her. Slowly rising up from within it was a snowy dragon covered in feathers. One might mistake it for a giant bird at first, but the horn atop its head, the long neck and tail, arms with fours talons on each hand, and large wings on its back designated it as a dragon. If one were to measure up to the very tip of its head, it would be the equivalent of a four-story apartment complex.

The White Dragon was a holy-type dragon that could expertly cast Recovery and Defense Magic. It could heal all party members in a single breath and was often placed in the rear guard during wars in the Game Era. Like the Black Dragon, it was one of the larger varieties, so defensive positions could easily be pinpointed and crushed. The White Dragon did have a light-based breath attack, but you had to wait an hour before you could use it again.

After being brought back by the therwolves, the girls gaped in horror at the dignified White Dragon standing there. The barrels, the Flame Spirit bonfire, and their bedding were all directly beneath it.

The monsters that had brought them there thus far were low-level and more along the lines of simple protective charms. Unlike those, this one was a real type of protective measure. Even a horned bear would turn tail in the presence of a level-440 White Dragon.

Cayna had summoned it with the thought that they could sleep tight among its fluffy feathers.

"Hey now, are you guys okay? Come on over."

"Sh-she's asking if we're okay…?" Lonti wondered.

"It—it won't eat us?" Mye questioned.

"I summoned it, so it does whateeever I say. *Paw.*"

As the girls cowered in fear before it, Cayna held up her right hand. The White Dragon touched this with one talon.

After she had the dragon do "Other paw" and "Lie down," the girls finally drew near. When they managed to come under its spread wings and look at each other, Cayna gave a wry smile.

"Is this your first time seeing a dragon?"

As they started eating the bread, cheese, and meat skewers Cayna had made, the girls glanced up at the chin of the creature that blocked the night sky above them and glowed red from the bonfire.

At Cayna's question, they paused for a beat before nodding simultaneously. As if remembering an old memory, Mye replied as she pinched her brow.

"What I do know is mostly through hearsay. The leader of the knights spoke of them long ago."

"He spoke of them to me as well. Like how dragons always remain in old ruins in order to protect them…"

"The knight leader? Was he alive two hundred years ago?"

"He took the position several years ago, so I cannot verify his age. However, he is a dragoid."

"Hmm, is he strong?"

"Yes, very strong. He can break a boulder with ease."

Could he be a player?

She had questions, but none of them could be answered unless she met with the person himself.

"Do you usually go outside with the Academy like this?"

"No, not especially. Actually, I'm registered with the Adventurers Guild and take on requests such as herb gathering and hunting for small animals, but those are always day trips," Lonti replied.

"I see. Can you go out, too, Mye?"

"I always have a guard with me, but I have been outside."

"Sounds like you've got a lot to deal with."

"I believe I am fine with simply attending the Academy for now."

"I don't blame you. Oh, Lonti. Has Primo made any escape attempts lately?"

"Ah-ha-ha. Ever since you made an infamous name for yourself, we have had no such reports."

"'Primo'?" Mye tilted her head at the unfamiliar moniker.

Holding back a laugh, Lonti explained that they were talking about the prince.

"You mean that boy?"

"On the day he escaped, my grandfather just happened to meet Cayna and asked for her aid."

"The knights have indeed said it's been troublesome catching him each and every time. She was able to do so?"

"As we were chasing him, I partly called out '*Prince*.' I tried to stop myself, but Cayna heard me and started calling him Primo instead."

"Goodness!"

"I can walk on walls and water, so nothing can hide from me."

"I…would have very much liked to see that."

"Huh?"

Cayna picked up on Mye's interest in the words *on walls and water*.

"Magic for walking on walls is intended for personal use, so I don't see why you can't try it yourself."

"Hold on, Cayna! Please don't tempt Mye like this!"

"Tempt…? Well, I don't know if I'll be able to teach you, but I can give you a test if you're interested!"

The Skill Master habit of giving trials made her blurt this out, and question marks appeared over Mye's and Lonti's heads.

"Are we supposed to beat you in a battle?" Lonti questioned.

"Nope, that could never happen."

""You're deciding just like that?!""

Cayna waved her hand in flat-out rejection of the idea, and the two jokingly complained of such cruelty.

"C'mon, give me a break, guys."

"If we upset you, won't that upset Master Skargo as well?" Mye wondered.

"Hmm, good question. I'm not really sure."

She talked until the wee hours of the morning until the girls' nerves finally abated. There were a lot of weirdos back in the game, so it had been a long time since Cayna could laugh so warmly with others.

CHAPTER 4
A Reunion, a Monster, Subjugation, and a Clue

Back in the capital, a day after Cayna and the two girls had spent the night in the forest with the White Dragon…

One man among the rowdy bunch in the Adventurers Guild mumbled, "Oh yeah, I haven't seen that girl here in three days. Maybe she went off on another guard job somewhere?"

The party known as the Armor of Victory were frequent visitors to the guild. Each member was a seasoned veteran from the same village. They'd had a conversation with her on the day she took the horned bear request. The party had filled their purses a few days prior, so they were finding ways to laze around without blowing their money. Still, they were never ones to miss a good payday and made sure to stop by the guild.

Among their number, a young male knight who was sort of the brains of the operations made an educated guess.

"She took on a hunting request, but I don't think there's any need to worry about her."

"Looked like a pretty reckless girl. You sure she's okay?"

"Maybe it's high time we introduce her to a party?"

As the members all discussed Cayna, only their tank, a man dressed in armor, shook his head.

"As if anyone could ever stand up to her…"

These solemn words cut all conversation short. The man and his comrades looked at one another in silence, then he apologized with a wry smile.

"Ah, sorry. That's just the feeling I got. The words slipped out. Forget it."

"Hey now, Cohral. Sounds to me like you're not tellin' the whole story. You in love or somethin'?"

"Wha—?! Wh-who would love that girl?!"

The man named Cohral fumbled over his words and lashed out at the man who had poked fun at him. Since Cohral was their tank and occasionally the one who delivered the winning blow, the joker was no match for his rage and ran outside. The others called Cohral down, and he gave up on the pursuit. Recalling the difference he sensed in her the first time he saw her, he shuddered.

Leadale was once an online VRMMOPRG. This was where the twenty-something human character Cohral was born. His avatar looked pretty much the same as he did in real life; he only changed the hair and eyes to brown.

Due to sudden, unexpected circumstances, the wonderful land of dreams—where he met people who knew neither his face nor his name and had banded with him in times of trouble and grew alongside him—fell into decline.

Then, on the last day of service…

Uninterested in messing around with his friends, Cohral had climbed to higher ground where he could take in an unobstructed view of the blue sky and green earth.

However, before he knew it, he realized he was standing alone in the middle of an unfamiliar forest.

He couldn't contact the Admins. He couldn't message his friends. The Map function was disabled. Equipped with absolutely nothing and at a complete loss, he was found by a hunter from a nearby village and taken in.

There, he heard a fairy tale. It was about how the destruction of seven nations had ushered in an era of development that led to the formation of three new nations. In this world, over two hundred years had passed since the players' glory days.

After worrying himself sick in this first village he came upon, he decided to live on as Cohral. He departed the village and headed for the royal capital in Felskeilo with other aspiring adventurers and became one there.

Although he had initially started out with seven (nonplayer) party members, after ten years had passed, their numbers decreased to four. Some had died while others had left. He traveled all over in search of players like himself in similar circumstances.

However, after a decade, he had aged from a twenty-something greenhorn to a thirty-something middle-aged man. His desire to continue the search was fading along with his realization of how the years had passed.

Then, it happened.

Upon returning to the Felskeilo capital to get back to the basics, he met the new adventurer known as Cayna. The moment he saw this female high elf who knew nothing of the world, he was dumbfounded. After all, he couldn't use Special Skill: Search to check her level or stats.

However, this lack of information had reminded him of something: The inability to see the values of someone with a higher level than you was part of the VRMMORPG *Leadale*'s unique system. If this girl was one of the players he'd been looking for, there was a possibility there were others.

He would have liked to confirm this with Cayna herself, but the past ten years had made him a coward.

Upon indirectly gathering rumors about her, it became more and more clear she was a player.

Some said she walked on water. Since the magic that allowed one to do so was gone in this world, it was clear-cut proof.

Others also said she was the mother of Felskeilo's famed sibling trio.

He tried to confirm his suspicions with the siblings themselves, but as expected, it wasn't easy for an adventurer to get an immediate audience with the headmaster of the Academy and the High Priest. As a result, Cohral was only able to get in touch with Kartatz, the head of the shipbuilding workshop, but he was still unable to verify whether Cayna was a player.

His comrades noticed his obsession with Cayna and laughed that even a lout like Cohral could fall for a girl.

It was around that time when surprise visitors passed through the guild door. They wore white helmets and armor that both bore a griffin crest. Two of the Felskeilo knights.

One of the pair was an average human knight that you might see anywhere, while the other was a silver dragoid who carried a giant sword appropriate to his size.

The human knight looked around the guild and headed straight for the reception counter. He seemed to be asking the attendant about something, but no one was able to catch any snippets.

The dragoid standing by the entrance looked at Cohral and the others and asked them a question.

"Pardon me, but we're looking for something. Have you seen a well-dressed girl with light-peach hair?"

Most knights looked down on adventurers when they came across one another in town, so the latter weren't their biggest fans. The fact alone that the dragoid had prefaced his question with an apology made them warm up to him. Even so, the adventurers hadn't seen any such girl, and they all shook their heads.

Cohral noticed something else different about him, and his eyes widened.

He couldn't read the dragoid's level with Search.

A silver dragoid with a large sword.

Digging through his memories, Cohral remembered this man had been the subleader of his former guild.

The man's name was...

"...Shining Saber...?"

"Yes, that is indeed my name. Mm? Did I already tell you?"

"From the Silver Moon Horsemen...?"

"Wait...what? How do you know that name?!"

He locked gazes with the baffled dragoid, and as they stared at each other, their eyes grew wide with shock.

"You're Cohral?!"

"Saber! It that you?!"

They didn't know whether it was safe to say it'd been two hundred years out loud, but the former guild comrades shook hands firmly and rejoiced in their reunion.

Cohral's current party members and Shining Saber's knight partner watched blankly as the two grinned at each other. It was obvious that none of them had any clue what was going on.

Meanwhile, at the Academy on the opposite of the Ejidd River that divided Felskeilo...

Professor Lopus Harvey was experiencing unprecedented suffering.

He had a bucket in one hand. Inside was mulberry-colored

liquid that gave off an odd stench. The failed results of his nightlong efforts—his attempt at creating that brilliant something he had seen only once and hadn't been able to banish from his mind ever since.

That brilliant something was his mother-in-law's ancient arts. When he talked it over with his wife, Mai-Mai, she had said that her younger brother, Kartatz, an artisan by trade, might have some ideas. Kartatz then told Lopus that he needed something called Craft Skills, and new ones could only be obtained through Cayna's own skills.

"Could I ask Lady Cayna to give them to me?"

"...That's a tough one. Mum is kind of the one in charge of handling those techniques. Even if me or my siblings said we wanted them, I don't think she'd hand 'em over. The only other way to get 'em is by passing trials."

There seemed to be an infinite number of these trials. Some took a ridiculous amount of time, while others were very likely to kill you. Plus, if you wanted to undertake these trials, you'd have to go to some place called a Guardian Tower.

Lopus thought about meeting her and confirming this himself, but either the timing wasn't right, she was out doing a request, or they met but were too busy to talk.

He had made countless attempts of trial and error with similar ingredients as a last resort, but to no avail. Everything he created was a failure with no satisfying conclusions. All he ended up with was a growing mountain of garbage and an unfortunate waste of precious materials he had ordered from afar. He wasn't sure whether it was because he was lacking in creative ingenuity or if he didn't have the talent to produce such an item.

Having fallen into the depths of despair, he took his failures to the garbage site at the edge of the Academy that was nothing more than a hole in the ground and dumped his failures in. A blinking arrow and ??? dialogue box appeared, something any player would understand the moment they saw it. But those symbols proved utterly pointless without any players present to see them.

At least, it would have been pointless if oksorre root, logga eyes, and nweve tongue hadn't been mixed into the garbage heap.

As Lopus switched his train of thought to once again reconsider his recipe, a light surged up from the hole behind him. He turned around in surprise, but the light was so blinding that he couldn't look at it directly and had to shield his eyes. He saw several strands of narrow light rise up from the hole.

At first, they only surged up upward, but the very next moment, the white light formed into uppercase and lowercase alphabet letters and began to rise up and dance like bubbles from narrow-necked bottles of champagne. Before long, these letters were systematically lining up in the sky. The small letters became ordered horizontally while the big letters did so vertically. They were set at spaced intervals and fixed in place.

Next, beams of light extended from the letters. They drew both up and down and to the side while using the letters as a foundation. They formed a portrait-style rectangle that was like a 3D grid. It was a massive creation that was forty meters high and twenty meters in length and width. It could be seen from the Academy building, from the boats passing along the Ejidd River, and even from the castle.

Not even stopping to pause, the grid transformed even further. Inside, the original beams accurately raced around as if drawing. High above the school, they formed some manner of an enormous 3D model in midair.

A short, wide torso. Arms similar to fins with sharp claws growing on the ends. Short legs with thick claws that could support a bulky body. Lastly, a long beak, a birdlike head, and razor teeth that clacked together.

When the light finished drawing the never-before-seen, never-before-heard creature, it disappeared. The eyewitness students who had been holding their breath stared at it with wide eyes and were unable to look away.

Before he even had the chance to notice, Lopus, who was looking directly up at it from below, had dropped to the ground. He only realized long afterward that he'd been frozen in terror.

Nobody could have ever guessed what happened next, either.

Bones suddenly formed inside the beams. Not only that, it simultaneously constructed a rib cage with organs inside. Next were muscles to highlight its body and skin that covered the entire surface.

From the skin came feathers that burst forth like sprouts, and eyeballs formed in its eye-socket cavities before rolling around and glaring at its surroundings.

It felt like this all took a preposterous amount of time, but the monster was completed in less than three seconds. The 3D grid disappeared, and the space around the monster billowed with dust as it landed. Lopus, who was directly beneath it, missed being crushed by a hair, but the impact of the monster's landing along with the burst of wind blew him several meters away in a dust cloud.

"GWAAAAAAAAAAAWK!!"

It screeched a birthing cry and looked directly behind it like an owl. As if observing its surroundings, its neck twisted and turned to the left and right at 180-degree angles.

If one had to describe its appearance honestly, it had taloned lizard legs, the body of a penguin, and two pure-white claws each on a regressed pair of wings unfit for flying. The creature had the head of a dolphin with a slender, fanged snout. Its entire body was covered in short black feathers. If you ignored the claws and talons, it was basically a penguin. All in all, it was about twenty meters high.

It gained command of its short legs and went to take a step forward. However, it was tripped up by the Academy wall and fell face-first into the Ejidd River, creating a grand pillar of water.

If it had been human-sized, it would have only created a small wave, but the upper half of its massive body that fell in was over ten meters by itself. Naturally, something of that size and mass would produce a wave to match.

Those who just happened to be sailing by could only look up in horror at the giant tidal wave. Unable to do anything about it, screams and bellows rang out as they were capsized and tossed away.

"GWAAAAAAWK!!"

On the residential side of the river, the vicious penguin monster got its limbs working, jumped to its feet, and screeched once again.

Caring nothing for the people running away madly in fear, it went to take its historic second step, walked on a pier, lost its balance, and fell again. In a repeat performance, an enormous spray of water shot up and caused a tidal wave. The planks of wood that made up the pier as well as small boats and vessels docked there were all blown to smithereens. The wooden crates and people who didn't escape quick enough suffered the same.

When the monster rose and scooped up the remains of the piers, it seemed in a strangely good mood. It flapped its wings, gave a *"gwak, gwak"* as if pleased, and started clearing away the additions to the pier that were set along the riverbank in a playful gesture.

The people had stood there befuddled by the sheer unrealism of it all for some time, but these screeches seemed to give them the push they needed, and they scrambled to escape. The residents prioritized getting away from the Ejidd River, and even merchants left their wares behind. Unable to row to shore, those still on passing boats were rocked by wave after wave and tossed about.

Even within the Academy, there were students who insisted they had no choice but to fight the monster that had appeared on the grounds. However, upon the headmaster's admonishment that "There's no way anyone can hurt that thing!" the students all safely

evacuated to the noble district, where there was relatively less damage from high waves.

The church also evacuated its members who could not fight and divided the labor between holy knights and priests who could use magic to prepare for the monster that had now washed ashore. They were running about like mad.

The penguin's destructive rampage was clearly visible from the noble district, and the king and prime minister sent out knights to deal with the emergency on their hands. However, even the knights would need to cross the river if they hoped to oppose the creature. The waves remained too turbulent to allow boats to pass, so they could do nothing more than watch from the other side of the bank as the monster trampled everything in sight.

Amid the madness, Kartatz, Mai-Mai, and Skargo had somehow come together in the noble district. Since *some sort of problem* had arisen at the palace, Skargo headed there posthaste. Unaware that this issue was in part thanks to their mother, it was fortunate the three put their own safety first.

Although covered in scratches, Mai-Mai found Lopus among the evacuees and gave a long, deep sigh of relief. As her husband told her more about the monster's appearance, she looked to Kartatz and said, "Come to think of it…

"…Mother might've said something about a nasty place on the sandbar…"

"Hey now! Mum usin' the word *nasty* is no joke! Why didn't you pay more attention, Mai-Mai?!"

"Well, there was a lot going on! Skargo was going crazy, and then there was the whole situation with Caerick. I forgot until now!"

"Hold on, you two! Now's not the time for family squabbles! What're we supposed to do about that thing?!"

Lopus, the main cause of this ordeal, intervened and pointed at the penguin monster that was merrily wreaking havoc on the opposite bank. He had no idea he was the start of it all; he just knew he wanted to somehow help put an end to it.

Chastised by Lopus, the two siblings stared hard at the monster with tense expressions.

"This ain't good. That thing is way stronger than us."

"Act first and ask questions later. Let's at least get it under control, Kartatz!"

"Hold it, Sis. If we get its attention, everything behind us will probably become its new target."

"Ah…"

Behind them was the royal castle that had the Effect Skills BAM! Written SFX and Speed Lines for Emphasis cast on it. Looking upon her older brother's handiwork, Mai-Mai realized what she was doing and froze just as she was about to cast magic of her own. This all but confirmed to Lopus and Kartatz that Mai-Mai would have absolutely fired at the monster if Kartatz hadn't said anything.

"Guess we've got no choice but to head on over to the commoner district…"

Just as Kartatz murmured this, the monster pretty much finished destroying the pier and turned its attention toward the bank of the commoner district full of new toys to play with.

Meanwhile, within the commoner district, Shining Saber was having the knights under him evacuate citizens.

Other knights were present as well to aid in the search for those who did not escape.

Having issued his order, Shining Saber dashed toward the monster with a nimbleness that belied his large size. Cohral followed him for some reason, but there was an oddness the two had not yet noticed.

"Hey, what're we gonna do about that thing?!" Cohral asked.

"Ain't that obvious?! Crush it, of course!"

"Wait, what?! There's no way the two of us can do anything without even backup from the mages!!"

The monster scooped up piers with a *crack!* then crunched them apart and stepped on them.

The two then realized they had seen it before. There was a Point that constantly changed countries during Battle Events, and if you threw a special item inside it, an Event Monster would appear. You needed over twenty level 300 players at the very least to defeat it.

Shining Saber quickly put the brakes on and came to a halt. He stared at Cohral, who had objected to the plan and bumped his hand against his fist in understanding.

"Oh yeah, come to think of it, you were an adventurer. Sorry 'bout that. I was accidentally actin' like we were in our old guild unit..."

As the former subleader bowed his head admirably, Cohral couldn't shake the bad feeling he had and asked for confirmation.

"Will you go on this suicide mission if I don't stop you?"

"Ain't it obvious? Of course I'm gonna charge in. This, too, is my proud way of protecting the nation."

Nevertheless, believing one could rush in blindly wasn't a good idea. If he was going whether Cohral was there or not, he could at least lighten Shining Saber's burden. Although utterly stunned, Shining Saber's actions felt familiar. Cohral drew the large blade from his back. Sensing Shining Saber's smirk, Cohral thought that there was no convincing him of anything other than this idiotic attack plan.

"Cohral?"

"I'll follow you. It's not like I hate stupid suicide missions."

"Sorry. I owe you one. When all this is over, drinks are on me."

"Sounds like a plan. Alcohol always tastes better when someone else is buyin'."

Their shoulders shook with laughter. They gave each other a single nod, then started their dash toward the monster. Using a number of Active Skills to temporarily heighten their physical abilities, they kicked off the ground and soared to the tops of the houses. The men accelerated forward while zigzagging from roof to roof. Magic that gave them martial arts skills flowed through their bodies and left trails of green and yellow behind them as they pressed toward their target. Shining Saber was green while Cohral was yellow.

"The enemy is huge! Let's jab it in the head and flip it on its back!"

"Got it!"

Their accelerated movement added to their martial arts skills, and the two danced in the sky.

Weapon Skill: Double Crush

Weapon Skill: Pike Ring Attack

Almost simultaneously, two shooting stars pierced the monster's face and exploded. The penguin gave a screech of agony and somersaulted backward. As it fell in slow motion, Cohral and Shining Saber, who had descended from the sky with the trailing reverberations of their techniques, simply looked on.

As a result of the penguin's body being twisted around when it fell, the flapping arms came rushing in on them. Since the use of their physical skills made them rigid directly after attacking, they weren't able to dodge. The giant fins hit them like a racket against tennis balls and sent them crashing into a house far across the riverbank.

The river once again produced a giant pillar of water, a roar, and a tidal wave. In the commoner district, two streams of dust rose up from the house.

"Agh, shit! How were we supposed to predict that...?"

Lying in the ruins of a house with wreckage on top of him, Shining Saber sat up. His armor was crushed here and there, it had a crack in it, and the silver frame was stained with blood.

He urged his battered body to move and crawl out from where he landed. He made his way to where Cohral had fallen.

"Hey! Cohral, are you alive?!"

As he called out, he could hear the sound of something crumbling. However, there was no reply from Cohral. Shining Saber hurriedly pushed through the broken beams and piles of wreckage to uncover him.

After hacking through a thick central pillar, he finally saw Cohral. He suffered more damage than Shining Saber and had injuries all over.

"It really is over level 400. We only took it down by twenty percent," Cohral said.

"If it's risky for you, then go back to sleep. I'll take care of it."

Seeing him so covered in blood was a gruesome sight, but despite being beaten within an inch of his life, there was a fighting spirit in his eyes. One might also say the same of Shining Saber, but unfortunately, both were losing too much blood.

There was a large hole in the roof, and a breeze passed through. The capital sky spread out before them. In addition to the sky, they could also see the head of the arisen monster penguin who was clearly looking to go another round. They had a feeling it was growing closer and closer.

Unable to come up with a decent counterattack, the two began thinking that their only hope would be to risk their lives in one final assault.

Then the monster penguin's head exploded grandly.

They could hear it let out an agonizing yell, so it seemed like magic or something similar had struck it.

The two had no idea what was going on, and the area around them began to glow with a white light. The damaged armor remained as it was, but any injuries they sustained were healed, and the pain subsided.

"Honestly… Although your strength is the greatest of any knight, I cannot praise you for rushing in unaided."

Accompanied by a Glittering Backdrop, a beautiful elf man dressed in a blue priest robe appeared with a Peal of Bells sound effect. The white light was one of Skargo's midrange healing spells. It wasn't a full recovery, but it did improve the conditions of the two men, who were likely to lose consciousness at any moment.

"Skargo, huh? You really saved us there. We owe you one."

"It's not over yet. My younger sister and the mages are on the sandbar drawing the monster's attention. I need you both to attack it once more. I shall provide healing and protection."

The strange man audibly gleamed and sparkled as he spoke. Cohral's mouth hung wide open.

"Hey, Shining Saber. What's with this guy…?"

"Hmm? Don't you know? He's the famous High Priest with the mother complex."

"Pardon me, but who has a mother complex? I simply offer my mother dear endless love."

""Yeah, that's a mother complex!!""

The two quickly forgot the situation at hand and cut right in.

Shining Saber, his ally Cohral, and their healer/support Skargo moved through the commoner district to get east of the monster penguin. At present, it seemed that the mages had secured a position on the sandbar and were using fire- and wind-based Attack Magic to lure the penguin's attention north. The pachinko-sized hits against its huge body would irritate the monster, and it sometimes headed toward the river with a howl.

However, the problem was that if it got beyond the sandbar and went north, it would find the overly conspicuous castle.

"We really did only twenty percent damage, huh?" Shining Saber murmured as he looked up at the monster penguin.

Cohral hung his head miserably. "We were ready to give our lives for that attack, too. Hearing you say that makes me give up all hope…"

Even though the two of them only carved out that much damage, it could have been worse. What they lacked was durability.

Shining Saber's armor had become useless, so he threw it away. As for Cohral, both his weapons and armor were a total loss. Even if he was told to do the same attack over, he couldn't do anything without his sword.

As the penguin approached the shore, giant fireballs would occasionally come flying in and explode at its temple from the east. With a threatening "GWAAAWK!" it wandered in different directions.

To the west, Mai-Mai was by herself, but she had things under control for the time being. The penguin was led around left and right in a two-sided attack.

Even so, everyone knew that these attacks alone wouldn't resolve anything.

Each did as Mai-Mai instructed, but their MP depleted before the enemy could get in the desired position. Skargo and Mai-Mai were the only ones with MP Healing. Furthermore, although Mai-Mai had more MP than the average mage soldier, she had to consider if her consumption was outweighing her recovery.

The attacks coming from the sandbar grew less frequent, and if the attack coming from the west ceased, the monster penguin would turn its curiosity on the commoner district.

Just as Shining Saber was firing himself up and saying "Guess we've got no choice but to take each other out," a mass of something crossed over their heads.

It was a lump of stone that was ten meters in diameter.

As the people gazed up at it in confusion and wondered what it was doing there, the flying rock slammed right into the monster penguin's face!

It wasn't just a direct hit. Right before making contact, the rock sank down a bit and hit the monster with a scoop-like uppercut from below that sent it flying. Left with no other choice but to dance through the air like a bent shrimp, the penguin landed in the river on its back. The fall sent up an enormous splash that produced giant waves all around it.

""Huh?""

Shining Saber and Cohral watched with slack jaws. They looked behind them, observed the partially sunken penguin, looked behind them again, then forward.

Among them, only Skargo's eyes glinted with a *gleam!* and he murmured, "Just in time."

At any rate, although the flying rock that came out of nowhere had hit the monster with a harsh blow, it was still alive and well. Its neck wobbled unsteadily, and it managed to get up. The head alone swayed from left to right, but the rest of it seemed to move with no issues.

"It's still goin'?" Shining Saber asked.

"More importantly, where did that rock come flying in from just now?"

Recovered from his stupor, Cohral glared at the monster. As Shining Saber glanced around, he noticed Skargo with his arms crossed and a composed expression.

"What's up? You know something about this?"

"Yes. The threat is no longer imminent."

Skargo continued to sparkle audibly as Cohral and Shining Saber exchanged confused looks. Strangely enough, on the opposite side of the monster, the mage soldiers were shooting Mai-Mai odd glances as she told them the battle was over.

Just as everyone's minds raced with confusion, a crash of thunder suddenly roared down from the cloudless blue sky.

Only a few people instantly covered their ears. Most sat down and averted their eyes from the thunder that rumbled through the pits of their stomachs and the flash that swallowed the monster whole.

Struck by lightning, the penguin remained upright and was charred to a crisp. Furthermore, a fiery pillar rose up beneath its giant body and turned the monster into a megatorch. The flames that brightly lit up the surrounding area had no effect on anything else. It was swallowed up by the river almost as soon as it appeared.

All that remained was a pitch-black, charred corpse. Even that fell apart almost instantly and disappeared into particles. Those who witnessed the mysterious phenomenon were unable to process what just happened and could only look on in confusion.

Why did the monster appear?

Why did the monster destroy the town?

What was the lightning and fire that destroyed the monster?

Everyone involved was full of questions, but they could sense the danger had passed. Some collapsed with relief. Some had their head in their hands in an effort to process what just happened. Others already set about preparing to rebuild. The townspeople who had initially been swept away by despair followed the lead of those who stepped forward and started taking action themselves.

Only Cohral and Shining Saber had any idea what the lightning and flames were.

"That was..."

"It was top-level Lightning and Fire Magic, wasn't it?"

Since this world's system of magic was completely different compared to the game world, they knew this spell had come from a player.

Skargo and Mai-Mai alone knew exactly who had cast it.

Let us return to when the monster appeared.

It all began with a message sent to Mai-Mai and Kartatz via Telepathy from an unknown sender. All it said was *Cayna is approaching town from the east.* Since Telepathy was only possible through blood relatives, the two found this incredibly suspicious.

The sender was dubious, but Kartatz at least thought it was for the best that Skargo didn't receive the message. If his older brother had heard such a thing, it was easy to imagine him rushing out at top speed. The High Priest turning his back on the monster and racing through the town would have undoubtedly sparked even more panic among the people.

Things being as they were, Mai-Mai suggested leading the monster into the river and having Cayna finish it off. It was Kartatz's job to convey this to their mother. Skargo left to aid Shining Saber, the knight leader who was the one other person who stood a chance against the monster. As a former palace mage, Mai-Mai gathered the mage soldiers and took on the role of diverting the monster's attention with magic. The one silver lining was that their foe didn't possess long-range magic.

Kartatz crossed the river in a small boat near the noble district's eastern gate and headed out toward the main eastern road from town. Fortunately, as he was passing through the eastern trade route not far from the Felskeilo capital, he was able to safely meet up with Cayna.

Cayna had finished her request and initially planned to take it easy on the way home. However, Li'l Fairy was forcefully pulling her hair and clothes and urging to go faster.

"Right. We better hurry back."

"Huh? What's wrong, Cayna?" Lonti asked.

"Something bad might be going on in Felskeilo."

""WHAT?!""

Thinking that fairies likely had some sort of sharp intuition, Cayna prioritized getting home as fast as possible. She once again summoned the two therwolves, had Lonti and Mye get on them, and ordered the beasts to take them near Felskeilo's perimeters.

Suffering a headache at the thought of what might have happened over the past two days, she swiftly returned home. On the way, she met a frazzled Kartatz, who told her the shocking news.

"Someone summoned an Event Monster?!"

"Y-yeah. Mai-Mai and the others are holding it back right now, but they can't keep that up forever."

"At level 300, one or two people don't stand a chance. What're they thinking?! Kartatz, take care of those two for me, okay?!"

"Huh, what? M-Mum?!"

Cayna left the two girls with Kartatz before racing off to the incident in question. She found the Event Monster caught in a wave of pincer attacks near the commoner district.

Unlike the battle with the bandits, Cayna determined that there was no need to show any mercy or care for it and quickly summoned her Silver Ring. Keeping herself hidden, she used both Double Spell and Boost to throw a giant boulder as well as rain down top-level lightning and fire for good measure. A penguin monster that was level 400 at best was a small fry compared to the almighty power of a Skill Master and a Limit Breaker.

After Cayna secretly unleashed her power, the unknowing citizens began to calm down. They declared the lightning and fire that had saved the town as a divine miracle, and all lifted their grateful prayers to the heavens.

When Cayna met up with Lonti and Mye, she tilted her head as she noticed the abject surprise on their faces upon witnessing the state of the town.

"What's wrong with these two?"

"Seeing your magic must've shocked them, Mum."

They were now close enough to Felskeilo that they could see the eastern gate.

Kartatz already understood his mother by this point and wasn't especially startled. However, seeing a pillar of lightning blast down from the sky along with a pillar of flames to match had apparently sent Mye's and Lonti's emotions through the roof.

"D-did you do that by yourself, Cayna?" Lonti asked.

"In retrospect, I should've used my Arcal Staff."

"That's not what she's talking about, Mum."

At any rate, she thanked Kartatz for looking after the two, and the group passed through Felskeilo's eastern gate looking completely innocent.

However, the situation was more complicated than that, and Kartatz got straight to the point.

"By the by, why's the princess with you, Mum?" he mumbled.

"Just turned out that way."

"……"

The dwarf held his head in his hands, and Mye and Lonti shuddered as Cayna eyed him mysteriously.

"Um, is this really all right, Cayna?"

"Huh? Should I have told him I helped you run away from home?"

"Waaaah?! Why did you say it out loud, Cayna?!"

Kartatz's face twisted in agony as he watched Mye flap her arms about in a panic. Between them, Lonti timidly tried to explain.

"Ummm. I'm terribly sorry, Master Kartatz. We got Cayna tangled up in our own personal affairs."

"Nah, don't worry about it. I can't tell Mum what to do."

"Whaaat? Are you saying you don't care what I do? That makes me so sad."

"I'm begging you, Mum. Stop talking."

Cayna giggled at her son's glum face and patted him on the head. Kartatz's shoulders slumped now that he lost his "dignified elder" status in front of Mye and Lonti.

Lonti smiled awkwardly as she watched this warm, familial exchange. Mye further told him, "You normally appear so stern, but it seems you can lose your composure, too, Master Kartatz." Then the dwarf turned away with his arms crossed.

Cayna fixed her teasing smile from Kartatz to Mye and said, "Next time you need a guard, offer a reward and go through the Adventurers Guild."

"Huh? I'll have to pay?"

"I accepted this time because Lonti was with you, but I'm not taking part in any more princess kidnappings."

"How very calculating. I'd expect no less of you, Cayna," Lonti said.

"You're better off paying Agaido," Cayna replied.

Since the town was in chaos, the people passing by paid no mind to their conversation.

Tilting his head with a "Geez," Kartatz was relieved to see his mother being the same as always—all too quickly letting things slide that any normal person would question.

"Well, that's how Mum is. Unless you announce *I'm an important person!* from the start, she'll take you for all you've got. It's a good thing Mum was on your side, Princess."

"If someone tells me from the get-go *I'm a super-amazing noble,* I'll hex them into a piggy."

Cayna followed this nonchalant remark with a "heh-heh" and thrust out her chest proudly.

Watching this full display of confidence, the two girls turned to Kartatz to clarify the true meaning of Cayna's statement.

"Would she really do that?"

"Does Cayna hate nobles?"

"She does what she says. If you flaunt your authority in front of Mum, the only result will be destruction."

As Kartatz, who normally looked stern anyway, answered them with dead seriousness, the color drained from the girls' faces.

They had seen the monster burning up in a pillar of fire from a distance and been utterly dumbfounded. When they imagined the same thing happening to a normal person, they shuddered.

Based on what they heard of the situation from Kartatz while they were waiting, the battle formation had consisted of a top-class lineup of mages, Mai-Mai, the determined knight leader, and Skargo. Even though such a team had been unable to take down the monster, Cayna had finished the battle in three magic strikes. The difference in power was clear, and Mye shivered at the thought of making a true enemy of her.

However, although she found her scary, Mye couldn't bring herself to reject her outright. She knew how carefully Cayna had guided and guarded them the past three days. She had also quelled their fears during the night, spoken with the girls during their travels, and issued proper warnings.

"Hey, looks like someone came to greet us, huh?"

Cayna pointed at the four human-shaped shadows ahead. Two were the worse-for-wear Shining Saber and his knight subordinate. There was also Cohral, who was similarly in rough shape, and Skargo, who held a round object. They waited at the corner of an empty street for the group.

"Your absence has caused your father much worry these past two days."

"I'm very sorry. I was careless."

Mye and Lonti, who had been handed over to Shining Saber, accepted their scolding with bowed heads.

As Cayna watched from the side, Skargo handed her the round object. It had a different shine compared to money and was lighter than it looked. It was about the size of a mature watermelon.

"Hang on, this is the divine metal orichalcum! Why're you giving me this?"

"It seems the monster dropped it, Mother Dear. Apparently those two did not need it, so they relinquished it to you."

Cayna frowned and looked at the pair. Neither had weapons nor armor. Their bodies were covered in wounds, and they were splattered with dried blood here and there. Given that Cohral had made a strong impression on her when they met at the Adventurers Guild, such shabbiness moved her to tears. She felt that these two needed it more than her.

Cohral noticed her gaze and smiled awkwardly.

"We don't have the skills needed to process that. You were the one who beat the monster, right? We figured you should have it."

"All righty, then. I'll make something out of it. What sounds good?"

"You can make something with it?!"

"Yeah. I already have enough weapons. It looks like you don't have a sword, so how about I go with that?"

"That's one huge favor. I'm not going to pay a processing fee afterward. Got it?"

Unable to ignore Cohral's suspicious expression, Skargo decided to step in.

"Cohral. Mother Dear has bestowed her kindness upon you, yet you treat her with such rudeness?"

"N-not at all. It's just that you gotta be on your toes as an adventurer. Sorry, miss."

Struck with fear at the Wolf Glare effect that Skargo was directing at him, Cohral bowed his head to Cayna. Cayna bopped Skargo on the head.

"Hey now."

"But, Mother Dear…"

"It's fine, so go ahead and get back to work. There are a lot of injured people, right?"

She gave her reluctant son one scolding look of *I said no!* and he agreed to return to his duties. As he unwillingly left like a crestfallen dog, Shining Saber burst into laughter, and a giggle escaped from Mye.

"There's something Shining Saber and I want to talk about with you later," said Cohral. "Do you have any free time tomorrow?"

"Tomorrow? That shouldn't be a problem. Kartatz, show me where that Black Hare of Inaba shop is later on."

"The heck is that?" Kartatz replied.

"Do you mean The White-Tailed Black Rabbit, Cayna?" Mye asked.

"Oh yeah, that's it. I'll also go see Mai-Mai while I'm at it."

After Mye, now flanked by two knights, corrected Cayna's error, the girl gave a polite bow and said, "I appreciate all your help." Shining Saber glanced between Cayna and the princess with a degree of shock.

Cayna shook Mye's hand lightly and left with Kartatz. The dwarf looked at his mother, who treated even royals so casually, and racked his mind over how she was always able to take everything in stride.

"Anyway, what business do you have in a noble restaurant?" asked Kartatz.

"I accepted a request to gather food ingredients."

"And why did the princess end up coming with you…?"

"Good question."

Kartatz had a bad feeling about Cayna's pleasant smile and feigned ignorance, so he decided not to ask any more questions. After all, he suspected that if he did, the same cold eyes Mai-Mai told him about in private would fall on him. The idea of his mother eyeing him up like that sent shivers down his spine as they crossed the river.

Having completed her request, Cayna headed for the Academy. Kartatz still had business to take care of at the factory, so they parted ways there.

Incidentally, the surviving vessels had all been gathered together and were operating as normal. The way people kept moving ever forward even in the wake of chaos touched Cayna, and she couldn't help but think about how incredibly resilient humanity was.

The buildings on the sandbar had only suffered some structural damage after being hit with water, but it seemed that about half the people who were washed away after stepping outside and witnessing the monster were missing. They couldn't search for those swallowed up by the river, so the soldiers dispatched throughout the town raced about and worked with the townspeople to clean up the port district.

"…Why are you hiding, Mai-Mai?"

"U-um…well, how shall I put it…?"

Now at the Academy, Cayna gave a wry smile as her daughter greeted her from behind Lopus. It was to be expected, considering that the two hadn't met since Cayna sent a declaration of obliteration via Mai-Mai's son.

Fully expecting her mother to blow her to smithereens the moment their eyes met, Mai-Mai was conversely unsettled by Cayna's lack of reaction.

"Well, the way you had me give a letter to someone you didn't even tell me was my grandson did make me angry. Still, I was glad to see they're such good kids."

"Oh…"

"Besides…," Cayna added as Mai-Mai put a hand to her heart in relief, "I actually had more fun with them than with you. They're kind, honest, and also pretty helpful."

"I'm sorry, Mother! I'm so sorry!! Don't abandon me!!!"

As Lopus watched Mai-Mai cling to her mother's waist in tears, he realized: His wife's wickedness was genetic.

As Cayna stroked her fussy daughter's head with a gentle smile, his eyes met hers. The reassuring look she gave him made his heart skip a beat.

He was a bit charmed by her, and he vowed he'd die before his wife ever found out.

"…So where'd it happen?"

"A-ah, right this way."

Remembering the task at hand, Lopus shook his head and led Cayna to a corner of the school grounds. The Academy wasn't all that vast, so they arrived quickly. However, their surroundings were dug up as if they'd been sent through chaos and acted as a vivid reminder of the blast. The monster had descended on the area and sent tidal waves crashing down, so it was only natural.

It was invisible to the other two, but Cayna could see *that* clearly.

An indicator of a Collection Point that matched those of the Black Kingdom hovered in midair with a ? ? ? dialogue box.

Although normally shy around people, Li'l Fairy left Cayna's shoulder and flew over to it. Upon trying to touch it and seeing her arm go straight through, she gave a fearful look and returned to the safety of Cayna's shoulder. She must have thought it was a ghost of some sort, but Mai-Mai and Lopus didn't see this, either.

Cayna did recall hearing something about a liquid being the

catalyst item here. Kee had this recorded in the log, which only further confirmed it. Lopus had mentioned something about a large quantity of failed experiments that contained unknown liquids, so she guessed that these had included Key Items. Creating these Key Items required no skills, and the materials could be acquired by trading with NPCs. The source of the chaos had been accidentally created by almost miraculous odds.

After a bit of thought, Cayna tried striking the Collection Point with blast magic and gouging out the earth, but the sign still didn't disappear.

The couple couldn't disguise their disbelief when Cayna suddenly burst into action.

"M-M-M-M-Mother!"

"Wh-what is it? What's wrong?!"

"Hmm. Nope, it's not going anywhere. Maybe I can get rid of it if I blow away the sandbar?"

The outrageous statement sent Mai-Mai and Lopus into a fit of trembling. After all, they knew it was Cayna, not an act of god, who had taken out the monster in one strike.

Her finger to her forehead, Cayna's expression was tight as she thought long and hard. The couple took a step backward. They were, of course, riddled with fear.

"Mai-Mai?"

"Y-yes! What is it, Mother?"

"Make sure no one comes near this place. Tell that to the knights and any other big shots. If this ever happens again..."

"Wh-what should we do?"

"...We'll have no choice but to blow up the entire sandbar and sink it into the river. To prevent anyone from abusing it."

"Yes! I will set up a barrier, isolate it, and throw every last person who gets near it in jail!!"

Mai-Mai snapped to attention and, in response to her mother's appeal, quickly ran off to begin the proceedings.

Cayna gave a "Pfft!" at her all-too-rapid retreat, then turned to Lopus, who had remained deep in thought with a glum expression the entire time.

"I get the feeling you want to ask me something."

"...I do. The reason all this happened was because I wanted to make the same potion you did."

"Pardon?"

Cayna pondered Lopus's sudden statement. After a moment, she pressed her fist against her palm in understanding.

"Ah, you want the skill for Potion Creation I, right?"

"Yes. I heard from Master Kartatz that you are in charge of these 'skills.' Do you think you could allow me some?"

"Hmm, normally you'd have to pass a trial. You don't seem like a bad guy who would abuse it, though, so sure, why not?"

Taking out parchment and ink, Cayna produced a glowing orb and began Scroll Creation. In no time at all, she handed Lopus a single scroll certificate written in the ancient language of the region.

"It'll all depend on if you can really *read into it*, though, 'kay?"

Lopus appeared to understand this baffling statement. He gave his thanks and took the scroll.

◆

Then, the next day...

Shining Saber had said they would meet up in the plaza in front of the Battle Arena in the afternoon. First, Cayna ate lunch, then she left the inn and made herself scarce for the time being. When she returned to the inn, she dusted off her hands with a sense of accomplishment and murmured, "That should do it!" As she once again made her way back toward the Battle Arena, she found Shining Saber and Cohral already waiting there.

For some reason, only Cohral looked completely exhausted. He sat tiredly on a nearby boulder. He looked just like those sports players who burn themselves out, and Cayna looked to Shining Saber for clarity.

"Why is Cohral the only one who looks worn-out?"

"Well, we got summoned to the castle as 'heroes' and were busy there all morning... Y'might say all that etiquette took it out of him. We did get reward money, though."

"We said you should be summoned, too, Cayna, but Skargo was vehemently opposed, so the matter got dropped."

The reason for this was probably something along the lines of *Mother Dear is a high elf. If she was to be summoned by a human king, it would create friction between the elves and humans and create a troublesome situation.*

The people had recognized everything that had happened as an act of god, so it seemed that Skargo was acting as if it had been an invisible hand.

The princess had testified as an eyewitness, but the prime minister apparently claimed there was no way such a powerful mage could be permitted in the castle and put a halt to this for the time being.

That must've been Agaido...

Even without the princess's testimony, he was a remarkable figure who sent out shadows to keep tabs on Cayna's movements. Even she thought it unwise to let him catch her talking with fellow players and thus sniffed out and tied up all his shadows. Since she had tied them up with rope and left them on a roof, no one would think anyone special had done it, even if they were discovered.

Cayna had put up such warnings, but although she was certain no one could escape Kee's sight, she created a large Concealment Barrier around the plaza as well.

His eyes wide, Shining Saber voiced concern over the trailing shadows.

"You think someone's followin' us, miss?"

"The old self-proclaimed prime minister refused to see me and is sticking close by. It'll be a real problem if he hears us talk like this."

It was true that, as an outsider, Agaido really wouldn't have any clue what they were saying. However, it wouldn't be good if he mistakenly thought they were plotting something.

The two men nodded in agreement and started off by introducing themselves.

"Anyway, I'm Shining Saber. No need for formalities with me. I was the subleader for the Silver Moon Horsemen Guild. I'm level 427."

"I'm Cohral. I was in the same guild. I'm level 392."

Shining Saber beat his white armor with a *clang!* Cohral's busted metal armor from the day before was replaced with spare leather armor.

Cayna felt as if she'd heard the name of the guild before, and her memory hit upon a cow-spotted dragoid.

"The Silver Moon Horsemen? Were you in the same guild as Kyotaro?"

"Did you know our guildmaster?"

"Well, in a way. My name is Cayna. You can call me miss—or whatever else you like. My guild was Cream Cheese."

""BWUH?!""

As soon as they heard the name of her guild, the two men nearly fell out of their chairs. When Cayna saw Cohral slowly retreat with a vaguely tense expression on his face, she said, "Ah, you must know about the members of my guild."

"I got no clue," Shining Saber asserted.

"Seriously…?" Cohral questioned.

Her guild was so famous that anyone who didn't know of it was considered a sham. Even Cayna, who had been a member of the guild, was aware of this. Moreover, all eighteen members were Limit Breakers with the authority of a Game Master. Since everything in the guild's sight had been deemed bad enough to warrant an account ban, the guild's name itself became synonymous with fear.

It was here that Shining Saber seemed to realize something.

"Wait! You said you're a high elf who knew our guildmaster? Could you be the Silver Ring Witch?!"

Three angels suddenly appeared over Shining Saber's head. They blew trumpets loudly and twirled around as they tossed white feathers over him.

This was Cayna's Special Skill: Oscar—Roses Scatter with Beauty.

"Gah, this skill is…"

"Correct!"

A disquieting air suddenly settled in, and Cayna's mood darkened. Her twisted smile was filled with a sense of danger, and with a humorless tone, she opened up her Item Box and took out a staff. The sharp-eyed Cohral realized what it was and took a step back with a wail.

"Gwah, the Arcal Staff?! What're you plannin' to do with a thing like that?!"

"I hate that disgraceful moniker. You can forget it right now, but if you don't…"

Noticing the glassy look in Cayna's eyes as she slowly readied her staff, the men nodded so violently that their heads might have come off.

She watched them suspiciously for a moment, then put away her weapon with a sigh.

"I'll immediately knock you out the next time you utter that vile name again."

"Okay. I get it, so stop lookin' at me like that!" Shining Saber exclaimed.

"In other words…you're a Limit Breaker. And also a Skill Master."

"Yup, that's right. I'm Cayna, the Third Skill Master. Normally, I'm transferring skills to people who pass my trial, though."

Sensing their lives were no longer in danger, Shining Saber and Cohral let out a deep sigh of relief and slumped their shoulders.

Given that the strength of this particular item largely depended on the magical power of the caster, for someone like Cohral, who had a nearly 700-level difference, one direct hit would likely turn him to ash. Shining Saber was in a similar boat and couldn't hide his blank bewilderment. For now, they were openly relieved she had laid down her arms.

"Oh, I got the goods I promised yesterday, Cohral."

"You say it like it's contraband or something…"

Cayna took a large sword out of her Item Box and handed it to Cohral. He checked its stats and was flabbergasted.

"WH-WHAT IS THIS?!"

"What's goin' on?! What'd she give you?"

Shining Saber peeked in from the side and took the sword. He checked the status for himself and gulped.

"The Holy Warrior Soul Valhalla?! Isn't this the best sword out there?!"

"Well, it does boost your stats all across the board and has holy attributes. It won't break so easily next time. I also had diamond and corundum on hand and upped its grade, so I really put my all into it."

The men's faces clearly said, *"Put my all into it" doesn't begin to describe this.*

Cayna puffed out her chest and gave a self-important "heh-heh!"

After all, in the world of the game, such an item could sell for seventy million gil. In the modern world, this was approximately seven hundred thousand gold coins.

"Damn, I want ooooone! Hey, you got any more?!"

"I'm out of material."

There was actually more in the stash she had taken from Opus, but she kept that to herself. As Shining Saber stamped his feet in frustration, she understood it was a weapon swordfighters would give anything for.

"Shining Saber, you have a weapon, don't you?"

"I'm borrowing it from the knights!"

The conversation looked like it would turn to weaponry for some time, but Shining Saber regained control of himself and forcefully changed the subject halfway.

"Anyway, there's a lot I want to talk about. I've only been in this world about three years…"

"It was that recently, Subleader? I've been here over ten."

"Now that we're talking about it, I've only been here two months. More importantly, what's going on with *Leadale* shutting down its servers?"

At Cayna's question, the two men looked at each other with puzzled expressions.

"Hold on. Don't you know anything about it?"

"Nope. My last memory was around the end of May."

"*Leadale* ended service on New Year's Eve. Why would someone who logged in half a year earlier be here?"

"Well, I did die while playing the game."

""Ah, I see… WHAT?!""

Cayna scolded the pale men for acting as if they'd seen a ghost and briefly explained that she'd become bedridden due to an accident. From what she could surmise, her consciousness had escaped to the game world after a lightning strike interrupted the machine that kept her alive.

Cayna told them the short version of her story: how she had woken up at her last save point, the remote village near her tower.

After hearing all this, Cohral nodded in understanding.

"There were rumors going around for a while about someone who'd died while playing the game. That was you, Cayna?"

"Uh, what? I sparked rumors? I'm pretty sure my uncle wasn't the type to go telling everyone."

After word about someone dying while playing the game got around, the parent company apparently put heavy pressure on *Leadale*'s Administrators. Before anyone knew what was going on, it was decided that the game's service would end.

From what the players determined, they couldn't do anything about it. According to Shining Saber, who had played until *Leadale*'s termination, he had formed a slapdash party and went on a bunch of raids. By the time he realized the service period had already ended, he was standing alone in the middle of the road. There was no trace of his other party members.

"Hmm. I'm not really getting the whole picture here."

"I got no clue idea what the deal was with the Admins or the parent company. I told you all I know."

"In that case, why don't we try asking Li'l Fairy for more details?"

""Li'l Fairy?""

Shining Saber and Cohral looked at each other upon hearing such an odd statement.

The fairy was hesitant to reveal herself, but Cayna managed to coax her out. The men's eyes grew wide.

"What is that?!" Shining Saber exclaimed.

Startled by the booming voice, the fairy who had trouble even showing herself quickly escaped back onto Cayna's shoulder. It seemed that only players could see her.

Question marks raised over their heads, and Cayna quickly explained this and that. Shining Saber then held out his hand in curiosity, but the terrified fairy refused to come back out.

"Opuskettenshultheimer? Never heard of him," Shining Saber stated.

"He was also known as *Leadale*'s Kongming…"

"Agh, that guy. I remember the one time I avoided a huge tree that was falling down, got my legs tripped up on the rope attached to it, and was dragged all the way down a mountain. When I got to the bottom of the valley, the tree fell on me, and I died…"

As Cohral fell into a pitiful depression at the memory, Shining Saber put a hand on his shoulder and shook his head as if to say he had the same recollection. The two stared into each other's eyes before grabbing each other tightly and bursting into tears.

Left out in the cold, Cayna looked upon the unsightly scene and spoke candidly:

"What is this, a comedy routine…?"

""WE SHARE THE SAME PAIN!!""

She was too exasperated to tell them that a little brotherly love was all well and good, but now wasn't exactly the best time to be coming out of the closet.

After their sentimental moment, Cayna added them both to her friend list. As long as they had exchanged names, they could contact one another wherever. However, without the Admins as backup, they weren't sure how much of a distance that connection could handle in this world. Not only that, even though each person had the functionality, it was unknown how it continued to work. It was far better than the forlornness Cayna had felt when she first arrived.

"Come to think of it, I've been wonderin'. That guy's your son, right?" Shining Saber asked.

"You did say you came here two months ago. What about your kids, like Master Skargo and Master Kartatz?"

"Oh, they're from that thing—y'know, the Foster System. Mai-Mai had kids during the past two hundred years, so now I have grandkids... Thanks to that, I've got people calling me Grandmother and Great-Grandmother at my age. I'm already used to it, but..."

"So that's where those Effect Skills come from...," Shining Saber commented.

"Yeah. I don't know why, but Skargo has a natural talent for Oscar—Roses Scatter with Beauty."

"That reminds me..."

Cohral took a good look at Cayna as she explained with a tired expression and a shrug, and he put a hand on her shoulder. Although it was hard to recognize in Shining Saber's dragoid features, sweat trickled down his face.

"...I had two foster kids. They were sorta like my apprentices," said Cohral.

"...Shoot, I remember makin' an elf younger brother and an elf best friend."

"If they were elves, Shining Saber, then they're probably still alive. As for you, Cohral, if you go searching, you'll probably find a Cohral swordplay school, right?"

"Agh, that's one school I do NOT wanna see..."

Cohral held his head in his hands and moaned. Realizing it was his problem, too, Shining Saber started worrying over what he'd do if he met those people in person.

Glad to see that they were just as frazzled as she had been, Cayna simply looked on as a spectator. Cohral quietly approached her as she casually observed them.

"Hey, Cayna. There's a skill I want..."

"I'm not promising anything, but which is it?"

"…Healing Magic."

"You don't have it?!"

Shining Saber had cut in with a look that said, *What is this guy, an idiot?*

Healing Magic could be very easily obtained through online and offline Events. These quests were simple and could be completed by anyone in less than an hour. It was rare to find anyone who didn't have it. Both Cayna and Shining Saber were shocked to meet someone so unusual out of the blue like this.

"Well then, please take on a trial. It would be a disgrace to me as a Skill Master if you asked for it and I answered with *Sure, here you go.*"

"Agh, that's so stingy. Can't you just give it to me? We're not in a game anymore."

"You'll be fine. Even without that skill, you're still leagues above other adventurers."

"Tch. Dammit, c'mon. Help a player out," Cohral cursed as he mumbled and grumbled.

"So where's your tower, Cayna?" Shining Saber asked after brooding for a moment.

"Hmm, well, if you go a little south of the outer eastern trade route and past the country's borders, it's a silver tower in a forest. It's often considered the easiest of all the Skill Master trials."

At the very least, it was far preferable to Opus's hellish tower full of death traps. The players who attempted his tower would call it the place where you can find 108 ways to die. Many of her online friends had criticized it as the most brutal of the thirteen towers. Since the most casual movement could send you to your death, it was called the House of Murder and Malice.

"That's pretty far…," Cohral stated.

"Yeah, no kidding," Shining Saber agreed.

Cohral still grumbled, and Shining Saber wasn't able to leave the capital whenever he pleased. Cayna pointed at the Battle Arena behind them.

"Incidentally, that's Kyotaro's tower."

"What?!"

"It—it was this freakin' close the whole time?!"

"I don't know what the trial will be like, but we should be able to get it to work. He's not around anymore, but I can use it since I'm in charge of it now."

This would be discovered later on, but the trial of the tower was Fight Two of Your Own Clones. Cayna told the two the state of the Guardian Towers—and how they were now on standby due to a lack of magical power. She also told them she was currently searching for each one's whereabouts and asked that they contact her if they found one or stumbled upon any leads.

With a smirk that said he was up to something, Cohral jumped at the opportunity.

"Got it. In that case, you better trade me that skill if I find one!"

"So that's how it's going to be. Okay then, fair enough."

"Aw yeah!"

"Man, come on. What are you, a kid…?"

Cohral struck a victory pose and hopped up and down. Shining Saber looked like he was done with it all. It should be mentioned that Cohral was just barely in his thirties.

Cohral whipped out a map and pointed to a coast near the border of Felskeilo and Helshper.

"There's a fishing village along this shoreline. The villagers free diving for fish there say there's a palace in the ocean. That's enough compensation for you, right?!"

"If it's in the ocean, it must be Liothek's."

After pondering this with a strained look on her face, Cayna used Scroll Creation to create Simple Substance Recovery: Dewl. She passed it to Cohral.

He had expected her to fight him a bit more and felt rather let down. Shining Saber noticed Cayna's long face and guessed the reason.

"Do you not know how to swim?"

"Um, yeah. I can't. I never really got to swim in real life, either."

"Seriously? At your age?" Cohral questioned.

"Hey, Cohral, mind your own business, would ya?"

Shining Saber prodded Cohral into silence. As the two glared at each other, Cayna came between them with a ball of fire in one hand.

"What is fighting because of me going to solve? If you don't listen, I'm going to let loose on both of you."

"All right, then. I've learned Healing Magic, so come at me!"

Before anyone realized it, Cohral had used up the scroll and was acting strangely wound up. Cayna put her hand to her head and thought, *If they can't tell what kind of spell I just used, it's not much of a threat, huh?*

Shining Saber crossed his arms, gave a sigh, and warned the oblivious Cohral.

"I don't even know if you'd be able to recover from a hit like that."

"Huh? Really?"

Inside the fireball floating in Cayna's hand was a fiery beast with a lionlike mane. Igua Beast was a spell that, once released, would chase its target to the ends of the earth and bite into the neck until the victim went up in flames. Whether it be through the sky or sea, it could go anywhere with homing-type capabilities, so unless you used Teleport right before a direct hit, it *would* find its target. Since Cayna had been too strong for her guild's advance guard during Battle Events and didn't have much to do, it was the one magic she could show off.

"I'm sorry. I was wrong. Please forgive me."

"Uh, no, it was just a little threat. There's no need to apologize…"

She'd been more concerned with the Guardian of the tower than swimming.

Liothek, the Sixth Skill Master, was a girl and a player who removed herself from all that was cute and pretty. If anything, she'd made a hobby out of collecting anything creepy-cute and grotesque. The statement *She primarily summons arthropods and amphibians* painted a pretty good picture.

Given that her personality preferred mollusk and crustacean types over dragons, the thought of how many disgusting things she might have spiraled Cayna into a depression.

"Ah, well, I better get back to work, then. I've been away long enough already. Come to the castle if you need anything."

"Yeah, I guess I'll get back to my party, too. Later, Cayna. Stop on by the guild again."

"Come to the castle, you say… Even if I go, will they let me in?"

The sun had descended significantly, and evening approached. Looking up at the sky and realizing how much time had passed, Shining Saber clanked his sword against his back with the notion that their meeting was adjourned. Cohral followed his lead and left as well. She saw them off with a nod and a small wave and felt a pang of jealousy at the sight of them congenially walking side by side.

"That sure seems nice…"

As she watched on enviously, Li'l Fairy popped out from her shoulder and rubbed against Cayna's cheek. She seemed to be trying to console her. When Cayna held her in both hands and stroked her head, the girl smiled comfortably.

"Yeah, you're right. Thanks."

She smiled at Li'l Fairy, who admirably reminded her on occasion that she wasn't alone.

It was because of this that Cayna had dropped her guard.

She gasped as her partner Kee reported *"Behind you..."* and followed through with a powerful left-hand strike in the indicated direction.

The blow rang out with a *thunk*, and there was a pathetic cry of "Eep?!" as something blue went flying.

"Uh, huh? ...Wh-what the—?"

Since the silver bow assimilated into her left armband was actually a rare item, its toughness was guaranteed; even without transforming entirely, it was a suitable shield and weapon. It had apparently struck someone sneaking up on her from behind.

When she turned around, she found Skargo curled in a fetal position on the ground and foaming at the mouth. Cayna noticed the height difference between them and thought the arrow of the armband must have mercilessly drove into his stomach.

"Oh shoot. A-are you okay, Skargo?"

"He was not quite fast enough..."

She hurriedly cast healing magic and gave Skargo a light shake. An instant later, he jumped up like a grasshopper and grabbed Cayna's shoulders tightly. Not knowing what in the world was happening, she stared at him in astonishment. A Jealous Aura enveloped Skargo as he howled, "Are you all right, Mother Dear?!"

"...Huh?"

"I, Skargo, heard you were having a clandestine meeting with men, and I dropped everything to come save you!"

With a Katsushika Hokusai–Style Breaking Great Wave and Surreptitiously Added Capsized Boat backdrop behind him, Skargo turned in the wrong direction and raised his arms vigorously to the heavens.

"Hey, um, S-Skargo?"

"What in the world were those men threatening you with?!

Furthermore! Yes, furthermore! Why was one of them the leader of the knights?!"

Skargo turned back toward Cayna with a Blinding Flash of Lightning in the Darkness as Ominous Black Birds Fly About background and clutched at his heart.

"No matter how fine a person the leader of the knights may be! He is not worthy of Mother Dear!"

"Um, hellooo? Earth to Skargo…?"

Cayna got the impression he was seriously misunderstanding something and tried to calm him down, but it was no use. Although he had said he came there to save her, for some reason, the conversation was heading in a completely different direction.

"I shall never entrust my mother dear to such a man!"

Realizing he was too far gone no matter what she said, Cayna took a certain staff out of her Item Box and held it aloft.

"That villainous Shining Saber! How dare he act cold toward other women yet try to lay a hand on my mother dear! He dares call himself a knigh… Um…M-Mother Dear?"

"…Yes, whatever is the matter?"

"Wh-what do you intend on doing…with that raised staff in your left hand?"

"If it's raised, I'm obviously going to bring it down, right?"

"It seems like I'm directly under where it's going to land…"

"Oh my, what a coincidence. Perhaps you ought to settle down?"

"………"

"………"

"I'm terribly sorry."

"As long as you understand."

She felt a wave of relief as Skargo meekly bowed his head. Even though he had come to some strange misunderstanding, the fact that her son was worried about her made Cayna smile.

Skargo had expected wrathful lightning to fall on him, so he looked at her blankly when she smiled at him.

"Has something happened, Mother Dear?"

"No, nothing at all."

She tugged at the sleeve of his robe, and with a light wave of her hand, Skargo obediently bent down. She patted his head, and he tilted his own with a Question Mark Over Head effect. Ever since their reunion, Skargo had rarely seen his mother in a good mood. His fear of being jabbed like the other day abated, and he felt a bit relieved.

"How long have you been watching Shining Saber? You didn't hear what we were talking about, did you?"

Cayna's gentle expression changed in an instant, and Skargo could hear a dangerous note in her voice. He shook his head and completely denied having heard anything; he had apparently come across Cayna while returning from the most recent meeting to discuss the damage the monster had caused. It was rare to see her having such a good time, so he had followed her without thinking in order to find out more.

Skargo apologized for this. The barrier that had been set up prevented him from getting closer, but watching Cayna have such a pleasant chat with the knight leader and adventurer had apparently filled him with jealousy and unease. Not realizing that his internal assumption of *That bastard thinks I'll give him Mother Dear?!* was wrong in every way, Skargo had mentally blacklisted Shining Saber as a threat.

Cayna was also a bit to blame for having so much fun talking to other players that she ignored her surroundings. That was why Kee had been the one to warn her she was being trailed, and it was Cayna's magical interference that had removed Skargo from the barrier.

From the very beginning, the highly visible Skargo wasn't greatly affected by the Concealment Barrier. Cayna thought it might be because he was a blood relative, but she decided to keep an eye on any issues regarding the barrier. Since the Battle Arena employees wouldn't be able to notice the surrounding area, either, if she left the barrier up, she made sure to release it.

"Well then, I think I'll head back to the inn and take it easy…"

Cayna gave a big stretch and sensed something odd about Skargo, who seemed to burn with a sense of purpose. She tugged on his robe.

"Ah! What is it, Mother Dear?"

"I'm going back to the inn, but make sure you do your work, okay?"

"Well, we have reached a stopping point in our medical treatment of the injured at church, so I thought I might take a short break. We have obtained some fine new leaves, so won't you have tea with me, Mother Dear?"

Cayna thought she could see an imaginary puppy tail wagging behind him. Since she wasn't in any particular rush, she accepted.

As she watched her son look so delighted that he might jump for joy, she thought that Mye's prospects were grim. He seemed to have no clue that he had the attentions of a princess, and Cayna held her head in her hands.

"What's going on? Why do you still look so stressed out?"

Mai-Mai entered a private room of the Academy without knocking as Lopus poured over the scroll, and he let out his several hundredth sigh of incomprehension. His wife was rather candid no matter how close she was with someone.

"Lady Cayna told me to 'read into it,' but I can't grasp the meaning at all."

He had already finished deciphering the scroll's writing. It spoke of recipe ingredients and the required magic. He had everything he needed to test it out, but that alone didn't guarantee anything was going to happen. He was at an utter loss.

Mai-Mai, on the other hand, perfectly understood problems that couldn't be explained no matter how hard one tried. Her mother, Cayna, and brothers would have gotten what she was saying, but as someone of the modern world, such concepts were beyond Lopus.

"Um, well, first, recognize *that* as your own. If you can use it after that, then it should be simple…"

"I've been listening this entire time, but I swear I don't get what you're talking about. Lady Cayna gave this to me, so there's no question it's mine. I'm asking how I *use* the scroll."

"Aghhhhhh, geez! How am I supposed to explain this?!"

As Mai-Mai gripped her head and writhed about in an eccentric display, Lopus considered it *same old, same old* and sank into his thoughts.

One might say they were a well-balanced couple.

The Item Box was the source of all clarity.

For those like Cayna who had player senses, their Item Box stored everything they owned. A screen would then indicate what was in their inventory. From there, they could tap USE and enjoy the effects of potions and the like without ever picking them up. This also applied to Foster Children, like Mai-Mai and those made on different accounts.

However, people like Lopus, who had absolutely no connection to the game, couldn't understand the concept of an Item Box. *Obtaining* and *using* the scroll were literally beyond his logical comprehension.

What it boiled down to was that he couldn't use it.

Furthermore, this scroll made by a Skill Master was definitively different from the skill scrolls obtained in Events. This problem made itself known here.

"Ah…"

"What the…?"

Just as the outline of the scroll in Lopus's hand began to fade, it suddenly disappeared with a burst of light. A drawback to this scroll was that it only lasted twenty-four hours after its initial creation.

Unaware of this, Lopus stared in shock at the light particles and the last remaining vestiges of the scroll. With an "Ah," Mai-Mai laid a comforting hand on Lopus's shoulder.

"Looks like the time ran out. When Mother makes things like that, they only last a day."

"Tch. And I finally had some answers…"

Mai-Mai nestled close to her husband as he dejectedly dropped his shoulders. She wanted to give him another scroll, but that was her mother's department. Cayna would mostly likely say he should take on a trial, so there didn't seem to be much choice outside giving up.

Helpless, she gently wrapped her arms around Lopus to comfort him.

CHAPTER 5

Intruders, a Duel, a Move, and Blood Ties

Cayna vacated her room at the inn for the time being, and since she was unsure whether it would be a long journey, she procured several days' worth of food, potions, and anything else she might need. She purchased lumber from Kartatz's workshop at a good price through a wholesale retailer and attended to various other remaining tasks.

Her first destination was the ocean tower she had heard about from Cohral. Since she had magic that would allow her to both move and breathe underwater, it didn't matter if she couldn't swim. Should she grow a bit lonely on her solitary trip, she learned from the Adventurers Guild that a joint force of Felskeilo and Helshper knights would be setting out in two days to take care of the remaining bandits. Cayna considered joining their ranks and accompanying them halfway.

Since Cohral was also in the Guild, she pestered him for more info about the coastline. He naturally insisted on monetary compensation, and she obliged. He looked elated—apparently, he'd needed money to repair his armor.

"Hmm, I should've gathered info ahead of time," she mused.

"Mm? Something happen?"

"I moved out of my room at the inn, so what am I supposed to do for two days…?"

"Gettin' ready is pretty tough, huh? Ha-ha-ha-ha!"

She sulked at Cohral's smile. It then struck her… She could stay at Marelle's place. On the way back from her last trip, she had only checked on Mimily, so she decided to pay the village another visit.

"Do you have somewhere to stay?"

"Yeah, a remote village."

"Won't you get there by the time the cleanup force is returning home?"

"Heh-heh-heh. My dear Cohral. Who do you think I am? My tower is over there, and I can return here in an instant with Teleport."

Cayna puffed out her chest and wagged her finger with a "Tsk, tsk, tsk" in a needless display of importance.

"Ew, gross! At least suffer a little like the rest of us!"

"Isn't it a little late for that? If you tried it once, you'd know I'm right."

At Cayna's high-handed attitude, Cohral tried to reach out and poke her head. She dodged with ease. No longer joking, he repeatedly extended a hand to grab her, but she nimbly evaded each attempt.

His comrades lukewarmly watched over this sudden game of tag. However, it wasn't long before the receptionist Almana angrily called out, "Please don't horse around in the guild!" and brought it to an end.

"Hah! Your level and speed are no match for me, young Cohral."

"Dammit, I'll get you for this!"

Cohral shook a fist at Cayna, who had now pulled down her eyelid and stuck out her tongue at him, but his friends pulled him away with a "Now, now," in an effort to calm him.

As she watched him get dragged off, Cayna regained her composure and murmured "Well, guess I better get going" and went on her way.

Prior to leaving the capital, she once again searched out the prime minister's spies and tied them up. Before the man observing her in the shadows had a chance to realize it, he lost sight of his target when Cayna snuck up on him and knocked him unconscious. It was his second slipup, and he started wondering if he should find a new career.

Cayna used her own ring to travel to her Guardian Tower in the remote village. The Guardian at the Battle Arena had approved of her, so she made sure not to use the Ninth Skill Master's ring to prevent accidentally winding up there.

Then she received some *very* curious information from her delinquent wall Guardian.

"Someone was here?"

"Yeah. They showed up after you left, Master. Maybe a couple days ago. 'Bout three people, I'd say. They hesitated in the forest below and ran off. Bunch of gutless wimps."

"Oh, well then, maybe they could have been players?"

At the very least, she didn't think by now anyone would come on business to a place rumored to be the home of a scary, ancient witch.

If one had enough patience, the trial in Cayna's tower was easy enough for even a low-level player to clear. If they hesitated in the forest maze and decided not to enter, they either came looking out of curiosity or went back to prepare for the long trial.

It was all speculation, so Cayna set the problem aside for the time being. She'd have the Guardian tell her if anyone came again, and she could use Search on visitors to find out if they were players.

Everything would have been so simple if the Guardian could confirm these things by itself, but unfortunately the Guardian was an overseer of the region, not an intercom or concierge. The most it could confirm was whether someone entered the forest or tower. Besides, a wriggling, moving wall Guardian would be pure horror.

After telling the delinquent just to contact her if anyone came along, Cayna descended the tower and headed for the village. At the entrance, there were two covered wagons stopped beside the workshop that had stood there the last time she visited. Since the village had no stables for them, the horses munched on the grass nearby.

Thinking that the villages really seemed to be flourishing, and there even appeared to be more people, Cayna headed toward the inn.

"Ah, Miss Cayna!"

"Hello, Lytt."

As Cayna came across Lytt carrying a bucket of water in front of the inn, she felt all the tension fall from her shoulders. The girl lowered the bucket, and they bowed to each other.

"I was thinking of staying at the inn for two days. Do you have any rooms available?"

"Uh-huh. We're surprisingly busy, but I think it'll be okay."

"If you're saying it's surprising, I take it things aren't going all that well…"

Lytt brought the bucket into the inn, and Cayna followed. Marelle, who was busy cleaning the tavern, greeted her.

"Hi there, Cayna. Been nearly a month since I last saw you, huh?"

"Long time no see, Marelle. I'll be staying just two days, if that's all right with you."

"You're free to drop in whenever. No need to be shy now; stay as long as you like."

After paying forty bronze coins in advance for her two-night stay, Cayna asked about the bustling atmosphere.

"Have you been getting more people here again lately?"

"Oh, you mean those covered wagons? They say it's that bathhouse you made. Students from Otaloquess even came to study it."

"Otaloquess… They came here from that far south? How are rumors even there…?"

Cayna had learned basic geography from Elineh. Of the three

nations, Otaloquess to the south (also known as the former Red Kingdom of Questria and the Blue Kingdom of Aulzelie) was famed for its superior magic techniques. She also heard that they'd had the same high-elf queen since the nation's founding and that Felskeilo's Royal Academy had modeled itself after them. However, Mai-Mai had said that since the Academy didn't have enough magic instructors, they couldn't dedicate themselves solely to magic.

Despite the southern Red Kingdom of Questria being entirely made up of desert, it had transformed into a lush, dense forest like the Blue Kingdom of Aulzelie that occupied the same territory. The climate was a perfect tropical rain forest, and Cayna heard the temperatures were high all year round. She thought that a desert becoming a jungle within two hundred years was one mystery too far.

"Students, huh? They're not giving Mimily any strange looks, are they?"

"They're all male. Mimily is in the women's bath, so they haven't seen her. Now that we're bringing her meals to her, I don't think she'll catch anyone's attention."

Although they were watching out for Mimily's well-being, it seemed that the villagers were very much used to the mermaid doing their laundry by that point. It didn't seem like she'd have to deal with any unnecessary stalker issues.

As she drank Marelle's lukewarm tea and recalled times both past and present, Cayna locked eyes with a male and female werecat entering the inn. The man had brown hair and ears and wore leather armor. He had the look of a swordfighter and carried a sword at his side. The woman had beautiful black hair and ears, wore leather armor, and had a long bow across her back.

The woman stared at Cayna and briskly approached. Flustered, the man followed after.

"Hello, comrade."

"'Comrade'?"

"You're an adventurer, aren't you? Or am I wrong?"

"Oh, that's what you mean. In that case, a fine hello to you, too. What can I help you with?"

The female werecat appeared to think about Cayna's question for a moment. Next to her, the swordfighter was poking her shoulder and uttering complaints of "What the heck are you doing?"

Cayna quickly used Search on them and found a bit of a surprise.

The woman, at level 70, was the weaker of the two, while the man, at level 80, was the stronger. Higher than Arbiter. She initially thought they were players, but since nothing indicated them as such, she judged they were from this world.

Incidentally, Search *did* display the nation a person belonged to. In Cayna's case, she had last belonged to the Black Kingdom of Lypras. Cohral and Shining Saber had been a part of the Blue Kingdom of Aulzelie.

"We came at the great scholars' request, but there's nothing here, and it's dead boring. We heard there was a tower of wisdom nearby, so we went with 'em to check it out."

It was then that Cayna understood. These were the visitors. They had been unprepared and were planning to come back with the scholars, but Cayna thought it was all for naught. The area around the tower was covered by a powerful barrier, so it rarely suffered outside attacks. However, there was also a set time limit between breeching the tower and arriving at the time, so all you had to do was stop in the middle and be sent back outside.

This loudmouth werecat girl was just like the players in the Game Era who had bugged Cayna for skills. The idea that there were still people like that here made Cayna want to burst out laughing, but she held her tongue.

"So how about coming along? You can ride on our big names once we take the tower."

"No thanks, I'm good."

"………"

To keep from blowing her cover, she flat out rejected them with a great big smile.

I want to laugh so hard right now.

"It will only aggravate them."

They're the ones already picking a fight.

"Well, yes…"

Apparently not expecting a refusal, the werecat woman froze with a shocked expression. Behind her, the man gave a look of apology for her rudeness and mouthed *Sorry* with a raised hand. The werecat woman's face twisted with disgust, and spit went flying as she rattled on.

"Listen here! We're famous adventurers in Otaloquess! You better realize that working with us is an honor! Think of what it could do for your own reputa—"

"No thanks, I'm good."

The woman looked on in disbelief at this word-for-word repeat rejection. Her eyebrows slowly raised with rage, and with one look at Cayna, she furiously raced up the inn stairs.

"Sorry about my little sister."

The man briefly apologized with a quick bow of the head and followed after.

"Adventurers like them seem hard to get along with…" Cayna looked toward the stairs with shock.

"Perhaps they are famed adventurers not for their skills but rather their impressive egos?"

Even Kee sounded surprised, and Cayna couldn't help but nod in agreement that this was likely the case.

"Sorry you had to put up with that."

"Why are you apologizing, Marelle? Adventurers come in all types, so you're bound to run into ones like them at some point."

As Marelle took her cup, Cayna reassured her that there was no need to worry. If she wanted to talk about bad, then the players who tried to steal her skills by force back when she was a Skill Master were a million times worse. They'd been so full of themselves, but their reactions when they failed were adorable.

"Oh, right, please listen to this, Marelle. My daughter, Mai-Mai, is *so mean*."

"I still think hearing a word like *daughter* come out of your mouth sounds ridiculous."

"Wha—?! *You're* so mean!"

"Yes, yes, I'm sorry. What about your daughter, now?"

"So you see…"

Cayna wiped away the dark atmosphere by recounting what had happened in Helshper. She recounted for Marelle how Mai-Mai had kept the truth about her grandchildren from her, how the three girls had gone hunting for a horned bear, and other such events for the remainder of the morning.

Not only was Marelle dumbfounded that Cayna had grandchildren, she was also shocked to learn they were involved with Sakaiya. After relishing a delicious, long-awaited lunch made by Marelle, Cayna promised Lytt she would recount her adventurer stories over dinner.

Cayna then headed over to the workshop by the village entrance where the technicians for whom she had drawn an illustrated explanation of the water wheel's mechanisms lived. She cheerfully greeted the villagers she passed on the way and ran into Lottor, who was carrying several rabbits.

"Yo there, Miss Cayna! You came back?"

"It's been a while, Lottor. Are you done hunting?"

"Well, I can't say I've been all that busy. You on another request?"

"Just taking a short break. I'll be leaving for a far-off place the day after tomorrow."

"There's no real reason to come to our nothing village… If you're already visiting this often, how about moving in?"

Lottor had meant it as a joke, but Cayna was silent. When he looked at her, she had her arms crossed and was deep in thought.

"…It's a possibility."

"Hold on, Miss Cayna. Are you serious?"

"I'd been considering setting up a base of operations somewhere, so you might say this is a windfall. I'll speak with the village elder later."

She was serious from every angle. In that case, even if he'd meant it as a joke, Lottor figured he should run it by the elder first.

With this in mind, he parted ways with Cayna and decided to head for the elder's house before returning to his own.

Setting aside Lottor's proposal until she discussed it with the village elder later on, Cayna initially went to see firsthand how things made with Craft Skills changed once people got their hands on them. At the workshop entrance, she called out to a dwarf who was crouched down, working on something.

"Hello."

"H-hello… You're the young miss from earlier, right? What can I do for you today?"

"I'm here to talk about the picture I explained before. Is anyone else around?"

She wanted to discuss some pretty confidential matters and asked that no one else come inside. The dwarf agreed immediately and led Cayna in. There, he brought out a woman and two more dwarves.

They started with basic introductions.

The bespectacled, sharp-eyed human woman was Sunya. Of the dwarves, the largest and brawniest was named Lux. The next biggest was Lux's apprentice, Dogai. The smallest (who still reached to about Cayna's chest) was Lux's son Latem. They were apparently a family who ran an engineering workshop and had contracts with Helshper merchants.

Cayna was surprised to find out that Sunya and Lux were married, but when she heard that Latem was Lux's son from his previous wife, it all made sense.

"Well then, Miss Cayna. You mentioned that you wished to discuss some sensitive matters. What might those be?"

Sunya seemed to be the delegate Cayna would be negotiating with, and Cayna continued. Lux and the others were all about production, so they were entrusting the business matters to Sunya.

"I explained on paper before how the mechanisms of the well work, but I can provide you with a full version for a fee."

"What?!"

""What was that?!""

This was the last thing they'd expected her to say, and it was far beyond anything they would have hoped for. Sunya looked utterly bewildered. Lux and the others seemed even more surprised. Their mouths were wide open, and they stood perfectly still. This moment of silence pressed on, and Cayna couldn't hide her smirk.

Lux was the first to recover.

"H-hold on, miss! We're very grateful to research your device, but is it really all right to transfer your own technique privileges to someone else?"

"Huh? What's that?"

Cayna had no idea what this sudden mention of technique privileges was. After all, usually someone who passed the offline quest could create the mechanism in question. Plus, it had no purpose outside the quest anyway. Cayna tried confirming it the other day, but it seemed that Shining Saber and Cohral could use it as well.

In the world of the game, it was treated as a prerequisite skill needed in order to obtain other skills. However, since it was only used when building fortresses, it pretty much gathered dust.

Sunya understood by Cayna's reaction that she didn't know what they meant, and it reconfirmed to her that perhaps the elf's offer to hand over a technique so precious in their modern world for a fee wasn't the wisest decision.

Cayna, on the other hand, was so dumbfounded by how far techniques had deteriorated that she gladly handed it over to them for research purposes.

In addition to monetary payment, her other stipulations were that they never name her as the contributor and never turn it into anything used to kill people. Of course, how things developed after Cayna passed it to them would all depend on the other party's discretion.

"...Understood. We shall follow your two conditions. However, in regard to the monetary fee, I'm afraid we cannot provide such a large amount. We will conduct negotiations and verify the matter with our partner merchants, so would you mind waiting for a short while?"

"Umm...is it really so valuable? That thing?"

It was just a simple, human-powered device that turned gears and used a caterpillar track to draw up troughs of water, so she wondered how much they were possibly willing to pay. A large question mark appeared over her head.

"Yes, well, if we include its future usefulness and diffusion...I believe we are looking at around ten gold coins."

"Bwagh?!"

Cayna sputtered when she heard the number that was twenty

times more than she'd expected. For that price, she could stay at the inn for seven years without lifting a finger. Although Cayna's standards for currency exchange were out of line with the modern world as usual, Sunya herself was completely serious.

"Are there even any merchants who can provide that much money at the drop of a hat?"

"I believe the merchants we are contracted with will be able to accommodate it."

Cayna had a bad feeling before Sunya even said anything. Knowing full well she was on the mark, Cayna went ahead and confirmed her fears.

"...Like Sakaiya?"

"Yes, indeed. We are supported by the master of Sakaiya."

"You're under Caerick's direct supervision, then. In that case, there's no rush to get the money. I'll ask the kid for it myself."

"What?! A-are you an acquaintance of the master?"

"Yeah, well...you might say we're business partners, I guess?"

Just to be safe, she wouldn't mention that he was her grandson. After all, it'd be a pain if Sunya and the others bowed their heads every time she stopped by. If the other villagers found out, and they all prostrated themselves before her, it would break Cayna's heart. Having a blood connection to a big name directly correlated to increased stress, so she decided to keep mum about that matter alone at any cost.

Unsurprisingly, as soon as Cayna called Caerick by name and referred to him as the kid, they knew exactly what the connection was between the two. They had apparently said nothing out of consideration. Cayna, who wasn't really a fan of hierarchical relationships, judged that they had their own reasons for doing so and continued pretending not to notice.

"Well then, why don't we get crackin'?"

Just as she said "As for the materials...," a log that would have required two adults to carry appeared in front of Lux. One could only assume it came out of thin air, and several more of the same size popped up in a similarly odd fashion. A single log must have weighed four times more than Cayna.

Their eyes widened in wonder at what mysterious technique could allow one girl to prepare such a large volume.

Paying no heed to their uneasy gazes mixed with fear, Cayna cast the spell to process the wood, then used Craft Skill: Water-Drawing Mechanism.

Everything had been split up into pieces last time, but this formula put everything together all in one go. The rectangular planks came together to create the caterpillar track, and there were two conspicuously big wheel gears powering it on either side. This was connected to a gear box with a crank one could use to transfer energy, and within mere seconds, a water-drawing device identical to the one used by the village's well was complete.

Sunya and the others stopped what they were doing and stared as they witnessed this entire process happen in midair. To be honest, such methods were incomprehensible in the modern world.

"Hmm, I guess the caterpillar track didn't need to be this long if it's going to be inside."

Cayna had measured the initial device so it would reach the bottom of the village well, but the extensive length of the track seemed a bit cumbersome here. The wells in the village also had preservation magic cast on them, but considering the workers here would likely disassemble the device, she decided to forego this.

As she gave a gesture of *It's all yours*, they finally moved forward. The parents, their child, and their pupil all raced at the parts that interested them most, and Cayna felt like she'd just given children a new toy.

Sunya awkwardly withdrew to the back of the workshop and returned with several documents.

"Well then, Miss Cayna. Could you please sign these?"

"Um, sure. Here and here?"

Since coming to Leadale, Cayna hadn't had much opportunity to write her own name. Besides signing in to lodgings, the only other time had been when she registered for the Adventurers Guild.

She didn't have a last name here, so she simply signed it *Cayna*.

"Well, I guess I'll head to the village elder's house nex— Huh?"

"Hello, Lady Cayna. So this is where you have been."

Cayna was stupefied to see the village elder approach her with a questioning murmur, but as soon as she saw Lottor grinning right behind him, she understood what was going on.

"Geez, Lottor. Isn't it unfair to talk to him before me?"

"Nah, it's faster this way, don'cha think?"

The village elder smiled as he stroked his peppered beard and permitted Cayna to build a home within the village.

"In that case, shall we all build your home together, Lady Cayna?"

"Ah, there's no need to go that far for my sake. As long as I have a plot of land, I can build it myself."

Of course, there had been a build-your-own-home offline event in the game, but those usually involved huge fortresses. The basic Building Skill had several house templates, so she planned on going with one of those. Wandering here and there as an adventurer was fun and all, but she also wanted one place where she could relax. Marelle could also teach her methods of housekeeping that didn't involve skills. Since Cayna had spent most of her life in a hospital, she dreamed of having her own home.

The village elder proposed a place farther within the village that received plenty of sunlight, and the villagers who had gathered approved as well. Long ago, the pioneer who founded the village had built his house there, and no one had thought to build on it since.

"What?! Is it really okay for me to have a place like that?"

"Lady Cayna, although you are not from this village, you've done so much for us, have you not? It would be shameful of us to not repay you at a time like this."

As the elder said this, the other villagers nodded simultaneously in agreement.

"That's right. If Cayna's around, we can expect better game from her than Lottor!"

"Hey now! I'm gonna lose my job as a hunter, ain't I?!"

"No one's sayin' that. We'll just have better banquets."

"A nice excuse, but we don't have the money to pay for all our husbands' drinking."

"Whaaat? I wanna kick back for a day..."

Several of the men groaned, and everyone burst into laughter. It wasn't a flat-out refusal, though, so Cayna decided to gratefully accept their feelings.

After that, the women of the village gave her an overview of items necessary for daily life, such as one goat per household and a barn. If she was hoping to plow the fields, they said they would give her a corner of one of the fields that several families were managing together. Kee stored away all this information for use after the house was built.

She could buy a goat someplace in advance, and she could make most of the furniture herself as long as she had the materials.

The problem was coming up with something she could also share with the villagers.

It was true that ever since she made the bathhouse for them, they had said not to worry about it. However, she couldn't just depend on them and investigated the matter further.

The quickest solution would be to simply take on a huge job at the Guild and put that money into the village. However, since Cayna was oddly famous in Felskeilo, there was a good possibility she might earn other adventurers' animosity.

There was also the matter of Mimily. It all depended on the mermaid's wishes, but Cayna dearly wanted to put a large aquarium in the house for her to live in.

"I've gotta think of something…"

"Well then, why not go hunting with me for now? That way, you can eat some good, rare food and find plenty to sell, right?"

"That's true. Maybe I should be a hunter like you, Lottor…"

He put his hand on her shoulder. Grateful for his proposal, Cayna accepted.

"I knew it'd turn out like this!"

That night in the dining hall, the tavern was quickly transformed into a welcoming banquet for Cayna. Of course, Lux and his family, the two Otaloquess palace mages conducting magical investigations in the bathhouse, and their four adventurer guards were invited despite knowing nothing of the events leading up to it. It was dangerous for Mimily to be around those who didn't know her circumstances, so Lytt brought food and alcohol to the women's bathhouse for her.

The villagers lined up tables and chairs beyond the dining hall and commenced with the festivities. They forcibly put Cayna in the seat of honor, and adults packed around her to pour her alcohol.

Here and there, exhilarated villagers placed their arms around one another and sang with full vigor. Realizing she couldn't beat them so she might as well join them, Cayna shouted a loud, desperate "Cheers!"

Even so, she had things she wanted to do. Marelle would likely complain later, but Cayna used the Poison Nullification on her arm-band to prevent herself from getting drunk.

However, she could occasionally feel a strong, malevolent gaze focusing on her, and when Cayna traced it back to its source, she found the girl who had charged at her that afternoon glaring in her direction. When their eyes met, the werecat girl once again frowned with displeasure and turned away. Cayna couldn't figure out what in the world she was so unhappy about.

As the banquet wore on, and increasingly more people were growing unsteady with drunkenness, Cayna stood up. Since the villagers had shown her such hospitality, she thought she'd show them a bit of a spectacle.

Reading the room, Marelle clapped her hands to pull everyone's attention toward Cayna.

"Hey now, everyone. Cayna has something to say!"

"Sorry about this, Marelle."

"No worries; it's the least I can do. C'mon, you better say what you want fast."

"Right. Well then, everyone. Thank you kindly for throwing me such a wonderful banquet tonight."

Cayna gave a low bow, and cheers and clapping erupted. One could not say who, but a number of people gave a look of *How crass* and turned their heads away.

Wheat flour, fruits, eggs, and other ingredients had been set on a table. Naturally, for the people of the village, they had a good idea of what was going on; Cayna had ways of taking ingredients and creating finished products as if it were nothing.

The ones who *weren't* aware of this were the Otaloquess guests who had just arrived in the village and weren't yet familiar with her. They took one look at the mountain of ingredients on the table, grew bored, and returned to their private conversations with one another.

Even their faces would change to a shade of shock after Cayna's next move.

"Right here and now, I shall produce a dessert found only on aristocratic tables."

The second she said it, she cast Cooking Skill: Cake.

She held her hands in front of her chest, and an orange-colored magic ball of fire formed within. It swallowed up several ingredients on the table. The fireball changed to a sphere of marble and disappeared. Soon after, cake appeared in Cayna's hands. The fluffy sponge cake had layers of red berries and cream. The top and sides were decorated with pure-white cottony icing.

One might normally call it a basic cake, but for the villagers who had neither seen nor heard of such a refined, noble dessert before, there was no greater work of art.

On top of that, the sweet fruity scent wafting from the cake enchanted them, and they swarmed on Cayna as if they were being drawn in. She stood before them and made cakes of red, orange, and yellow. Using what she'd learned from television, she cut pieces of cake for the villagers while using a cloth to wipe the warm knife she had received from Marelle.

Marelle, Lytt, Gatt, and Luine were the first to taste it. She soon offered it to the village elder, his wife, and Lottor.

Lytt immediately dug right in. When she did, her eyes grew wide, and she froze. When Cayna worriedly asked if maybe she didn't like it, Lytt shook her head and proclaimed, "It's soooo yummy!" with a great big smile.

As the inn's and elder's families savored their first taste of the sweet cream and fluffy texture of the sponge cake with wide eyes, Cayna set to work. Since everyone had unanimously agreed it was delicious, she used all the ingredients she'd procured beforehand and created one cake and pie after the other.

She offered some to Li'l Fairy as well, but the girl sniffed the aroma and gave a bright smile. Apparently, she really didn't need to eat or drink.

It wasn't long before the villagers polished off Cayna's desserts.

"We'll have to make sure Mimily has some later, too."

"Right! I'll take it for you, Cayna!"

"Great. Why don't we go together, then?"

"Sure!"

After a pleasant conversation with Lytt, Cayna made berry, ruche, and nanafruit cakes and set them aside.

The attentive guests from the southern nation had been keeping an eye on the whole affair from a corner of the dining hall, and they observed each person's eyes go wide with shock.

They didn't know the village's political or hierarchical system, but they chuckled at the people's extensive surprise.

…If only they could have just stayed surprised.

Someone who couldn't read the enjoyable atmosphere stood up.

"Unacceptable! H-how could I ever stand for th—?!"

Just as she was about to continue a stream of insults, her older brother put a hand over her mouth. With a "Hgwhh?!" she began to flail.

Upon hearing her very first utterance, every villager present turned a cold, piercing stare upon the siblings and scholars. The collective glare of *Who do you think you are, ruining our good time?* sent the Otaloquess group running full speed to their rooms.

The brother had pinioned and knocked out his sister and, with an apology of "Sorry to disturb your festivities," withdrew to the second floor.

"What the heck was that…?" a shocked Lottor murmured. Every other villager shared his sentiment.

Despite having their parade rained on, the villagers continued enjoying their rare, sweet delicacy with relish, and the revelry continued.

As the party drew to a close, Cayna escaped the inn with Lytt and headed toward the bathhouse to give Mimily her cake. The three then sat alongside one another in the bath and aimlessly looked up at the steam-filled night sky.

"Hmm. Land dwellers certainly do think differently from us merpeople."

"…'Land dwellers.'"

After hearing about the strange occurrence at the banquet, Mimily nodded sagely. She had lumped humans and every other race as land dwellers, and Cayna frowned. The mermaid seemed to know something about the werecat girl's hysteria.

"That person probably overlapped Cayna's image with someone else. That's why she said it was unacceptable."

"'Someone'?"

Not understanding what she meant, Cayna tilted her head. Mimily continued with an example.

"There might be someone precious to her who looks just like you. Rapid-fire ideas like *They would never do such a thing!* may be running through her mind. Don't you think?"

Cayna thought of her cousin and imagined if she had a rude look-alike. Yes, she sensed this was likely what was going through the werecat's mind.

"I totally get it! I'd be mad, too, if there was a Not–Miss Cayna!"

Next to them, Lytt looked at the night sky and raised her arms to prove her point. Cayna and Mimily smiled.

"I, too, am glad you are the one who saved me, Cayna."

"Th-thanks, you two." Cayna's cheeks reddened at their unabashed affection. She thought that she probably wasn't imagining the water growing hotter. "Still, you really hit on something, Mimily."

"Ah yes. I've been on the receiving end myself, after all. I certainly understand how it feels."

As Cayna watched Mimily cross her arms and look away with a nod, she seemed to be hinting at a dark past. She thought she heard the mermaid whisper, "Back then, with Mother...," but decided to pretend she hadn't.

As if attempting to dodge the issue, Mimily coughed and turned to the plate at the edge of the bath with a straight face.

"Well then, this must be the food all land dwellers crave!"

"I don't know about *all* land dwellers, but it's cake. *Cake.* It's a dessert."

"Everything Miss Cayna makes is delicious!"

Next to Cayna, Lytt bent forward with a sigh and praised it wholeheartedly.

On the plate was a berry shortcake. The berries were as big as grapes. There was also a ruche mousse. Ruche were fruits that had an orangey flavor. Last, there was the nanafruit chiffon cake. Nanafruits tasted very similar to bananas.

"Everyone ate the rest. I'll have to pick up more fruits when I'm in Felskeilo."

"But fruit is so expensive..."

Lytt had only seen fruit a handful of times. Since Elineh's caravan required magical tools to keep them fresh all the way to the village, the unit price was high. Thus, the most sweetness that the villagers tasted was honey and small wild berries.

"Don't worry, Lytt! I'll take you to Felskeilo someday and show you all sorts of things!"

Cayna gave sad Lytt a big hug to cheer her up. Pressed against her small chest, Lytt simply gave a dry laugh of "Ah-ha-ha" and murmured, "I won't get my hopes up."

Meanwhile, Mimily carefully approached the cake with the fork Cayna had given her. She gulped, took a plentiful scoop of cream off the berry shortcake, and very slowly raised it to her mouth.

As the sweetness melted on her tongue, a sharp glint came to her eye like a bird of prey. She stabbed the very center of the berry shortcake and tried to shove as much in her mouth as possible. Mimily squeezed out every ounce of sweetness as she squashed the cake with her tongue and swallowed. She enjoyed it despite the slight choking sensation. After her body finished trembling, and the last notes wore off, she eyed her next prey—that is, her next cake.

Upon devouring that cake in a similar fashion, Mimily noticed an empty plate and two pairs of eyes staring at her in shock.

"You coulda at least enjoyed it a bit more...," Lytt said with a note of disappointment.

Cayna, on the other hand, had a slightly different take.

"You looked just like Scylla turned Kuchisake-onna devouring its prey."

"That's so mean!"

Mermaids in particular took great offense at being compared to Scylla, hence Mimily's reaction, but Cayna then replayed the scene for the two of them. After all, the way she savagely gobbled up the cake was like none other than Scylla itself.

"Woooow! How did you do that, Miss Cayna?"

"It's a skill that lets me replay any scene I find impressive only three times."

"How about me? Do I get a turn?"

As Mimily hung her head in self-loathing in a corner of the bathtub, next to her, Lytt was begging Cayna to do the same thing for her cake-eating experience.

"Hmm. I can't remember something I didn't take much note of. Next time, okay?"

"Whaaaat? I wanted to see me, too."

Lytt gave a mournful moan, and Cayna said "Sorry about that" in apology.

This peaceful scene continued (despite the dark clouds rising from one corner) until Luine came over and asked Lytt how long she was planning on lazing around while everyone was still cleaning up.

The storm Cayna thought she'd avoided once again made landfall after the banquet was over. She was helping Marelle and the others tidy up. Lytt and Luine rubbed their eyes sleepily as they carried plates, and Marelle did the dishes. For whatever reason, Cayna was helping wipe the tables.

"Sorry about this, Cayna. You're the guest of honor, yet I'm still having you do the dirty work."

"I don't see the issue. I'm a part of this village now, too, so we all work together."

Luine called out to Cayna while carrying enough plates to look like she was attempting a world record. Smiling wryly at the girl's strength, Cayna washed out her rag and went to answer her. Lytt was also at her side making herself known by tugging on the older girl's sleeve, and Cayna answered this with a smile. The moment she saw Lytt's grin, it made her whole world. It was indeed a small happiness, and the thought of the days continuing on like this made Cayna's heart dance.

However, that happiness was short-lived.

Kee's close-range warning system pointed her toward the stairs, and she saw the werecat girl racing down it. She charged at Cayna, stopped just in front of her, and glared with enough malice to bore a hole through her. Apparently hoping to continue from before, she thrust out her chest and made her declaration.

"I'll never accept you!!"

"What's up with this crazy lady?"

Luine voiced exactly what Cayna was thinking.

The girl turned her stare on Luine, and as one might expect, such a look from an adventurer was enough to strike fear in an average girl like Luine.

Stepping between them, Cayna handed Luine the cloth, activated several of her Active Skills used in Battle Mode, and stared down the girl opposite her. Scaring her longtime friend Luine had set Cayna off. After all, now that she heard from Mimily that the werecat was venting her personal frustrations, Cayna wouldn't stand for it.

The girl took a step back at Cayna's threat, which surprised even her. She probably never imagined someone with as much excessive pride as her would show fear.

Upon seeing the werecat's expression and deciding she'd had her revenge, Cayna burst into laughter.

The glint gradually returned to the werecat's eyes, but she couldn't keep venting her misplaced anger forever.

"How can someone as low as you wield the same ancient arts as the queen?!"

"...Ah, I get it. I guess you're not a Foster Child or anything, huh?"

Cayna's relaxed attitude suggested she'd hit upon something, and the werecat raged with fury. After directing her bloodlust at Cayna for a while longer, her hand went for the short sword at her side.

Cayna would have preferred to avoid bloodshed in their current location, but honestly, she thought talking wouldn't get them very far, either. If her foe made a move, she could suppress her with ease.

"So if you're not going to accept me, what will you do?"

"We will duel!!"

"......Huh?"

Cayna took some time to break this down, stew it over, and slowly process the information. The situation had grown more troublesome than a mere counterattack, but she realized the definitive truth of the matter and answered honestly.

"No thanks. I don't bully anyone weaker than me."

"Who you callin' weak?!"

It was only natural. The difference in power between a level 1,100 and a level 70 was obvious. It was like an ant picking a fight with a nuclear missile. Cayna's reaction was a matter of course. If this were the game world of *Leadale*, it'd be like her launching a concentrated attack on a new player who only joined two or three days prior. Such actions weren't anything to be proud of.

However, her foe didn't realize that. Immediately being declared weak sent the werecat into a fit of snarling, and her position shifted into one that suggested she might lunge at any moment.

There was a high-pitched keening that made her want to rip her ears right off. Sure enough, Cayna's head slowly began to throb.

"I will have you kneel before me."

"Oh, I see… I'm pretty sure that's impossible, though."

Cayna gave a tired look and shrugged at her laughably high self-confidence; she hadn't even agreed to the duel, yet the girl already looked raring to go.

Finally, she accepted the situation before her. Perhaps in a good mood, the werecat gave a proud look as she fell back and disappeared.

Her brother then appeared from the shadows of the stairs. Unable to hide that he, too, was clearly fed up with all this, he looked at the ceiling before approaching Cayna and bowing his head.

"Sorry about that. My sister said some pretty ridiculous things."

"Y-yeah… It's fine, don't worry about it. I kinda already agreed to it by this point. What was that all about anyway?"

"I'm seriously sorry. She loves and admires the queen, so when she saw you using the same techniques, she got offended. Well, there's no need to hold back, so give her a good whupping."

"That doesn't really seem like something a big brother should be saying. Oh, I'm Cayna. What's your name?"

"I'm Cloffe, and that was my sister Clofia. I'd like for us all to get along, but…"

"Yeah, she and I aren't exactly there yet."

Cloffe's and Cayna's sighs overlapped. The reason was easy enough to guess.

Cayna gently patted Luine's back as she eased away the fear of the werecat's overwhelming aura.

"Hey, are you okay, Luine?"

"Y-yeah… Thanks, Cayna."

"Luine! You okay?!"

Marelle, too, had been frozen on the other side of the counter and now dashed forward. As Cayna watched the still-trembling girl fall into her mother's arms, her shoulders relaxed.

From the shadows of the counter, Lytt timidly looked around the tavern.

"Th-that was scary."

"Indeed it was. The mean demon lady is gone now, though, so everything's okay."

Cayna stroked Lytt's head comfortingly, all the while staring sharply at the ceiling.

Then, early the next morning, the duel in question was held on a main road near the village. The witnesses were Cloffe and Lottor, who just happened to be passing by on his way to pick berries. Unfortunately, this activity took place at the same time Cayna was leaving the village.

"*Sniff…* I just wanted to look for berries this morning…"

"Like I said, I'll help you once we're done with this. Please cheer up, Lottor."

Cayna had persuaded him to wait there by promising to accompany him after finishing the duel quickly. Hearing this made Clofia seethe next to her, but Cayna paid her no mind.

They weren't able to hold the duel in the village since Clofia's weapon was a bow, and Cayna primarily used Attack Magic, plus Cayna didn't want to bother the villagers with a personal vendetta. Furthermore, Clofia's energy was at a fever pitch before the duel even started, while Cayna couldn't have cared less.

"Well, I'm ready when you are," Cayna said to Clofia with the calmest of expressions, despite not having so much as a wand on her.

I'm counting on you, Kee.

"Understood."

With Kee helping out, Cayna found the will to give it her A game from the get-go.

"Understood. The duel between Lady Cayna and Clofia will now begin. Does either party take issue with the use of lethal attacks?" Cloffe asked.

"None here!"

As Clofia replied with a powerful nod and her bow at the ready, Cayna waved her hand casually and kept her tone light.

"Sure, no problem. I've gotta hurry and finish this up so I can go berry picking."

She was fully aware this would only get Clofia more riled up.

"Well then, begin!"

Cloffe swung down his raised hand, and the battle commenced.

Clofia made the first move with some smugly shot rapid-fire arrows, but they all stopped in midair a few centimeters from Cayna.

"What…?!"

"Oh my, are you planning to go easy on me? You'll never hit me that way, though."

Clofia leered as Cayna put her hands on her hips and tilted her head in surprise.

"D-don't you underestimate me! **Break Ball!**"

The very next instant, a prickly ball of fire came hurtling forward, yet that, too, was blocked midair by some unknown force right in front of Cayna.

"Wha—?!"

"That's some pretty weak magic. At this rate, you'll never get past my Divine Spirit barrier."

"Divine…?!" their referee Cloffe exclaimed in surprise.

Next to him, Lottor wasn't really sure what was going on, but he had been watching the battle in amazement the entire time.

According to Skargo, Divine Spirits were one step above the spirits that Cayna summoned. Cayna herself knew nothing about that, but he seemed to be talking about Kee.

Kee was the one who acted as her source of knowledge and advice and served as her protector of sorts. That was why if so much as a piece of paper blew her way, he put up a force field to nullify all attacks. Since Clofia also had no way of knowing what was even going on, Cayna openly faced her evil arrows with no preparation at all. Kee's force field blocked every last hit.

Finally, just as Clofia went to draw her sword, she tripped over her own feet upon witnessing Cayna raising her arm straight into the heavens and glaring at her.

Clofia realized that the magic condensed above Cayna's hand was enough to make one's hair stand on end.

Magic Skill: Load: Laguna Vala Giga

"Tear her apart!"

The water spears shot from Cayna's hand and made parabolas

that spread out in four directions. They changed trajectory half-way, converged on a single point, and instantly froze together in front of Clofia. The icy mist scattered across the area, solidified, and transformed into a beastly jaw big enough to swallow a house as it descended on the werecat.

It hadn't even taken a second for it to travel from Cayna's hand to right in front of Clofia's face. Her eyes wide with shock, it looked as if the icy maw would eat her up and kill her right then and there. It put her head between its teeth, and the tip of its fangs were almost at her throat when it stopped.

Cloffe had told Cayna to "give her a good whupping," but it didn't mean he wanted to see his own sister die. He had averted his gaze, but when he turned back to look, he saw Clofia collapse to the ground in shock, pale-faced. Her eyes were unfocused, her teeth rattled, and the icy maw had turned to crystals and crumbled.

"If you ever hurt the villagers, I won't show any mercy!" Cayna said, hands on her hips and cheeks puffed out in a show of how mad she was.

Cloffe raced over to his sister, who was now curled up in a fetal position and trembling.

With the hostilities having only ended moments before, Cayna waved her arms as if to clear the air, gave Lottor a push from behind, and went to leave.

"Come on, Lottor, let's get going."

"H-hold it. Is it really okay to just leave those two?"

"It's fine. The duel is over."

As Cayna further hurried Lottor on, behind her, Cloffe bowed his head silently.

She passed by the area again an hour later with Lottor after they'd finished their berry picking and were on their way back to the village. Clofia was gone, but Cloffe alone stood there straight and tall.

"Hey, where'd that girl go?" Lottor asked.

His tone had been amiable, but Cloffe simply shook his head and said, "I sent her back to our room at the inn." He then turned to Cayna and asked if he might borrow some of her time.

Confused by his strangely polite tone, she nodded awkwardly. He put a hand to his chest and replied, "Thank you."

"Well then," said Lottor, "I'll be going on ahead to the village, Miss Cayna. Gotta give the proprietress these berries."

"Oh, right. Sorry for dragging you along."

"No worries. See you later."

Cayna waved Lottor off, then turned to face Cloffe, wondering exactly what he wanted to talk about, when she was met with an astonishing sight.

Cloffe was down on one knee like a vassal before someone important.

"U-uhhh…"

Unsurprisingly, this made her face twitch. She instinctively took several steps back and reeled at the troublesome truth that now awaited her.

"Wh-wh-wh-wh-what is it, Cloffe? Why are you on the ground?"

"Yes, ma'am. You are as kind as they say. I, the humble Cloffe, am deeply moved."

"Uhhhh, d-didn't I give her a good whupping like you said? What part of that was nice?"

"Regardless, you did not deal the final blow even at the very last second. You could have easily taken my sister's life."

"Just how savage do you think I am?!"

Her retort was spur of the moment, but Cayna suddenly realized something odd.

"Huh? 'As they say'? Who told you about me?"

"From the ruler of Otaloquess, Her Majesty, Queen Sahalashade. We have come here on secret orders from our sovereign."

"Hmm? Why do I feel like I've heard that name somewhere before?"

The name of the southern nation of Otaloquess's queen rang a bell, and Cayna tilted her head. As she tried to recall where she had heard it, Kee presented a related conversation from the log:

"My dear Cayna, I have followed your example and taken on a Foster Child as well."

"Oh, you too, Sahana? Are they going to be your child?"

"Yes, she is a fellow high-elf girl named Sahalashade. If you two should ever meet, please come to love her, would you?"

"Um, how am I supposed to love an NPC...?"

"This has nothing to do with Eternal, so please don't say anything."

"...Right."

"Come to think of it, that was the name of Sahana's kid..."

Sahana was a former player who was in the high-elf community and whom Cayna had registered as a younger sister. She remembered Sahalashade being the name of her attention-seeking Foster Child who was the closest thing to a baby squirrel. Eternal was registered as the oldest player in the high-elf community. He was probably the sole male high-elf player in the entire game. After all, there had only been six high elves left last time she checked, so it was easy to remember everyone's names.

Wait, hold on. If Sahana was my "little sister," and this is her daughter, that makes me her aunt... That's why I'm being treated like royalty?!

Cayna's emotions dipped straight into melancholy at the thought of the incredible mess she was now involved in. She also now understood Cloffe's behavior. First of all, she herself was a high elf, the royalty of the elves. It was one thing to be served by elves, but the fealty of a werecat was normally unfounded.

"Come to think of it, you said something about secret orders, right?"

"Yes. Well then, please allow me to explain in further detail. A short while ago, shadows from numerous nations reported sightings of an adventurer named Cayna in Felskeilo. The queen was exceedingly intrigued by this and sent us to gather more information. We haven't been observing your every move, of course. We have simply been compiling the rumors spreading nationwide. After close examination of this data, Her Majesty confirmed you to be the real Cayna and sent us here."

"Wow... I can't say I'm all that shocked, though. Is your sister one of these shadows, too?"

"No, she is not. She came here for the same public reason as the adventurers and scholars and merely accompanied me."

Their purpose of researching the ancient arts had apparently been a front. The real goal was to find and solicit Cayna.

She was surprised that the ruler of an entire nation would go that far. Really, she wanted to tell them not to put her through such trouble. She had big tasks, like finding the Palace of the Dragon King and building her home, both of which demanded her full attention. When Cayna considered her to-do list, this problem didn't seem like anything to get worked up over.

"*Sigh*. Well, tell this to your queen for me, okay? 'I don't plan on coming to Otaloquess.'"

"Understood... Huh? My queen's wish was indeed to greet you in her kingdom..."

"I still have a lot of things to do. I have to find my friend's tower and build a house. I also have to repay the villagers for their kindness and thank Elineh and Arbiter. My kids are in this country as well, and I want to see my grandkids. Even if I have adventuring business in Otaloquess, I don't plan on going to the castle to see the queen. Tell Sahalashade that."

Cayna understood that she should care about the queen as her niece, but she simply didn't have time at the moment. Sahalashade was like a memento of Sahana, and Cayna thought she should visit her at least one time at some point, but in terms of priority, she was near the bottom of the list. She decided to visit her niece once things had calmed down, even if she had no idea when that would be.

Cloffe wasn't sure what to do about this flat-out rejection. The primary goal of his mission had been *Do whatever Cayna wishes*, so for now, he considered his task finished. Even so, there was no question that repeating Cayna's answer before the queen, who had issued his orders, would require nerves of steel.

Cloffe floundered a bit and wanted to stop her, but he and the other shadows who had been dispatched to Cayna's usual haunts had one last important goal.

That was: Do not upset the target under any circumstance.

When his fellow shadows had questions over this, the queen replied, "If my aunt Cayna doesn't hold back, she could burn this entire nation to the ground."

If Cayna herself heard this, she would have furiously replied, *What kind of crazy game of telephone are you playing?!* Since he'd caught a glimpse of her power during the duel with his sister, Cloffe exercised restraint and swallowed down any further remarks that might get her going again.

Even in the best light, Clofia was an upper-tier adventurer, and Cayna had sent her spiraling into fear with a single burst of magic.

If Cayna unleashed the full extent of her power, she'd destroy everything in seconds.

"Well then, I suppose I'll head back to the village. Care to join me, Cloffe?"

Even though he was kneeling before her, Cayna acted like her usual self. However, there was something oddly nebulous about her gaze, and he shuddered. He stood up, brushed the dirt off his clothes, and informed her that he'd return after a round of patrolling.

"No problem. Um, could you tell your sister I'm sorry?"

Cayna relayed this request to Cloffe with a smile that said she wasn't especially worried.

"I shall be sure to do so. Whether she will listen is another matter, however."

Cayna murmured, "Did I scare her too much?" to which the grim-faced Cloffe gave a small nod.

"Hmm. Okay, then. She's actually pretty interesting, now that I think about it, so tell her we should meet up again sometime."

"I cannot imagine she would do so upon hearing such snide remarks. You truly are a curious one, Lady Cayna."

"Well, it's better than fighting each other, right?"

"…Understood. I would not anticipate any replies."

Since Cloffe always had a small grin anyway, it was hard to read his expression. He sounded amused, though, so Cayna gave a solid nod.

After that, Clofia never left her room, and Cayna returned to Felskeilo via the Battle Arena ring.

The next morning, Cayna returned to the Felskeilo capital.

Since she would be traveling alongside the subjugation forces, she decided to gather her supplies while the sun was still high.

First, she used Teleport to visit Sakaiya in Helshper.

Since the trip back meant she'd have to travel to the village after returning to her tower anyway, she decided to leave basic items in her inn room after telling Marelle in advance. If she set her own house as a main base, she'd be able to fly to the village with ease. However, since any other destination had to be something conspicuous like a castle, using Teleport had some drawbacks. The only other option were the Portals set in each area long ago to act as relay points. But even if you compared the old maps against the new ones, the Portals didn't exist in this modern land of Leadale.

Just to be safe, she went someplace near the Helshper capital and made sure not to leave a single trace.

"Maybe I should just build a tower as my own landmark?"

"It would undoubtedly be taken over by bandits."

"Well, what if I place a dragon or a golem, and…?"

"It would no longer be a relay point but rather a stronghold, correct?"

Cayna couldn't argue with Kee's logic, so she scrapped the idea. If she did build it, adventurers sent to check out the suspicious structure would likely run into unfortunate accidents.

"Next we'll have to find or dig up magic rhymestone. I want to bury it with quartz sand and make window glass."

"It appears we need a host of ingredients."

Cayna continued chatting with Kee as she kept going through the Helshper capital. Any outsider would believe she was talking to herself, but she paid this no mind.

Magic rhymestone was an ore that collected magical power, and it served as the battery that kept magical tools running. Its effectiveness varied depending on size, but since it allowed a user to cast simple spells multiple times without the need for a charm to sustain its life span, it was quite useful. Not only could it provide light, it could turn a barrel into a refrigerator if you used Freeze, and it could also make that very same barrel become a washing machine if you used Spin.

In the world of the game, one could obtain these via Dig Points, but it was unknown whether those still existed. Honestly speaking, this kind of ore wasn't something you could find just by mining in the mountain.

There were three ways to find magic rhymestone:

Do a thorough search of the area and discover magic rhymestone mines.

Summon a rock worm and search for it that way.

Take it from worm-type magic beasts who love tough boulders and stash both ore and other rocks in their nests. One grew to be twenty meters tall and five meters in diameter, so it was an annoying beast that lived almost entirely in holes. The jewel worm collected only the greatest treasure, but such a catch was geared toward eccentrics. A vast span of land would collapse whenever a jewel worm appeared during Events, so players didn't know much about these monsters.

Cayna was grateful for this modern world, since the chances were good that she would be able to find a rhymestone later on without any digging.

"…At any rate…"

As soon as she arrived at Sakaiya, she was greeted with the same sight as before.

One could boldly declare by this point that this street ran on Sakaiya's prosperity alone. The bustling mass of people was a mix of laborers' shouts along with the sounds of customers and small-business employees. On top of that, the one-story Japanese-style tiled house was completely different from any other house around it. Amid the crowd, there were even tourists with open guidebooks who had nothing to do with business.

On either side of Sakaiya were shops that had gone under—the direct opposite of Sakaiya's prosperity. It left nothing other than the impression that Sakaiya was a greedy merchant from a period drama who rose up with the power of money.

"*Caerick* and *Caerina* are both taken from parts of my name, right? Could it be that Mai-Mai missed me for two hundred years?"

Kee gave no reply as she murmured this to herself. Instead, another voice called out.

"…Great-Grandmother?"

"Oh, Idzik. It's been a while."

The elven young master had been accompanying the workers but stopped and stood in the middle of the road when he noticed Cayna. He trotted over to her, gave a bow, and happily asked what brought her to Sakaiya.

"I came to deliver a letter. Caerick said he sent a family of crafts-people to a village near the Felskeilo border, right?"

"I'm afraid that sort of matter is outside my jurisdiction. Let us have Father confirm it for you."

Idzik issued several work-related orders to the kobold maid right behind him before leading her into Sakaiya.

"I'd rather have you prioritize your profits, to be honest."

"Father grows afraid when you are disrespected, Great-Grandmother. My aunt is here as well."

"Caerina's here?"

She had repeated him unintentionally, but Sakaiya was Caerina's home. It wouldn't be strange at all for them to run into each other.

Cayna was led to a Western-style room with wooden flooring and suitably dignified furnishings. Personally, she thought the garden with the lush view of strange plants and a gourd-shaped white-sand garden had a sweeping view.

Also unlike the room she was led to before, Idzik knocked on an already open door. When the siblings asked what he wanted, and he proceeded farther inside with Cayna in tow, they hurriedly corrected their posture.

"Father, Aunt Caerina. Great-Grandmother is here to see you."

"Hey there, you two. Long time no—"

""G-Grandmother?""

Cayna looked at them as they spoke in unison and trembled with fear.

"Well then, Great-Grandmother, do enjoy your stay. I shall bring you some tea later on."

"It's okay; don't worry about it. Thanks for all your help, Idzik."

Caerick and Caerina were both clearly acting suspicious as they watched him give a bow and retreat. Caerina wasn't as much, thanks to her knight training, but Caerick's flustered look was another story. Even so, just as she thought there wasn't much point in a big merchant who built a major distribution system trying to hide anything, Caerick frowned.

"G-Grandmother. It's been quite some time. How may I help you...?"

"You both seem pretty upset about something. Is it something you can't tell me?"

These few words were right on the money, and the thudding of the pair's hearts jumped up an octave.

Caerina invited Cayna to sit next to her, and Cayna passed Sunya's letter to Caerick. They were surprised to find out that the new technique their craftsmen reported about came from Cayna herself. As Caerick briefly read over the letter, his eyes widened when he saw his grandmother's name as the provider of the technique. After reading it over again, he looked at Cayna across from him hesitantly.

"Could it be that the mechanism described here is an ancient art?"

"Yep. If they have that, they should be able to find plenty of uses for it, right?"

She hadn't expected to hear that Craft Skills went by the bombastic title of ancient arts in this modern world. There were only a few textbook patterns available to create with. If current technicians improved upon it, they could use it for more than just wells. This was also one form of dependence on magical tools, but small villages excelled at getting by on labor alone.

All sorts of items that players had made in the Game Era swarmed towns and fields. Cayna thought it might be interesting for others to research even a fragment of these techniques and mechanisms and give them new life.

"If I had to pick, though, I'd say Opus is better at this negotiating stuff."

"Grandmother?"

"Oh, it's nothing. Nothing at all."

She had grumbled without thinking and quickly covered her tracks.

"Anyway, what made you want to get involved with a Felskeilo village, Caerick?"

"I thought it might give me some new business concepts. Based on the reports, there were a number of things I was highly interested in. However, I never imagined they would be your doing, Grandmother…"

He spoke rather proudly. Caerina, however, held her head in her hands and gave a long, long sigh.

"Do take care, Grandmother. Once this guy has his sights set on something, he never lets go. He'll sink his teeth into it until he understands its workings inside and out."

"…Dear sister. Might you please stop making me sound like a lid snake?"

"It's the truth. When we were younger, you took apart several of the tools Father bought for you, did you not? Parts were scattered throughout the house each and every time."

The siblings glared at each other with a *What was that?* and a *What did you say?* but both turned away with a gasp when they heard giggling.

Hiding her mouth behind her hand as her shoulders trembled, Cayna nodded and gave a laugh that implied *You two are so similar.*

Embarrassed, Caerick said, "The tea is late," and stood up. Once her brother had run off, Caerina grew clammy as she waited with Cayna, who was grinning from ear to ear.

It wasn't long before Caerick returned, and once the maid he'd brought back served them tea, he hesitantly sat down.

"So what were you two talking about?"

As soon as they returned to the subject at hand, the siblings fell into a gloomy silence. Cayna's curiosity sent a swirl of Intuition around the pair. Caerick's earlier despair caught her interest, and she was intent on discovering their secrets.

The siblings saw her expression and, as if sensing danger, averted their gazes. Caerina brought the sword leaning against a chair closer.

"Anywaaaay. Are you two in some sort of trouble?"

"A-ah, no, well, a-about that… Ha-ha-ha-ha."

"…Caerick, you idiot."

No matter how eloquent a merchant he was, Caerick put Cayna's fearsome anger above all else and failed to hide distress. Caerina sighed and face-palmed at her brother's *Something is totally up* response. She had been planning to keep it from their grandmother, but now that the topic had been broached, she decided to disclose *that* herself.

"Um, Grandmother. About the bandit leader you captured before…"

In that moment, Cayna's face fell terribly.

Although she had handed him over to the country, he was still originally a player. There was no way it wouldn't concern her.

Caerina hesitated a bit, as if worried she might have chosen the wrong words. Since she'd already gotten the ball rolling, there was no turning back time. She continued until the very end.

245

"There was a public beheading the other day, and…"

Cayna's face fell even farther.

Because of what he had done, there was no question the country's response was just. However, the grandchildren were worried their kind grandmother would feel responsible for the monstrous villain.

It was clear that Cayna had created a chance for a player to be killed. But even so, the problem was that there was a player who would do such things in the first place.

Nevertheless, such a statement was strange coming from someone who had tried to kill them right then and there. Or perhaps it was more accurate to say she had impatiently determined that doing so on the spot was the only proper punishment.

Honestly, Cayna was slightly grateful Caerina had stopped her. After all, despite his heavy sins, he had been one of the few fellow players.

Cayna put this aside, and the conversation continued.

"Publicly…"

"Huh…?"

Caerina wrestled over what to say, and Cayna's eyes shrank to dots. Here was the gist of what she was timidly trying to explain:

The guillotine swung down during the public execution. However, the bandit leader did not die.

Cayna's concern grew as she took in these snippets of explanation that sounded as if even Caerina wasn't exactly sure what she was saying.

His head was cut, but he didn't die… Have players always been that hardy?

"For a player to die, their HP must fall to zero."

She speedily conversed with Kee in her mind and came to a conclusion. The most likely reason he didn't die was because damage was based on the HP system.

In the game world of *Leadale*, the difference between life and death lay between zero and one. Normally, even if your head was cut off, as long as one HP point remained, you wouldn't die.

Not having HP dispersed across every part of his body had probably kept him alive. The Punishment Collar had dropped his stats and level to a tenth of their normal power, but HP and MP were unaffected. Although defense did drop, demons boasted a high amount of HP. For someone like Cayna, who knew Opus, it was only natural that they were extraordinarily hard to kill. Especially when they had skills like Continuous HP Regeneration.

That aside, this naturally caused a major panic during the execution. After all, his head never fell from the guillotine.

Having no other choice, the nation postponed his sentencing for the time being and exhibited the royal family's authority over the people by putting a similar criminal's head on display later on. A number of vassals who had been disturbed by the bandit leader's failed execution forced him to work in the coal mines as a lifelong prison sentence instead.

There seemed to be a growing pile of problems, but Cayna felt relief all the same. She still had a hefty amount of concerns, but everything beyond that was for the country to deal with somehow.

Feeling a bit calmer and back to her old self, Cayna gratefully patted Caerina's head for telling her such confidential information.

"G-Grandmother... I'm not a child anymore..."

"You're still my granddaughter. C'mon, Caerick, over here. I'll pat your head, too."

Cayna beckoned him over with a wave of her hand, but Caerick backed away while shaking his head. When he noticed her look of dissatisfaction, he quickly made a break for it.

"I-I-I-I'll go get your payment! Please wait just a moment, Grandmother!"

His footsteps receded and disappeared.

Cayna blankly watched him run off while still patting the blushing Caerina's head. Her granddaughter didn't forget to mention that her brother was merely shy.

As she looked out over the relaxing garden, Cayna imagined herself as a young child. Was this what parental love felt like? She remembered the way her own mother would stroke her head.

"I wish I could have learned more when I was little..."

"If I had met you when I was younger, I'm certain I would have been a bit different as well."

They bonded over conversations of what-ifs and softly smiled.

Caerick returned shortly afterward, and Cayna accepted the payment. She had the entire stash of gold coins changed to silver since her Item Box didn't have an automatic conversion feature. Within the Item Box, it indicated her gil earned during the Game Era, which was calculated in all silver. Unless she prepared additional purses for gold and bronze, they wouldn't go inside the Item Box.

"Sheesh, it really is such a pain."

"Not at all. As a merchant, such work is what I desire more than anything."

"I know what you mean. All we need are our bodies, right?"

"There are nobles who believe they can buy such things for the right price, so I ask that you not recklessly expose me."

"...If you say that to Grandmother, I have a feeling all the nobles will be gone by tomorrow..."

Caerina suspiciously looked away from Cayna with a murmur, and Caerick's cheek twitched.

"How rude! That's the sort of thing Opus would do! I'd just change them into pigs!"

As Cayna gripped a fist in front of her, Caerick grimly asked that she not declare things like that.

"Who is this Opus you were talking about earlier, Grandmother?" he asked.

"Hmm... A bad friend?"

At the words *bad friend*, Caerina couldn't help but imagine someone with the same might as her grandmother, and she was left speechless at the idea that there were two Caynas. If there was indeed another like her, the truth was that they would be completely unstoppable.

"Well then, I don't want the knights to leave me behind, so I'll guess I'll get back to Felskeilo."

"The knights?"

"Yeah. I heard we're teaming up with the Helshper knights to crush the bandits' stronghold. I'll be accompanying them up until the halfway mark. You wanna join me, Caerina?"

"My duties are within the capital at the moment. I'm afraid I cannot take part."

"I see."

"Did you accept such a request from the Adventurers Guild, Grandmother?"

At Caerick's question, she waved her hand with a *No, no, nothing like that.*

"There's a fishing village on the way there. I've got some business to take care of."

"I see. So it has something to do with a previous matter you've been entrusted with. I understand. As for your inquiry from the other day, I'm afraid I've had no luck. I apologize."

"Ah, don't worry about it. I had a feeling I was barking up the wrong tree. I'll take it slow and search at my own pace."

As she might have expected, finding a land dweller with a

connection to the mermaids was probably impossible. Cayna sighed at the thought of having to check each and every gulf.

Cayna used Teleport to return to the Felskeilo capital. Her arrival point was outside the eastern gate. She was in the middle of a forest a distance from the main road.

The technique had a set range of about one hundred meters from the nearest gate. There was the danger of crashing into someone if she flew right into town, and the flashing light would put all eyes on her as well.

For the time being, she would tell her worrywart children where she was going.

First, she headed to the market to get a small amount of cake ingredients. She didn't know when her next opportunity to treat someone to delicious delicacies would be, but she had no intention of creating a huge feast the way she did with the villagers. Cayna filled half her empty Item Box space with food ingredients and the other half with two or three people's worth of camping materials.

Next, she asked the local kids if anyone nearby was selling stones. She had asked Caerick about magic rhymestone as well. He said that while the stones did exist, no one knew how to process them, so he wasn't sure if they would last in the long run.

She had searched for these stones and bought them up in Helshper as well. The kids would pick up pretty rocks from the side of the road and river, polish them, make them presentable, and sell them for pocket change, but even a few magic rhymestones had gotten mixed into the bunch.

Cayna searched out kids doing the same thing in Felskeilo, and she quickly found what she was looking for after asking them who hung out with Primo. She was able to buy a decent amount from other kids selling the same thing as well. However, since a single stone was less than a few centimeters long, she had to gather a large amount.

Cayna planned to take these later and process them into a decent size. For the time being, her only real option was to become the kids' number one customer.

Caerick had proposed having her create products from magic rhymestone and transfer the selling rights over to him. She said she would mull it over, but although they worked in close contact with each other, he seemed to have his heart set on opening a Sakaiya remote-village branch. Cayna had a strong feeling he was moving forward with plans to strengthen the village on his own.

She next headed over to her eldest son Skargo's church, but he seemed to be attending a meeting at the castle. It most likely concerned last-minute details and adjustments to the knights' departure the following day. When she heard this sort of news from others, he truly did seem to be a man who worked hard for the good of his nation.

Even so, that grateful heart was smashed to pieces every time they met.

Since there was no way around it, she went over to the Royal Academy, bowed her head to the guards, passed through the gate, and entered the grounds. Word had already traveled among the teachers, so no one stopped her on the way to the headmaster's office.

"Mother?"

"'Sup, Mai-Mai?"

As Cayna knocked and entered the room, Mai-Mai put down the papers she was looking at and rushed to greet her mother. Her daughter charged forward with love for her mother in every fiber of her body.

"Why are you clinging to me all of a sudden...?"

"But you never pay attention to me like this, Mother."

"I don't think a grown woman with kids who has been married twice should be talking like that."

"Oh, Mother, you're so harsh."

Mai-Mai narrowed her eyes slightly at being looked down upon, and she reluctantly separated from her mother. Cayna, on the other hand, was a bit jealous of Mai-Mai's mature proportions. Thanks to the evils of character creation, there were no signs Cayna herself would develop any further.

Cayna thanked her daughter for the tea she brewed and took a sip of her twice-steeped black tea. The tea from Sakaiya was fine quality, but this had a delicate sweetness.

"Well then, what can I help you with today?"

"I'll be leaving Felskeilo tomorrow to search for the Palace of the Dragon King along the coast."

"Palace of the Dragon King? What is that?"

"Oh my, I guess you don't know it by that name. Basically, it's an underwater version of a Guardian Tower."

"*Sigh...* Before saying something like *I'm leaving*, wouldn't it be best to find a decent place to live first, Mother? You can't be a rootless blade of grass forever."

As Mai-Mai broached such a subject, the timing put a satisfied smile on Cayna's face. She nodded.

Mai-Mai hadn't expected her to respond so pleasantly to the suggestion and went on guard.

"Actually, I was planning on settling in a remote village after I looked for the tower."

"WHAAAAAAAT?!"

"What are you so surprised about? You just proposed it now yourself."

Mai-Mai's eyes were wide, and she nearly dropped her teacup, but Cayna's reply was matter-of-fact. She had expected this reaction from her daughter, and at this rate, Skargo would likely talk about building a church there.

"You mean you won't stay in the capital?"

"Nope. There's not enough nature, and it seems like I'd be more likely to get mixed up in the nation's problems. Besides, I'm afraid Skargo would swarm on me every day."

"Ha...ha-ha. It's true. He would do that..."

The fact that she knew so many people involved in the running of the nation was problematic. The High Priest and the prime minister. The headmistress of the Royal Academy, the head of the shipbuilding factory, the leaders of the knights. The prince and princess. She was blessed in terms of social connections. On the one hand, for having only arrived in this world three months prior, it was a distinguished lineup. On the other, in addition to also having a grandchild who was an influential merchant in a foreign nation and a niece who ruled a southern one, she was anxious about her chances of involuntarily becoming involved every time conflict arose.

She would inform everyone she'd probably hide away until things calmed down. Cayna thought Mai-Mai seemed fine with anything other than the depths of the forest that had kept her mother away until recently, and she gladly agreed to pass the message on to Skargo and Kartatz.

"She's always in a hurry," Mai-Mai muttered as Cayna said her good-byes and disappeared with Teleport.

"Still, there does always seem to be an uproar wherever Mother goes..."

Appearing in the capital and capturing the prince. Sending the High Priest flying and getting caught up in the trouble with Mai-Mai as well. Going up north and wiping out bandits, then returning home to find an Event Monster had popped up. Mai-Mai couldn't help but feel that she'd become the world's deterrent.

"Just because she'll be going to the ocean, that doesn't mean she'll find trouble...right...?"

253

She felt an uneasiness. Since Cayna possessed a rare power that could either involve her in chaos or cause it, Mai-Mai wondered if she'd see reports about changes in terrain along the coast in the coming days. Such clear images gave her an insuppressible headache.

Cayna used Teleport to return directly to the room she had set as her basic (throwaway) landmark point. Lytt was shocked to see her come downstairs when she should have been away. Marelle had no intention of disclosing a guest's circumstances, so she greeted Cayna as normal.

Evening was approaching, but the inn lacked the hustle and bustle of the previous night. Frankly, it was *too* quiet.

"It's pretty quiet, isn't it?"

"Oh, that's 'cause the scholars from Otaloquess went home. Guess they finished what they came here for."

"I—I wonder if those shadows really did just come here with an ulterior motive...," Cayna said.

"That cat boy was looking for you, since he wanted to say good-bye."

"Oh dear, it looks like I've done him wrong. You see, I thought if I left him any later than that...I wouldn't be in time for dinner, Marelle."

"You always know just the thing to say, that's for sure. Flattery won't get you a larger menu, though."

"Aw, that's too bad."

As Cayna bopped her own head and gave a look of defeat, Marelle disappeared into the kitchen with a smile. Still not understanding what was going on, Lytt looked up at Cayna.

"If you left the village, why did you come down from upstairs?"

"Hmm? Oh, um, I have a spell that lets me travel between big cities in a second regardless of distance, at least to a certain extent."

"Really? Wow, you're amazing, Miss Cayna..."

Not questioning anything, Lytt looked up at her with envy. Cayna flinched a bit and fell speechless. She would have liked to bring the girl along, but forming a party was out of the question.

Instead, Cayna thought about what made her happy—and hit upon an idea.

"Well then, Lytt, would you like to try flying?"

"What?! ...Like, in the sky?"

"Yup, that's right. The weather's nice today. I'm sure it'll be a beautiful view, and you'll get to see lots of things from far away."

"Um, but my mom..."

As Lytt tried to explain that she couldn't leave the inn without Marelle's permission, Cayna crouched down to her eye level and patted her head.

"In that case, let's ask Marelle together. If she says it's okay, will you go?"

"Y-yeah!"

Cayna and Lytt smiled at each other like sisters. Nearby, Lytt's real sister, Luine, had finished work early for once. She saw them, and her shoulders dropped.

"*Sniff.* Lytt isn't attached to me at all..."

"Miss Cayna is way better at relating to kids. She's really one strange girl," Marelle replied.

Epilogue

Several shadows shuddered in the darkness.

The location was within Felskeilo's city center. The roads were paved with stone, yet a dozen or so trees still lined the area. They were a head taller than a two-story building, and the branches and foliage that stretched out on either side provided cooling shade. It was a beloved plaza where citizens gathered in the afternoon as they pleased and enjoyed a moment of respite.

Mothers with young children met here for idle chitchat.

Elderly couples who passed down the leadership of their families to their children would stop by to enjoy a brand-new lease on life.

Troublemakers who had been kicked out of their old haunt due to redevelopment gathered under the shade of the trees to plan their tricks with a certain prince in disguise.

And once night fell, and there was only the moonlight to guide people, the shadows of the trees began to take on a particularly eerie quality. No one would willingly enter this place once it got dark, not even the patrol guards. They would rather go to neighborhoods full of rowdy bars than wander around the plaza at night.

By all rights, it was not a place where shadowy figures could run rampant. But no matter how frightened the guards were, they none-theless made their way inside.

For whatever reason, on this night they took only a quick glance around and made no attempt to enter.

Under one of those trees...

An unnatural shadow perched atop a branch among the foliage that reached toward the heavens. Normally, such a branch would bend at the slightest touch of a small bird resting its wings, yet even the weight of a human did not sway it. No one would be able to tell if anything was there even with the shadow present.

There were similar shadows on the treetops surrounding the plaza.

One was as big as three people. However, the number of arms it carried proved it was not human in any capacity.

Another had a figure whose humanity was also highly suspect. It had no neck and clearly lacked the fleshiness of a person.

Opposite these were two shadows that one would still call human-like. However, their ears were long and pointed, and they had horns. They were in no way human.

The silence carried on, until finally one of the horned, human-looking shadows spoke.

"It's about time we make ourselves known and get on the nobles' nerves. We'll use servants instead of sending out our own subordi-nates. Let's make quick work of them."

The speaker was a man of considerable age, his voice quiet enough that only the one beside him could hear. But even the leaves were silent tonight, and his voice therefore traveled far.

The odd shadows across from him nodded. The larger one went "Gu-gu-gu" as its body trembled with laughter.

"We can decide the methods, right?" the other, thinner odd shadow asked the raspy voice.

The humanlike shadow gave a small nod. "Off you go, then."

Upon receiving this brief command, the strange shadows disappeared into the treetops as if they had been swallowed whole.

Only two shadows remained. The long-earned, horned figure who had said nothing thus far looked over its shoulder. The soft contours of her body marked her as a woman.

"Are you all right with not meeting them?" she asked.

"It would be pointless."

His reply was curt, and he disappeared into the treetops just as easily as the deformed shadows. Her own shadow simultaneously vanished as well.

The wind blew through the trees and shook their branches as if it had only just remembered how to do so.

BONUS SHORT STORY
New Days

Mimily looked up, and before she knew it, all the energy had drained from her tense body. She stretched out her lower half and sank beneath the hot water.

"*Sigh...*"

"Oh, what's wrong?"

"Ah, no, it's nothing."

She put on a serene yet empty smile for the concerned woman bathing across from her.

"You can always tell us if something's the matter."

"She's right. A backwoods village like ours may not have much to offer, but we do what we can."

"We owe a lot to you, too, Mimily."

The other older women soaking in the bathtub nodded.

Mimily had never received such open gratitude and was at a loss on what to do. She had been treated as a pebble by the roadside back in her merpeople village, so she wasn't the least bit used to the good-natured nosiness she experienced here. It was an unfamiliar sensation.

"More than anything, we all depend a lot on Cayna."

"Definitely. After all, she's the one who gave our village a luxurious bathhouse."

"She made it right then and there without even the teeniest reward. It's a shame we can never truly express our thanks."

According to the ladies, Cayna had constructed this building in a single day. Furthermore, she didn't do it because someone in the village asked her to; she did it "because having one would be convenient." She heard that, thanks to this facility, the village had picked up the custom of bathing daily. Since bathing had constituted nothing more than pouring water over oneself in a washtub and wiping the body for as long as the villagers could remember, they had been shocked. For a mermaid like Mimily, who was constantly in water, it seemed unbelievable.

"Where is Cayna from?"

"Who knows?"

"She just came to the village one day and started staying at Marelle's."

"Come to think of it, Cayna doesn't talk much about herself."

"But…"

""""We do know she has three kids."""""

This last one alone was declared in an amused chorus, and the effect was astounding.

As far as Mimily knew, Cayna was frightfully strong, and at any rate, she was a rare high elf. In Mimily's world, high elves were like characters in fairy tales. Weaker, lower-ranked races like mermaids couldn't possibly compare.

The practice seemed to be rather uncommon in this world, but from Mimily's point of view, Cayna's ability to employ spirits at will made her want to revere the girl as a sort of divine messenger.

That point alone already made the differences between this world and her old one perfectly clear.

However, Cayna was fervently searching for Mimily's village.

Now, she couldn't just say, *Our worlds are different, so you don't have to keep looking.*

Even so, Mimily herself didn't have many fond memories of her hometown and wasn't particularly eager to go back.

A certain common folklore had brought suffering to merpeople like Mimily for many years. This was the belief that "eating merpeople meat would grant one eternal life." The merpeople themselves only lived around two hundred years, so the idea that consuming their meat would give one immortality was ridiculous.

The merpeople had been protesting this rumor for many years, but even up until the present day, there was no sign of anything ever changing. Among humans and other land dwellers, it was said that the smallest piece of merperson meat was worth a fortune. The merpeople wanted to scream, *What a bunch of crap!*

However, no amount of screaming would change anything. It wouldn't sway human dominion over the world. Over the years, the merpeople were forced deeper and deeper into the ocean. Mimily and her sister, Lohli, who was one year older, were two of the very few children who would continue their bloodline.

Their clan had placed excessive hopes on the girls and crammed their educations to the brim from the very start. The sisters were initially supposed to get along and learn from each other. They helped each other, taught each other, and absorbed everything they needed to know about the merpeople.

It didn't last long, however, and the first rip in the seam was because of Mimily.

A shift occurred; she was constantly late to class, and Lohli ended up being the only one who did any studying.

Of course, it wasn't as if Mimily had simply given up. She fervently chased her sister and lost sleep as she poured over her studies.

However, the difference between them was so great that it could never be overcome.

It was amid this that Lohli confronted Mimily.

"I'm sorry, Mimily."

"...Lohli."

"It's not your fault. It's no one's fault. It's what we merpeople must do to deal with these circumstances forced upon us."

"Don't apologize, Lohli..."

"I'm sorry. I truly am."

"...Lohli."

Lohli's title as the next queen weighed heavily on her. The future of their people was at stake.

She couldn't afford to be looked down upon and cast Mimily aside.

Lohli also loved her little sister and never wished to abandon her. It was easy to imagine this had been a bitter decision to make. If the two deliberated, there was a chance they'd both be cut off from the merpeople community.

After that, Lohli prepared to be the future queen, and Mimily was excluded from any education that would teach her to carry on the next generation of the clan.

However, despite having now found herself in a state of limbo, Mimily was made to cultivate seaweed for the time being. After all, the clan had no room to allow surplus members time to play. There were voices who labeled Mimily an embarrassment who failed to carry on the future of the clan and said she should be cast out as unnecessary.

The one who put a stop to this in the form of an exchange was Lohli. She asked that they permit Mimily to stay in return for Lohli rising to the throne and giving birth to their future queen. Lohli could no longer speak with Mimily, but she was happy to know her little sister was there. A single glance at Mimily put her at ease and gave her the courage to steadfastly lead their people.

Lohli then became queen at a young age, and she put forth measures to increase their continually declining population. At the very least, her reign slightly improved their prospects. The merpeople praised their queen, the queen supported her people, and they attained peace. Lohli was extolled as the savior of the merpeople.

However, all was not positive. Naturally, there were also holes and downsides to her plan. The main reason these did not come to come the surface was because Mimily took the brunt of the attacks.

"The queen's leftovers."

"Lazy freeloader."

"Human spy."

"Useless."

"A sacrifice the queen uses to dump the people's dissatisfaction."

They whispered these terrible things right in front of Mimily, and the heartless words struck her daily. The only reason she narrowly avoided being physically harmed was because of the people's promise with the queen.

Eventually, the risk of being poisoned became too great, and she was driven from her seaweed-cultivating job. Despite remaining in the village, she wasn't needed, and she lost a home to return to.

Mimily moved to the outskirts of the village and spent her days avoiding the eyes of others. She would only show up at a function if it was for the queen, and speaking with her was unforgivable. The merpeople spit venom right in front of her. If it earned them the queen's royal gaze, they would drive her out further. Mimily's heart grew more and more tired.

Then it happened. The black hole right before her very eyes sucked her in.

When she was tossed into that watering hole of unknown darkness and shallow freshwater, she thought it was some sort of curse. She ate rations of tiny fish and sung to pass the time.

Even so, it was leagues better than the merpeople village. As long as she was determined to keep on living, it wasn't so bad at all. However, the lack of exits did concern her.

That was when Cayna appeared along with her powerful entity. She had given the astounded Mimily a sidelong glance and used the Water and Earth Spirits to bring her to the outside world. After that, she gave the mermaid a place to live in a human village.

"Fortunately, I got some tickets for free nights at the inn, so I thought you could stay here in the village."

At first, Mimily feared she would become their next meal. However, the villagers greeted her warmly.

"Oh, so you're a mermaid?"

"I've never seen one before."

"Can I call you Mimi?"

They stayed this way even after Cayna left. Not one person treated her any differently. Mimily calmed down, but as she learned more about her situation, she fell into a depression.

Her home was thanks to the villagers' goodwill, and it was the money Cayna gave her that kept her fed. It would be strange if she *didn't* feel uneasy. Wasn't this the same as when she was called a lazy freeloader back in the merpeople village?

That was why she wanted to be useful. She didn't want a repeat of the last time.

It was only by coincidence, but showing Lytt her magical ability to control water turned out to be a lifesaver. At Lytt's and the village grannies' insistence, she started a laundering business. The fee was one bronze coin for one full, family-sized basket. The women of the village thought that Mimily didn't know the value of currency. The laundry fee was initially three bronze coins, but Mimily disapproved under the reasoning that she used borrowed items in addition to her own talents. The price was dropped to two bronze coins.

Lytt was also brought on board to help, and they split the shares evenly. From a village child's point of view, the pocket change was an extraordinary amount.

"This won't do. A little kid can't go earnin' that much. One bronze coin a day is enough."

"I agree. Earning so much makes me feel uneasy."

Both mother and daughter weren't thrilled, so the changes were made. Mimily would receive one bronze coin for each load of laundry, and her part-time helper, Lytt, would receive one bronze coin per day.

It started out as a convenience for the men and those living alone, but it soon caught on across the village. The work of a farmer's wife clearly wasn't an easy one, and half the village came to Mimily with laundry requests.

Since the barrels rose above an adult's waist, just peeking into the barrel was laborious work for someone like Mimily, who couldn't stand up straight.

However, that, too, was solved one day when Cayna suddenly dropped in.

"What're you doing?"

"Hmm? Ah, Cayna. Hello. As you can see, I'm doing the laundry."

"The laundry?! Why're you doing the laundry?"

Seeing that she had upset her savior, Mimily gave an empty smile.

After explaining the course of events, Cayna sank into thought. Meanwhile, Mimily's mind raced with the fear that she shouldn't have done such a thing in the bathhouse after all.

"And to think I went and saved up all that money during my trip so I could help you. I guess things just didn't work out."

"Huh? Please wait. Don't make my debt any higher!"

"Not to worry. I'm simply going to make a small room next to the bathhouse so you can do your laundry. A barrel with a bobbing neck like you see in those bamboo fountains would be good, too."

"Bamboo fountain? Please wait! Hey, are you listening to me?"

"Yes, yes, I'm listening. You've got absolutely nothing to worry about. I'm going to make you a fabulous workplace!"

"Whaaaaat?!"

Wood material that appeared from out of nowhere floated in the sky and transformed. As Mimily looked on in bewilderment, a room was annexed to the outside of the women's changing room. Four barrels that could be turned up, down, and sideways were put in place, and a magical device poured hot water into the barrel from high up. It was a perfect laundry room that even had a waterway for Mimily to move about with ease.

The mermaid wanted to thank her, but she held her head in her hands at the thought of how much more debt she would be in.

"…Honestly. If this is how it's going to be, I'm going to work my tail off!"

Burning with a sense of purpose, the mermaid may have reached an epiphany.

Mimily's emotions had dried up so much that she couldn't even cry. However, whenever she was busy, she began to feel thankful for those difficult times and broke out into a pained smile.

"I really do have to thank you, Cayna. Lytt and the other villagers as well."

After all, it was probably thanks to this warm place that she could tell herself it was okay to keep looking forward.

The story of how her business later caught the eye of a certain merchant who spread it across the continent is another tale altogether.

Character Data

Caerina

Mai-Mai's daughter.
Caerick's elder twin sister.
In other words, Cayna's
granddaughter.

Still a youngster by elf terms at just
shy of one hundred years old, she
serves as one of the instructors of
the Helshper knights. Her strength
is said to be the greatest in Helshper,
but she was no match for a player
leading a group of bandits.

A serious person who is equally
harsh on herself and others, yet her
fellow knights seem to admire her all
the same. She doesn't return home
much and spends most of her days
in the Helshper knights' lodging
house. Calls her younger brother
dumb and is so obsessed with her
work that she can never find love.

Caerick

Mai-Mai's son.
Caerina's younger
twin brother.
Has a son named Idzik.

A skilled merchant who runs
Sakaiya, a large company
that does business across the
continent. Spent about fifty
years establishing the commerce
network that fell to pieces after
the seven nations became three.
Considered the founding father
of the Merchants Guild. Enjoys
a little trickery and intrigue
in business, but don't mistake
him for a corrupt merchant.
Although he initially upset his
grandmother Cayna, once they
made up, he's enjoyed helping
her in all sorts of ways. His
greatest concern right now is
finding someone to take his
twin sister's hand in marriage.

Afterword

Hello. This is Ceez. Thank you very much for picking up *In the Land of Leadale*, Vol. 2. I'm pretty sure there aren't any other people like me who read the afterword first, but I'd be happy if you take this book up to the register.

This time, I've realized that I am absolutely *terrible* at time management. I'm really just reaping what I sow, but being a slow writer isn't a good thing. I must have repeated the process of writing, rereading, erasing, and writing some more at least a million times. By the time the cover illustration was done, I was only about 20 percent finished...

There are two new characters in this book who didn't appear in the Web version, so I did some rewrites. The task of fixing my original manuscript continued even as time closed in on me and created a daily cycle of quickly deteriorating health. Once I made the change, I couldn't go back. There was a lot of suffering involved, so I hope Mimily and Li'l Fairy grow on you.

Also the shadow of you-know-who finally appeared. Those who have read the Web version know exactly who I mean.

Tenmaso, thank you again for the cover art and insert and interior illustrations. At first, I was surprised to see you went with a pink cover. When I put it on my bookshelf next to Volume 1, I didn't think any spines could look more opposite.

Also I'm eternally grateful to my editor, who I caused so much trouble for by submitting my manuscript at the last minute.

Thank you as well to everyone else who has been involved in the publishing process.

Ceez

It's been a while since Volume 1.
I'm Tenmaso, the illustrator.

The scenes of Cayna eating are always so
soft and warm. It's easy enough to grab
meat skewers in town, but they usually
look really tough and chewy, and I
could always just make my own.
Food seems three times more
delicious in a fantasy townscape.

It was a lot of fun drawing all sorts
of races for this book, from
dragoids to
werecats to
demons and
mermaids.

Until next
time, then!

Tenmaso